G000138082

Acclaim for
Glamour Girls: Femme/Fe

"*Glamour Girls* is an original concept whose time has definitely come: femme girls who seriously get off on sex with other femme girls—with no apologies and no excuses. Rachel Kramer Bussel has scored again with this terrific collection of truly erotic lesbian sex stories. Featuring lots of pretty gals having sex in the kitchen, sex in the dressing room, sex in public restrooms, getting sexy lap dances, even having sex in their parents' basements; there are bisexuals, three ways, and the ever popular one-on-one scenarios. They're all in here and all the women are dressed up and ready to get down to business. But reader beware, just because these girls are feminine doesn't mean they're delicate. There is some hardcore lust unfolding in these pages. *Glamour Girls* is not only a satisfying read for the seasoned connoisseur of sex with feminine women, but it's also an excellent intro to girl/girl sex for the many bicurious women out there."

—Marilyn Jaye Lewis
Author of *Lust: Bisexual Erotica;*
Editor of *Stirring Up a Storm:*
Tales of the Sensual, the Sexual, and the Erotic;
Founder, The Erotic Authors Association

"In her introduction, the editor says: 'Femmes who date femmes occupy a unique place half in and half out of the lesbian world.' Not recognizable as dykes on the street, the heroines of the twenty-six stories in this anthology combine glamour with chutzpah and creativity in ways that are profoundly queer, unconventional, but convincing.

This book seems likely to become a classic, not only in the field of sexual fantasy. It would be a useful contribution to the study of gender, and the quality of the writing is only matched by the new light it casts on those who were defined in the 1970s as 'women-identified women.'"

"Femme' identity in these stories is broad enough to include lipstick and muscles, elegance and fiercely willful desire. These stories show female bonding in various sexual forms, and it does not look like part of a patriarchal agenda.

The erotic power of traditional feminine roles (artist's model, courtesan, entertainer, beautician, seamstress) is part of the magic in these stories. Several of the characters could be seen as archetypes, but none looks like a stereotype or a victim. In some cases, the service provider makes the rules and brings ecstasy to one as alluring as herself. These women are mirrors, foils, allies, and rivals to one another, and they don't all limit themselves to one-on-one interaction. Welcome to the world of women loving women loving women."

—Jean Roberta
Erotic Writer; Instructor,
Department of English, University of Regina

"Sugar and spice and everything nice—that's what femme/femme love is made of. Unfortunately for femme women who love and desire other femme women, not everyone sees the visceral heat of such a combination. As editor/writer Rachel Kramer Bussel points out in the thoughtful and engaging introduction to *Glamour Girls: Femme/Femme Erotica*, an anthology in praise of the new love that dare not speak its name, some consider the double-dose of sensual femininity to be nothing more than 'air on air.' She and twenty-five other writers unapologetically, articulately, and erotically disagree. This book is a thoughtful, frequently delightful celebration of the femme/femme love continuum. Whether a nervous novice removing another woman's clothing for the first time or a confident daughter of Sappho urgently pressing her painted lips against those of another, the femmes in this collection prove that they and their passion are more than merely 'air on air.'"

—Theresa "Darklady" Reed
Erotic Writer

NOTES FOR PROFESSIONAL LIBRARIANS AND LIBRARY USERS

This is an original book title published by Alice Street Editions™, Harrington Park Press®, an imprint of The Haworth Press, Inc. Unless otherwise noted in specific chapters with attribution, materials in this book have not been previously published elsewhere in any format or language.

CONSERVATION AND PRESERVATION NOTES

All books published by The Haworth Press, Inc., and its imprints are printed on certified pH neutral, acid-free book grade paper. This paper meets the minimum requirements of American National Standard for Information Sciences-Permanence of Paper for Printed Material, ANSI Z39.48-1984.

DIGITAL OBJECT IDENTIFIER (DOI) LINKING

The Haworth Press is participating in reference linking for elements of our original books. (For more information on reference linking initiatives, please consult the CrossRef Web site at www.crossref.org.) When citing an element of this book such as a chapter, include the element's Digital Object Identifier (DOI) as the last item of the reference. A Digital Object Identifier is a persistent, authoritative, and unique identifier that a publisher assigns to each element of a book. Because of its persistence, DOIs will enable The Haworth Press and other publishers to link to the element referenced, and the link will not break over time. This will be a great resource in scholarly research.

Glamour Girls
Femme/Femme Erotica

Glamour Girls
Femme/Femme Erotica

Rachel Kramer Bussel
Editor

Alice Street Editions™
Harrington Park Press®
An Imprint of The Haworth Press, Inc.
New York • London • Oxford

For more information on this book or to order, visit
http://www.haworthpress.com/store/product.asp?sku=5328

or call 1-800-HAWORTH (800-429-6784) in the United States and Canada
or (607) 722-5857 outside the United States and Canada

or contact orders@HaworthPress.com

Published by

Alice Street Editions™, Harrington Park Press®, an imprint of The Haworth Press, Inc., 10 Alice Street, Binghamton, NY 13904-1580.

© 2006 The Haworth Press, Inc. All rights reserved. No part of this work may be reproduced or utilized in any form or by any means, electronic or mechanical, including photocopying, microfilm, and recording, or by any information storage and retrieval system, without permission in writing from the publisher. Printed in the United States of America.

"If You Can Make It There, You Can Make It Anywhere" was previously published in *Best Lesbian Erotica 2001* (Cleis Press, 2000) and in *Erotic Stories* (Cleis Press, 2004).

"Scary Date" was previously published in *Hot & Bothered 4*, edited by Karen X. Tulchinsky (Arsenal Pulp Press, 2003).

"Looking, Really Looking, at a Painting" was previously published in *Zaftig: Well Rounded Erotica* (Cleis Press, 2001).

"Cinderella's Shoes" was previously published in *Best Lesbian Erotica 2003* (Cleis Press, 2002).

"The Game" was previously published in *Blue Sky Sideways* (Rosebud/Masquerade, 1996).

"Lap Dance Lust" was previously published in *Best Women's Erotica 2003*, edited by Marcy Sheiner (Cleis Press, 2002); *Mammoth Book of Best New Erotica*, Volume 3, edited by Maxim Jakubowski (Carroll and Graf, 2004); *The Good Parts: Pure Lesbian Erotica*, edited by Nicole Foster (Alyson, 2005); and online at www.cliterati.co.uk, 2003.

"The Manicure" was previously published in *Paramour Magazine* (Fall/Winter 2000), edited by Amelia Copeland; in *Best American Erotica 2000*, edited by Susie Bright (Touchstone, 2000); and in *Sex Toys*, edited by Berbera and Hyde (Mondadori, 2001).

"Alicia" was previously published in *I Don't Really Love Sex* (Sex Mag Ich Eigentlich gar Nicht) (Maas Verlag, 2005).

"Two Girls in a Basement" was previously published in *Best Lesbian Erotica 2005*, edited by Tristan Taormino (Cleis Press, 2004).

PUBLISHER'S NOTES
The development, preparation, and publication of this work has been undertaken with great care. However, the Publisher, employees, editors, and agents of The Haworth Press are not responsible for any errors contained herein or for consequences that may ensue from use of materials or information contained in this work. The Haworth Press is committed to the dissemination of ideas and information according to the highest standards of intellectual freedom and the free exchange of ideas. Statements made and opinions expressed in this publication do not necessarily reflect the views of the Publisher, Directors, management, or staff of The Haworth Press, Inc., or an endorsement by them.

This is a work of fiction. Names, characters, places, and incidents either are the products of the author's imagination or are used fictitiously, and any resemblance to actual persons, living or dead, business establishments, events, or locales is entirely coincidental.

Cover design by Lora Wiggins.

Library of Congress Cataloging-in-Publication Data

Glamour girls : femme-femme erotica / Rachel Kramer Bussel, editor.
    p. cm.
  ISBN-13: 978-1-56023-534-7 (pbk. : alk. paper)
  ISBN-10: 1-56023-534-9 (pbk. : alk. paper)
  1. Lesbians—Fiction. 2. Erotic stories, American. I. Bussel, Rachel Kramer.

PS648.L47G58 2006
813'.01083538'086643—dc22

                                                                            2005026042

Contents

Editor's Foreword

Alice Street Editions provides a voice for established as well as up-coming lesbian writers, reflecting the diversity of lesbian interests, ethnicities, ages, and class. This cutting-edge series of novels, memoirs, and nonfiction writing welcomes the opportunity to present controversial views, explore multicultural ideas, encourage debate, and inspire creativity from a variety of lesbian perspectives. Through enlightening, illuminating, and provocative writing, Alice Street Editions can make a significant contribution to the visibility and accessibility of lesbian writing and bring lesbian-focused writing to a wider audience. Recognizing our own desires and ideas in print is life sustaining, acknowledging the reality of who we are, as well as our place in the world, individually and collectively.

Judith P. Stelboum
Editor in Chief
Alice Street Editions

© 2006 by The Haworth Press, Inc. All rights reserved.
doi:10.1300/5328_a

Introduction

Rachel Kramer Bussel

I'm a femme who likes other femmes, dates other femmes, loves other femmes, and fucks other femmes. This may mean different things to different people; for me it's had a very powerful effect on my sexuality, the way I see the world and myself, and I wanted to explore this concept within the world of erotica. Femmes who date femmes occupy a unique place half in and half out of the lesbian world; we can bond with our straight sisters over the makeup counter, ask strangers to tell us if something matches, be taken for straight on sight. We may look one way on the outside but feel utterly different on the inside. We are not just femmes but we desire those like ourselves, causing plenty of room for lust as well as doubt (Is she prettier than me? Am I simply being narcissistic? Am I playing into some male ideal of beauty?).

Although this is not an exclusive preference for me, I've always been drawn to glamorous, decadent, decked-out women, curvy lovelies with seductive smiles. Femmes were the first women I noticed, even though the first woman I dated was a soft butch. I think femmes have a universal allure, a siren call that can catch almost anyone off guard; at our best, we can flirt and tease and taunt with the best of them, but when it's other femmes who set our hearts on fire, things get a little more complicated. I wanted to create a book filled with women who are like me in some ways, women who go after fellow femmes, who have been on both ends of the femme pleasure ride, and some who are not like me, who'd surprise me, who'd show me varied, often surprising ways of being a femme who's into other femmes, because contrary to popular belief, there's more than one way to be that kind of girl.

Published by The Haworth Press, Inc., 2006. All rights reserved.
doi:10.1300/5328_01

1

Mostly, I wanted to reflect the varied, rich realities of femme-on-femme desire, ones far removed from the "girl-girl" porn images so clearly implanted in the public brain. I wanted to see and read hot, authentic, girlie-girl sex that confounded the stereotypes of both butch/femme and femme/femme, including "curious" women and women who didn't know where to place themselves on the lesbian spectrum, because their appearance does not match the mainstream vision of "lesbian." And I wanted to do so in a way that would in no way detract from butches, androgynous women, bois, transmen and transwomen, and any number of queer folks who are not femme-identified, because this book is above all a celebration and an exploration. It's about why we look the way we do, what we do once we look the way we do, and what lurks underneath our outer layers, in our hearts, minds, and pussies, but it is not at all about denigrating anyone else's identity in the process.

I also wanted to put to rest the notion that femme/femme desire is simpler, easier, or less worthy than any other kind of hard-fought identity. Simply because we may look a certain way, we are treated as the "dumb blondes" of the lesbian world, hit with the harshest of stereotypes from those we might have considered kindred spirits. In a *New York Magazine* article on bois, a gender identity embraced by a growing number of dykes and former dykes, someone named Sarah was quoted as saying, "Femme-on-femme is stupid to me. It's air. It's air on air. It just seems like Cinemax fluff . . . long nails, you know." I hope this book proves that indeed, femme/femme is not "air." Far from it. This book features women who will hiss and claw at you for suggesting that their desires are "air" simply because they may not be your own. These women do not (always) have long nails or fake laughs; they know how to fuck other women, they know who they are, removed from the media glare, and they often have to be stronger than their sisters to feel proud of who they are, because they don't have any true role models, any real source of validation except their femme lovers. They have come to terms with who they are (for the most part) and what they want, sometimes at desperately inconvenient times, and even if they have to be a little sneaky to get it, ultimately, they do. Sometimes their desires take them by surprise, and what seems like a natural progression from friendship to longing and lust leads them down unexpected roads, just like in real life. Sometimes we may think we are "straight" until our heads are turned by a fellow femme and we find we cannot unturn them, cannot push away this deep longing that lurks within us.

You'd have to clearly rethink the notion that femme plus femme equals a big zero after reading this collection, filled with fierce, fabulous, beautiful, intelligent, and passionate women who seek out what they want, and often have to go undercover. We can't always go to the lesbian bar or dance or reading and pick up another femme; even if we do, people might point or stare or whisper, and one or the other might worry about how it looks or what it means. We often find each other in specifically nonlesbian spaces, where our presence is a delightfully secret surprise shared only by those in the know. One advantage of being a femme is this ability to be ephemeral—to exist in female-only spaces without raising suspicion, places such as the sorority house in Michelle C.'s "The Crush Party," places that might not welcome such women if they knew them to be lesbians.

Other stories show that femmes can be sex workers and dykes, and can combine the two in necessary and surprising ways. In "The G-String," Jen Collins explores a wonderfully complex sexual trio, where jealousy, lust, and history, not to mention striptease, combine in an explosive way. In Lori Selke's "Diary of a Lost Girl, Part 1," a girl is inducted into her sexuality by her father's mistress, who straddles the line between mother and lover, worker and free being, caught between many worlds. Khadijah Caturani skewers myths about bisexuality as well as sex work, in this case porn, in "Schooled by a Straight Girl," as the lesbian narrator gets more than her fair share of shock at being taught a few hot lessons by her "straight" co-worker. My own "Lap Dance Lust" explores the visceral erotic power of those who use their flirtation skills and their bodies to earn a living. These authors show that sex work is not only filled with femmes who want femmes, but also with complex motivations and outcomes, a world where compromises are made and life may not be easy, but one that also gives us access to parts of our sexuality heretofore unknown. In the midst of a very straight world, especially that of sex work, we often find each other, seeking out girls like us who truly get it, circumventing the conventions around us (often in total secrecy) to fulfill our most cherished needs.

Which brings me to one of the main themes that cropped up throughout the stories I read—straight and bisexual seduction. Many stories I read involved girls with boyfriends who longed for something more, or were curious, or who wanted the warmth of another woman like themselves. I did not want to discount these stories, because I know that they are valid and real, that they are often the first time a woman has let herself consider the possibility of being with another woman, such as in Tenille Brown's "Dressing Desire."

I received many submissions that played on the student/teacher theme, perhaps because teachers are one of our primary icons of femininity. Many offered overly simplistic, stereotypical views of this relationship, but Anna South's "Zenda" provides a complex, nuanced look at the power dynamics between a college professor and her student, each one trying to outguess the other and figure out their erotic quirks.

This book is nothing like air, and these stories show that femmes with femmes do not have to be a substitute for anything else—butch/femme, boy/girl, or the porn term and look of "girl/girl." These characters are none of these—they are their own breed of fierce, fast, bold, brave women. By going beyond—as well as into, on top of, under, and around our appearances—*Glamour Girls* presents a vivid portrait of femme desire, which incorporates how we look into how we define ourselves into who we seek out into how we fuck.

This is a celebration and exploration of sameness and difference, of how women who may look alike may or may not think, act, and desire alike, about looking beyond the surface, about attractions that run deeper than lipliner. Femmes can be mercurial, passing and blending, their ability to fit right in a mixed blessing. Often taken for straight or "bicurious," being a femme can also gain us access to privileged female spaces, from kitchens to bedrooms to sorority houses, able to live among those who may have no clue about the true objects of our affection.

And as for those "bicurious" babes such as the budding femmes of "Two Girls in a Basement," which Cheryl B. so accurately describes, the ones who know there is something slightly different about them even though on the outside they look just like all their friends—they are prominently featured in this book. This is partly due to the large number of submissions I received in which girls with boyfriends discovered something missing from their straight relationships, or found something within themselves to act on, partly due to the nature of femme/femme desire, which may spring from a wholly queer setting, or may be more complicated. Regardless, I'm less concerned with whether these women are newfound femmes, lesbians, or bisexuals, as I am about exploring the fantasy and reality of femme/femme desire outside the mainstream heterosexual boundaries of such lust. Because in the straight world, no matter how much we get off on and with other women, all we really desire is a nice, hard cock, which we know isn't our truth, even for those who identify as bisexual. Masculinity, whether in male or butch form, doesn't have to be part of our lesbian construct of desire, and we should not have to solely be defined by its absence. These women are unapologetic about wanting other femmes. These aren't flings or fantasies necessarily, nor are they lifelong relationships, but they do show that there can be heat, passion, conflict, and lust between fellow femmes, that we are not necessarily in competition with one another.

And while this is a celebration of femme dykes, I would be remiss if I did not mention the seemingly eternal erotic mainstream (read: male) appeal of even the mere idea of two hot babes getting it on. Many of us know this and play with it, flirting by accident or design, simply because we can. Being a femme, being simply a woman, grants us a slightly elevated status, which can work for or against us; for femmes who revel in our femininity for ourselves first, we know that this often draws unwarranted amounts of attention from men, but this is not a reason to simply discard our coveted cloak of femininity, but rather to embrace, explore, and expand it. The powerful erotic allure of femmes with femmes goes beyond the straight titillation factor into something primal, the exhibitionistic thrill of being fetishized whether we like it or not. This duality—femme/femme desire and male appreciation of this desire is why "If You Can Make It There . . ." is one of my favorite erotic stories. The sexual display is not for the male cabdriver, but he can get his vicarious thrill while the two women knowingly engage each other, and him.

For many, having been ushered into the queer world within a butch/femme paradigm, their first time with a femme can be startling, scary, going against all that one was taught and believed about oneself. Just as many of us have no way of "learning" how to be a lesbian, we really don't have a way of knowing how to be a femme-loving-femme, and often we have to make it up as we go along, fumbling along for what makes the most sense and feels the truest to our hearts and bodies.

In short, there are infinite ways for femmes to like, date, love, and fuck other femmes. It's not a simple girl + girl formula, or something we're programmed to do by watching Madonna kiss Britney and Christina, or any other media construct (though of course it's a media field day when girls lock lips). These stories explore something much more powerful and daring, something bold and exciting, sexy and arousing precisely because it catches us off guard, throws off the tired old notions of what it means to be a girl, a dyke, a femme. The characters in this book will challenge and provoke you, tease and dare you, haunt you after you turn the last page. They are curvy and supple, brazen and pouty, wielding power and allure in the shape of lipstick and high heels. But watch out—unlike air, they just might attack you with one of their spike heels or long nails. And you just might like it.

– 1 –

If You Can Make It There,
You Can Make It Anywhere

A.J. Stone

For Wyatt

It's an early fall night when the weather hovers between thoughts of summer, hot and sticky, and then changes its mind and whips into the frenzy of fall. My skin reacts, stands away from bone, supported by fine hairs, and my nipples grow hard, as if touched by a finger or a tongue. It's late. A girl's night out, my friend Nathalie and I have splurged on a new and fashionable restaurant downtown just above Wall Street, a neighborhood as sly and mysterious as the weather. Nathalie and I have known each other for years. We roomed together briefly when Nathalie first came to New York. Now she lives uptown in an apartment which, until recently, she shared with Mark, her boyfriend of five years.

The restaurant is thick with businessmen on expense accounts, pungent with testosterone, cocks at attention and ready to pounce. Nathalie and I gossip and drink, round balloons of red wine, which pop down our throats and make us as giggly as sniffed helium. Two women in a room full of men, the first women most of them have seen all day apart from their dowdy secretaries or their female colleagues. Two women, dressed in revealing clothing—low-cut dresses that slip

Published by The Haworth Press, Inc., 2006. All rights reserved.
doi:10.1300/5328_02

and tease. A glimpse of nipple, a thigh unconsciously rubbed. Dresses of thin silk that slip into the cracks of our asses as we walk. Dresses clearly worn over no underwear. Dresses to frustrate. A few men buy us drinks, but we're not biting. I have another goal in mind: the blonde sitting across the table from me. Curiosity has been an unspoken dance between us for years, frustrated by our other obligations. Suddenly, we are single at the same time.

We skirt around the tension between us, pumping it up by discussing sex, the first time, the best time, the craziest time. Nathalie puts down her fork in the middle of the main course—medallions of black cod—and runs a hand through blonde hair. There is a moment of silence before she speaks.

"Remember the week Mark was away on business and we went out to that sushi place and got drunk on sake?" she begins.

I remembered that and passing out on Nathalie's bed.

"When I woke up, sometime around dawn, I had a terrible headache. I downed a couple of aspirin but I threw them right up. There was this . . . well . . . trick I'd learned in college. You were sound asleep . . . ," Nathalie faltered, embarrassed, the color rising in her cheeks.

"Go on," I urged her, one hand beneath my napkin, playing with my dress.

Nathalie plunges onward. She had pulled up her nightgown and masturbated while I slept soundly beside her.

"I was so afraid you'd wake up," she said and looked at me, then added, nervously. "I have to use the ladies room."

When she is gone, I signal for the check. I am not wearing any underwear, and I can feel a trail of liquid snaking down my thigh. Nathalie catches my eye as she makes her way across the room, but I cannot tell if her eyes are large with fear or desire. The eyes of the other diners follow us as we leave, their cocks thick and swollen. I can bet there'll be a lot of pounced wives tonight, visions of Nathalie and I beckoning forward more than one orgasm.

The streets are dark and deserted and shadowed. I weave down the street, dancing to too many glasses of wine echoing in my head, my dark hair as wild as a tussle beneath the sheets. A tune goes off in

Nathalie's head. She spins me and the world with me and I am thrown against a wall. A brief moment and then her tongue is in my mouth, tentative, slight, a drunken experiment. When she backs away, amazed at her boldness, she leaves me hungry, my nipples reaching out. We walk down the street laughing and I tease her about it.

"Do you want to feel my wet pussy?" I ask her, looking at her out of the corner of my eye, challenging her. She's unable to answer, but I can feel the lump in her throat. She's never done this before and frankly, neither have I, but the wine, the attention of the men in the restaurant, and her confession have made me horny and curious. I need to be touched, even if I do it myself. And, exhibitionist that I am, I want to be watched.

I lift my dress. Underneath I am wearing stay-up stockings. I circle my clit with my finger, beckoning her forward. First with my eyes and then, "Nathalie," I beg, my throat as thick and swollen as my cunt. She touches me, tentatively, her fingers brushing my hard clit. I moan and close my eyes, then will them open. I want to see her desire, her curiosity, as she sinks her fingers into me. Does she know that I've been wet all evening, willing her to do this? Does she know how many times my finger circled my clit at dinner, my eyes creamy not from candlelight but the look down the long slide toward orgasm? Her face is closed to my scrutiny.

I want her to sink her face into my pussy and I tell her. But she is hesitant. She has not yet found the audacity of desire. I won't push her yet, although I am eager to have her mouth on my clit, her tongue deep inside of me. I can feel an orgasm barreling down my body. I want to listen to my screams echo off the canyons made by the buildings. I want windows wide open and neighbors' heads thrust out, an audience to my cries. I reach out to touch her; she backs away, but not before I have cupped my hand between her legs. Her cunt beneath her dress is swollen and ripe. She is as wet as I am and I wonder if she stroked herself in the bathroom, bringing herself just to the brink of orgasm. Nervous, she wiggles her hips from my slender hand but not before I have pushed the front of her dress, light armor which only barely shields her naked cunt from my hand, into her. Her juices leave an imprint on the thin fabric. I suggest a cab, but they are difficult to find at this time of night and we begin to walk. She sucks on her fingers, tasting me for the first time, and I play with my nipple, hard through my dress, as she watches me, unable to look away. I tell her I want her tongue on me, rough and strong. I can see that her defenses are beginning to drop and beneath her dress her nipples are as tight as mine. At the corner, a taxi with its off-duty sign slows down for a red light and I step down into the curb . . .

☙❧

I roll my window down reluctantly. Instantly I know these two girls are drunk; their eyes are too bright. But I'm going uptown anyway and I figure I might as well make a decent fare off of it. They scramble in the back and give me two addresses.

It's late and I'm tired and I'm gunning for home and a few clicks across the porn channels before I pass out, my spent cock in my hand. The thought is enticing and I drive fast. It's strangely quiet in the backseat. And then I catch moaning. Damn, I think, two drunk girls. That's all I need, one of them sick in the backseat and an extra half hour while I have to clean it out, not to mention a little something less in my paycheck when they've got to take the whole car in for a shampoo. I glance up at the rearview mirror to check the backseat. The dark-haired girl, in a thin dress, coat off her shoulder, lies against one window, eyes half-mast, her hand lazily circling her nipple. The moans are coming from her mouth. I slow down, my cock suddenly hard and pulsing, straining to catch a glimpse of the other girl. I find her blonde head bobbing up and down, buried between the legs of the dark-haired one. I can't really see what's going on but I begin to guess, my imagination racing, as the dark-haired girl's moans direct her friend's movements. I raise my eyes and we catch each other for a brief moment in the mirror before she turns away. She must know I'm watching, listening, because she keeps looking up, her eyes seeking mine. I strain to catch her words as she begins narrating, her voice thick with lust. Lick me, suck my clit, she says. She pulls her dress down a little further and her nipple, pink and taut, springs free. Oh, a little sigh escapes from my mouth. I want my mouth on that nipple, to circle it with my tongue and bite on it and feel her clit jump against my swollen cock. Oh, yes, she moans, and every promise leaps out from her eyes. I'm imagining her, slick and tight, riding my cock. The cab slows as I stroke myself, pumping my cock in my fist, trying to keep my mind on the road. A red light up ahead brings my eyes back to the road. My cock throbs in my fist and it is all I can do to concentrate on driving. The light is green too quickly and I wish for another excuse to stop so I can use my other hand to pull at my balls, stretching the skin tightly over my cock. I search the rearview mirror for the black eyes of the dark-haired girl.

෴

The cabdriver agrees to take us both uptown with a first stop at my house and then on to Nathalie's and we scramble into the back. I have a goal that doesn't involve a second stop but I don't argue when Nathalie pipes in with her address. I get in first and Nathalie hangs back for a moment, as shy and eager as the new girl in school who dreams of being a cheerleader, before she scoots in beside me. Then she slams the door and by the time she has settled herself beside me I've pulled my skirt up and have begun playing with myself in earnest, my head leaning against the window, one hand manipulating my clit, the other hand pulling my nipples into hard points. For a moment, Nathalie can only watch in fascination, her mouth open. And then I see her tongue, moving quickly back and forth against her front teeth, debating. I push back the lips of my pussy, my clit swollen and red between them, as an offering.

"Please . . . ," my voice begs.

I want her kneeling between my legs, sucking at my clit so badly that I almost begin to weep. I know that I could bring myself to orgasm quickly. I also know how unsatisfying that would be.

"What do I . . ." Nathalie's voice falters, confused, worried about what to do in this unfamiliar, familiar territory.

I plunge my fingers into my cunt, hitting my G-spot, and for a moment there is nothing but my cunt, my fingers. I will myself reluctantly back to the present, back to the goal. My fingers are luminescent with my own juice and I reach over slipping them into Nathalie. Her hips press into my hand. She looks at me, then down at my fingers moving in and out of her cunt and then back at me and I can see the astonishment on her face. Nothing in her experience has prepared her for this, not Mark, three nights a week, not Joe, the best sex ever, not even Ian, the one-night stand who introduced her to anal sex. Her hips move in circles and her clit retreats and I can feel, from the way her muscles tighten, how fast her orgasm is building. But I don't want her to come just yet. That will be later, when I have time to explore her, tease her, stretched out on my bed. Right now, I want to pull her to the edge of desire, the place where all of her inhibitions disappear and there is nothing but body and want and need and hunger. She grabs my retreating hand and forces my fingers to her mouth, sucking each one slowly, telling me in silent language how much she wants me. I moan, pulsing in time to the motion of her mouth. With her other hand she begins to explore me, first tentatively, then more insistently, her fingers parting my pubic hair, pulling at the curls. Her head bends forward to examine me and I can feel her hot breath and I rise to meet her mouth. I groan, my eyes rising and briefly meet the eyes of the cabdriver in the rearview mirror. His eyes are large and dark and I recognize the look in them and know that his cock is hard in his fist. Another moan escapes my lips. Nathalie's tongue darts out, hard and pointy, and laps at my cunt, following my finger's lead, my pleas. My moans give her courage and she rakes at my clit with her teeth, pulling the lips down, her tongue exploring the crevices, my clit in her mouth being sucked like a small cock. She teases me, stopping and starting, knowing the rhythms of my cunt as she knows her own. I break the gaze of the cabdriver and watch Nathalie's movements intently as she inserts two fingers into me and I begin the slide into orgasm. I have only come like this a few times in my life, hovering between life and death, and when the explosions have ended, I pull Nathalie's head up and kiss her on the lips, tasting myself on her. When the cab jerks suddenly, I know that our driver has not been far behind . . .

⤳⤶

I try to keep focused on the road, periodically glancing into the backseat where the dark-haired girl has locked her gaze in mine. My hand moves with her friend's head bobbing up and down and I know how warm and wet that blonde's mouth would be, wrapped around my cock. The dark-haired girl looks away and I'm frantic, trying to catch her eye. My rhythm falters for a moment. But the growing series of moans from the backseat is a command my cock cannot resist. My hips buck upward, my foot jerking on the gas, and I empty myself deep into my hand, the dark-haired girl's screams a call that pulls my orgasm from me in violent spasms as I turn the corner to the first stop. . . .

∞∞

"Just below the streetlamp," I tell the driver, "then you can take her . . ."

Nathalie interrupts me before I have a chance to finish.

"No second stop," she says.

I look over at her as she springs out of the cab, already halfway up the steps to my apartment, and then I lean forward to check the fare. The driver and I catch each other's faces in the light, my mouth slick with my own juice, and then he catches my eye and an understanding passes between us. I reach into my wallet and press a bill into his hand. He closes my fingers around the crisp currency.

"My pleasure," he says.

The wine whispers the Sinatra lyric to me as I scramble up the steps. Nathalie pulls me to her, reaching over to suck on my earlobe. Then the door to my apartment clicks open and we are inside.

– 2 –

Scary Date

Trish Kelly

I met this girl at a party. She was short and retro-cute in a polyester A-line dress, Mary Janes, and white kneesocks. She had a way of talking that was almost too casual.

She knew who I was and wanted in on the action.

"Trish Kelly, if I made out with you, would you write about me in your magazine?" It was more a request than a concern. I told her that I usually only write about things that scare me, but I gave her my card anyway.

She called the following weekend and invited me to a screening of *Scream 2* at the discount cinemas.

Well, she was trying, and even though I have a rep for being an ultra-busy ultra-femme, I didn't have any other plans, so I went.

I put the bag of popcorn between my legs. I sucked the straw in my soft drink seductively. I leaned over to ask questions about the very complicated plot. The retro-cute girl ignored everything! When she managed to finish off the popcorn without so much as a hand brushing, I got quite pissed off. I should have known this would be a lame date when she said she didn't like to sit at the back.

On top of all this, Retro Girl made me promise to stay until the credits finished. She sat slurping her cola. "Pretty scary, huh?" she droned without even looking at me. We were the last people out of the theater and even the concession crew had gone home.

Published by The Haworth Press, Inc., 2006. All rights reserved.
doi:10.1300/5328_03

I had to use the bathroom and asked her to hold my jacket while I "powdered my nose."

In the bathroom, I reapplied my Outrageous Red lipstick, pouting my lips into the mirror. "What a fucking waste!" I muttered as I readjusted my breasts in the cups of my bustier.

I began my return to the hall where I'd left my lame date. She was gone. Annoyed, I made an attempt to crane my neck enough to see down the hall without actually moving.

From the opposite direction, I heard a quiet, but distinct "Boo."

I turned, my mouth open in something between shock and disgust, ready to explain that when I'd said she'd have to scare me, I was talking about a very sophisticated, intellectual scare.

But there was no time.

She shoved her whole fist into my mouth, pushed me backward through the door, and up against the sink.

"Now shut up," she ordered, her hand flying out of my mouth and hiking up her skirt. She tucked the front of her skirt into the harness of her strap-on. It was shaped like a porpoise, with only a small fin on top. She pressed her body hard against me, the sink cold against my thighs.

Her hands slid up my sides and pulled on the sides of my bustier. She pressed her body harder against me, and I had to grab the sink for leverage, my back arching and my pelvis bracing against hers.

She reached into the cups of my bustier. Her hands were hot little vice grips.

"There's a bottle of lube in my backpack over there," she breathed into my ear. "You are to get it out and lubricate my cock," she instructed, "then I'm going to fuck you in the stall." She released me and wandered to the stall.

I opened her pack and found a one-liter size of Probe. There were also vinyl restraints, a whip, and plain, old-fashioned rope.

"Don't touch anything else. Just get in here."

She opened the stall door and pulled me in, slamming the door shut with the weight of our bodies.

"But what if someone comes in?" I said rather weakly.

"The cleaning lady does the men's first. She won't be here for a while." Her hands went up my bare thighs and under my dress.

"No underwear. Figures," she muttered.

She opened the lube with her teeth and told me to hold out my hand. "Now, lubricate my cock."

I slid my hands up and down her porpoise, pushing it hard against her pubic bone.

She slid the lubed cock up my skirt and traced the lips of my cunt, zeroing in on my clit.

"You're not wet," she lied. She rubbed the length of the latex between my legs. She sat down on the toilet, pulling me toward her, grabbing me around the waist with one arm, while the other hand rubbed my cunt so hard my legs stopped working. Just when I was about to come, I heard a faint whistling from the hallway.

"Oh, yeah, she's right on schedule. We'd better hurry." She pulled me down on her cock.

"Hello, anybody in there?" the woman sang from the door.

"Just be quiet," my date instructed. "Yes ma'am, I'm having a little case of the upset stomach. I'll be out in a minute."

She pushed harder, and I moaned louder. She kissed me, swallowing each of my moans, simultaneously producing a constipated grunt for the benefit of the cleaning lady.

As I came, I reached behind my date, and flushed the toilet. She gave a huge sigh, and pushed me off her. I pulled down my skirt, and we exited the stall.

"Pick up my bag," she instructed.

"What?" I asked, not quite following.

"The bag over there."

"Oh, yeah, I guess we didn't get to use all that stuff," I said.

"Yeah, that's right," she said as she opened the door for the cleaning lady's cart, "but you've never taken SkyTrain with me before."

− 3 −

Diary of a Lost Girl, Part 1

Lori Selke

They all have their theories—the moralists, the social workers, the police, the politicians. They all have their lessons to be learned from my example. I make a very instructive lesson of the moral lassitude of youth, the unfortunate circumstances of women in this age, or whatever social ill you care to illustrate with the lurid details of my plight. Everyone has a story to tell of me, of my fall.

Everyone has their own version of the events that led to my current state.

It is time to hear mine.

My name is Lotte Gottingen. I am a fallen woman.

Barely a woman, I blush to admit, and unfamiliar with the rules and conventions of normal, respectable adulthood. Perhaps it is better to call me . . . a lost girl.

☙❧

It began with the housekeeper.

Her name was Rosa, and she was not much older than I was, a year or two maybe. She was hired by my widowed father to take care of the household, and she was very good at her job. Her very presence brightened our home. She was plump, rosy cheeked, plain but winsome, and affectionate. She was also quite hardworking. My father was nearing retirement, working only part-time at the accountancy

Published by The Haworth Press, Inc., 2006. All rights reserved.
doi:10.1300/5328_04

firm he'd founded, and resting his aging frame on the cushions of our
parlor room the rest of the week.

Motherless, I used to crawl into Rosa's narrow bed each night for
the comfort and warmth her ample body provided. We would lie together chastely, her arms around my shoulders. She would hum lulla-
bies in my ear. Sometimes she would let me undo her long, honey hair
and brush it out thoroughly before tying it into a simple braid for the
night. She treated me not so much like a surrogate daughter as like a
younger sister.

What I did not know then was that my father, in contrast, used her
much like he would have a wife.

What I do remember is my father appearing one night in the shadowed doorway as I lay curled in Rosa's arms. Rosa sat upright in the
bed. "What are you doing here?" she whispered to my father as she
hugged me to her breast.

My father said nothing, only stared at us both. I did not understand
the look in his eye.

"Lotte," she said in a curiously strangled voice, "go back to your
bed. This instant." Her hands, which a moment before had been caressing me, pushed me sternly out of my berth.

"Lock your door behind you, and stay put. You're not being punished," she added, her voice losing all iron. "Just, please. I will come to
you later and tuck you in. Be a good girl, a big girl for me."

My father's eyes smoldered with an emotion unfamiliar to me as I
passed.

It took me a week to gather the courage to ask Rosa what had happened on that night. When I did, she stiffened and tried to push me
away.

"I think it is best that you learn to sleep alone now," she said.
"You're almost grown-up. I shouldn't baby you. You'll become
spoiled."

Instead of acceding to her command, however, I curled up even
more tightly against her. "Please, Rosa, tell me. Why did father want
to see you? Why did you have to send me away?" I rolled over and
looked her in the eye; I tried to look stern, imperious, commanding. I
was the closest thing our little home had to a Mistress of the House-

hold, I told myself. In the absence of my mother, it was I who should command. "Tell me about it this instant."

Rosa stared at me for a moment in defiance, but a moment later her features softened. Something remained in her eyes, however, a spark or a glint, like a blade. I had never seen her eyes so hard before.

"You want to know what your father does with me, late at night? Or during the day, when you are away at school? You want to know my real purpose in this household, do you? Very well. You are old enough to know." She smoothed her plain gray skirt. "I am your father's whore."

I was dumbfounded. I wasn't even sure what the word she'd used meant.

Rosa wasn't looking at me anymore; her eyes had gone wild, and she stared past my shoulder, toward the door of her room. "Yes, that's right," she continued in a hysterical tone. "That he pays me to do the housework is only a cover. If only I'd known that when I entered his employment, I would have asked for a higher wage." Rosa laughed, a broken sound. She turned to me, eyes afire. "Let me show you what your father does to me, whenever he gets a chance at me alone. Then you will understand. That's what you want to know, isn't it?"

"Y-Yes," I stuttered.

Instantly, she leaped upon me, pinning me to the mattress, my hands above my head, clasped in her too-cruel grip. "What are you doing?" I cried.

"Yes, I'll show you what your father was doing with me," Rosa replied, and pushed my nightgown up to my waist.

After such a savage beginning, however, she turned strangely gentle. She spent a great deal of time stroking the white skin of my thighs, her hand never straying to my more intimate parts, not yet. She would alternate such caresses with a touch along my neck, a kiss upon my shoulder, and all sorts of affectionate gestures that soon had my skin afire, my nerves primed.

"Does it feel good?" she asked. I nodded. Her mouth formed a strange sort of smile. "It feels good when your father touches me like this, too," she said.

Her hand strayed to my breast. For a long moment, she merely drew her fingertips along the curve and swell to be found there, nothing more. But presently, her hand found my nipple; then, her mouth. I gasped as she sucked at it through the thin cloth of my silk nightgown, the nightgown my father had given to me on my most recent birthday. Rosa chuckled a little. "Yes, it's very nice, isn't it?" she murmured, hardly lifting her head to speak. I nodded, breathless.

"This is just the beginning," she said.

Soon her hand was worming into the cleft between my legs, and my own hand was covering my mouth to stifle the gasps I would otherwise have uttered. "Does it feel good?" Rosa kept asking as she pressed the heel of her hand against my mons, her mouth pouring kisses upon my neck and shoulder, behind my ear and on my cheek.

"Yes, yes, it feels marvelous," I finally cried. "Please, I am on fire!"

And I was, every nerve aflame, craving the merest brush of her fingertips along my skin. But Rosa's touches had grown progressively rougher. She had found my moistness and was spreading it along my nether lips, making me shiver with every stroke. My hips rose to meet her hand; my mouth opened in a wordless sigh. My knees parted. I welcomed her touch, her tender ministrations. How I adored them!

She lavished me with kisses, which kindled sensations I had never before known. My flesh unfurled beneath her hands, her mouth. I blossomed into a woman that very moment, or so it seemed.

And when I cried out in ecstasy, and bucked my body in the throes of pleasure, and my innermost moisture spilled out onto her hand, I looked into Rosa's fevered eyes with a new sort of love. The gaze she returned me mingled fear, shame, and exhilaration.

She lifted her hand to stroke my cheek; it was streaked in blood. When I looked at it quizzically, she smeared the stuff upon my lips, where it tightened as it dried. "Your virgin blood," she whispered. "I have taken your maidenhood, it seems."

I did not know it then, but that moment marked the beginning of my fall. Such a delicious moment, like the first bite of Eve's fruit.

I tasted myself, my blood and that other flavor, unfamiliar and yet unmistakably my own. I licked my lips clean, and then I kissed Rosa, yearning suddenly to taste her as well. Would her womanly savor taste the same as mine, or would she have her own sweetness?

It was as if a demon had possessed me. What else could explain my boldness? For now I was the aggressor, pushing Rosa down onto the thin mattress, pushing her nightgown up to bunch against her hips, spreading her plump thighs and peering at her womanly parts. I explored their pink furls first with fingers, then with tongue; I found her taste to be muskier than mine. I found the nub at the crest of her vulva that, when I flicked it with my tongue, caused Rosa to convulse in a spasm of pleasure. I found the cleft that was the source of her musky fluid. I even ventured a tentative lick or two near her other hole. Before long, I was buried to my chin in Rosa's glorious scent, her tender flesh, her moistness. She urged me on in husky tones, directing my tongue, my fingers, until she could speak no more, only howl her pleasure.

It was hours later when we finally collapsed, exhausted, into each other's arms. "You are a wanton," Rosa whispered in my ear. "An untamed creature. You are a wild thing, masquerading as tame. But you will not be able to keep this charade for long. You are no one's pet, destined to be no one's wife, or even mistress." She lifted her head and stared into my eyes. "I pity and fear you," she said. "And I also fear for you." She cradled me and kissed my hair, murmuring soft adorations to me.

As the first light of dawn crept through the bedroom window, I fell asleep cradled in my first lover's arms.

She would not be the last.

– 4 –

Poseidon's Paradise

Kiki Veronika

She swam over to near where I was standing, sipping my complimentary cosmopolitan, and waved at me. Her long, thin arm moved slowly and surreally through the water that encased her. I watched as she slid her hand down, over her pearly seashell bikini top and onto the hologrammatic material that began below her belly button and played chromatic tricks on the eye all the way down to the tail end. The hot pink-rimmed goggles that were suctioned tightly to her eyes allowed her to observe me watching her, and I wondered if through the thick Plexiglas she could see my cheeks turn a hue that matched her eyewear. She was hot. For a mermaid.

The bar was called Poseidon's Paradise. It was a newcomer in the big city. Inspired by the media hype it had been receiving, I had wanted to check it out for quite some weeks, but the opportunity had not presented itself. Until that night, that is. Complete with free cocktails and prime networking opportunities, the literary magazine launch party was the perfect chance for me to explore the scene and, hopefully, meet some people who could publish my creative pieces. Upon entering the roomy bar, I had been immediately captivated by the enormous fish tank that was essentially the entire wall behind the bar. It must have measured 20' by 40', or something close anyway. Gleaming water surrounded the usual fish tank adornments, including pink-and-blue rocks, plant life, and the cliché treasure chest—

Published by The Haworth Press, Inc., 2006. All rights reserved.
doi:10.1300/5328_05

only here, they were huge, life-size. And, slithering between the crevices of the leafy greens, circling the golden coins, and rising and plunging in rhythmic motion was the most beautiful creature I had ever seen. Long jet-black hair fanned out around her pale face and lent even deeper tone to her shocking evergreen eyes. The reviewers hadn't lied; this *was* an aquatic wonderland.

I wasn't sure whether to wave back at her. The other patrons seemed either oblivious to the waving mermaid or too image conscious to acknowledge how cool it was to be in a bar that had a life-size fish tank. I decided to play it cool and looked away from her, scanning the room for the friend I was supposed to meet, a fellow desperate freelancer. "Kiki!" I heard behind me.

"Oh there you are." Taylor greeted me with a hug. "You look great," I said. And she did. Her shoulder-length chestnut hair was pinned half up and fixed with a sparkly clip. A fitting yellow flower-print dress held her ample breasts close to her body, and espadrilles completed the look. I suddenly felt frumpy in the dress-over-jeans, Doc Marten-clad look I'd created for the evening. My waist-length blonde hair was parted in the middle and fell over my shoulders, creating a hippie-chic effect that now seemed very *un*chic at this bar. I wished I were wearing a skimpy bandeau top, maybe with a shimmer pattern that would match the mermaid's fins . . .

"Wow, this is fantastic," Taylor said, moving her head to the music. They were playing "Age of Aquarius."

"I know, look at that mermaid!"

Taylor glanced up briefly. "Yeah, but look at those hot guys!" She was boy crazy. "I'm gonna get another drink," she announced. I noticed that she had already drained her first cosmopolitan. Good. For a very straight girl by day, she could certainly become very gay when a few cocktails kicked in. Her boyfriend didn't mind that we sometimes made out, and I'd already been through getting my heart crushed by so many "sorry, but I'm straight" girls that I wasn't emotionally invested, just terribly physically attracted. Taylor walked to an empty space at the bar, where she was approached by an attractive man. No surprise for her. Great. I would be on my own for the evening.

I sipped the sweet liquor and looked back up at the tank. The mermaid was still looking at me. I smiled. She smiled, and small bubbles escaped from her lips and rose to the surface of the water as she mouthed something that I couldn't discern. I had never been a good lip-reader, and she was underwater, making it even more difficult to decipher. I mouthed back, "What?" conscious that I probably looked foolish to the patrons around me. She said whatever it was again, but I was as clueless as before. Confused and still awed by her aquatic sexiness, I fingered my long, golden locks and smiled shyly. The seashells covered her nipples but not much else, and I could see the water dash over her large, smooth breasts as she swam away.

Taylor approached me, stumbling a little. "I got his number," she slurred, "and he says he may be able to publish me." In a rush of hormonal charge undoubtedly fueled by the goddess in the tank, I pulled Taylor close to me and kissed her. Her mouth tasted like candy apple, and her tongue felt warm and capable as it swirled around mine. It was a long kiss. She pulled away first. "You're hot, Kiki." A guy tapped her on the shoulder.

"I overheard you talking with my colleague," he addressed her, as if I wasn't there, as if I hadn't just had my tongue in her mouth, "and I'd like to learn more about your work." Taylor's eyes brightened. It was no use. I just wasn't stacking up to hot male editors tonight. I turned and walked toward the corner of the room, where two empty sofas awaited. The oceanic atmosphere was further enhanced by the lighting, as images of bubbles and waves played upon the walls and furniture throughout the room. This place seemed too sexy for a business event. Or maybe I was just feeling horny. I surveyed the sofas, deciding which would give me the best view of the room, when I heard a voice behind me.

"Come sit with me." I turned to face a pair of enrapturing green eyes, eyes that I knew.

"You're the mermaid!" I must have sounded like a child who just met a costumed Mickey Mouse at Disneyland. "I mean, uh, hi."

She laughed, softly, and I almost expected to see bubbles arise from her lips. They didn't, of course, but she did still manage to take my breath away. "Over here." She took my hand in hers and pulled me toward a small loveseat set aside from the other seating and almost completely secluded from the rest of the room. I could feel the puckered ridges in her fingertips, evidence of her immersion in water for so long. We sat. She was clad now in a simple black knee-length dress, strappy black heels having replaced the shiny fins. Her hair was still wet and was combed straight back, behind her ears. The ends, which fell near her waist, sprinkled the sofa with droplets of water in an almost metric beat. Intimidated by her gaze, I looked down, but my eyes fell on her breasts, and I quickly looked up again, embarrassed.

"Um, aren't you supposed to be . . . swimming?" I asked awkwardly.

She laughed softly again. Her laugh was like cotton candy—sweet, light, and dissolving into the air like the puffy strands did on the tongue. "Mermaids get breaks too, you know."

I smiled. "You're beautiful," I said, my voice cracking a little. My bell-bottoms and Docs felt clumsy in contrast with her elegant ensemble. She was older than me, perhaps thirty-five to my twenty-five, but there was a sweet innocence about her that made me want to take care of her. Or something.

"It should be you in that tank, with this gorgeous hair." She ran her fingers down through my yellow strands. "You look just like an angel." I swallowed. I certainly didn't feel like one. I felt like sliding my hand onto her knee, under the hemline of her dress, and up, up, up, to . . . Her words cut into my thoughts. "I saw you kissing that woman. Is she your girlfriend?"

For a moment I was confused. "Oh, Taylor," I said, smiling. "No, she's just my friend. I mean, I like to kiss her, but she likes boys. I think guys are great and all, but I'm just more attracted to, I mean—" She put her finger to my lips. I inhaled chlorine and wanted desperately to taste it too but thought better of it. I must have sounded like an idiot, rambling on like that. I was sure she'd walk away.

"Then your friend won't mind if I do this." She put her hands on either side of my face and drew me toward her. She wasn't walking away. I didn't even get to complete the thought, *Oh my god, she's going to kiss me,* before her mouth was on mine, her lips suctioned over mine like her goggles had been over her eyes, her tongue probing the far reaches of my mouth like a diver on the search for a buried treasure. Our tongues encircled, my hot mouth warming her cooler one, and I felt a shockwave of heated attraction surge through my body. We pulled away and gazed at each other. I reached up to touch her hair and was surprised to feel for myself the cool, drenched strands even though I knew she'd been in the amplified tank only moments earlier.

"Your hair's so wet." I stated the obvious, for lack of anything sexier to say. She leaned in again, her cleavage beckoning me to explore what treasures lay buried in that depth.

"And that's not all that is," she whispered. I could overlook the trite play on words that sounded more like something you'd read in bad erotica than something that should actually be uttered in the moment, as I was focused more on what she was implying. I felt suddenly sizzling hot. Who cared if I was wearing a babydoll dress? I had made a mermaid wet. I was overtaken with lust.

"Show me," I returned. It was no challenge to begin the journey up her thigh with my hand, as I'd already practiced it in my head. I saw her shut her eyes as I did so. The flickering oceanic lights danced on her face. Her hands tensed up into small fists at her sides. I slid my hand into the crevice in her thighs, and she opened her legs for me. I reached up to where I knew her sweet wetness would be, anticipating that I'd pull aside her panties and . . . But she was wearing no panties. My probing fingers met with only a sea of moisture, and she was even wetter than I could have imagined. "Wow," I whispered.

She looked at me almost helplessly, and I began to circle my finger around her clit, using her moisture to stimulate her more. I could feel that her pussy was entirely shaved, which made my task—and probably her own of donning a skintight mermaid suit daily—much easier. She moaned. I moved my fingers rhythmically, making both of us hotter as I did so, and I pressed my body up alongside hers, until my mouth was close to her ear. "You are fucking stunning, do you know that?" She moaned again. "I said, do you know that?"

She turned her head to look at me. "I know that you are stunning fucking," she said, smiling coyly. "I know that I've wanted you since I saw you standing there at the bar, you sweet angel. When I saw you kiss that girl, I thought I might have a chance." Jesus Christ. *She* wanted *me*. Life blew my mind sometimes. My confidence level soared.

"You were right," I whispered into her ear, sliding a finger of my other hand into her mouth. Her red lips wasted no time in closing around it and sucking. Hard. "Except that I'm no angel." I could tell she smiled because her teeth brushed my finger and bit down a little. "That's nice," I said. "Bite on me." With another coy sidelong glance, she took two of my fingers in her mouth and played with them, with her tongue and her teeth. I gave her no warning and impulsively shoved two of my fingers inside her cunt. She gave a small cry and bit down hard on my fingers. "That's it, baby," I said, "take it." I coaxed her all the way back on the couch and lifted one of my legs over both of hers, straddling her. Now I was thankful that I'd worn jeans and not a confining skirt. I removed my sore fingers from her mouth and replaced them with my own mouth. We kissed deeply as I fucked her deep and hard. I shifted to allow her to spread her legs wider for me. Her breasts pressed and rubbed against my own chest, both our nipples hard and seemingly magnetically connected through the fabrics of our tops. When I could feel her tensing up, close to climaxing, I licked her earlobe and said softly, "I got to see you all wet in that tank, and now I get to feel you all wet here." Okay, so now I was using the cliché, but it still sounded hot, and she responded with a louder moan. "Come for me, sweetheart." As I said it, her body convulsed, and I could feel her constricting inside as a flood of her juices poured out over my hand. "That's good." Her head dropped back, and her breath came in gasps. I removed my hand and sucked on my fingers. Now my own fingers were puckered from moisture. I collapsed on top of her, and our fingers found each other's and interlaced on the velvet upholstery. The music and crowd in the background were barely audible above our breathing.

Finally, she lifted her head and laughed that sticky-sweet laugh again. "I'm glad you agreed. I wasn't sure."

"What?" I asked, confused.

She frowned. "In the tank before, when I mouthed to you 'I want you.' You understood."

Not letting on that this hadn't been a response to her request, but, rather, pure sexual impulse, I played it cool. "Oh, that. Yeah, you can say I wanted you. Hey, what's your name, anyway? That might have been useful about five minutes ago." I was trying to go for a little light humor in order to prevent the awkwardness that could ensue any minute now.

"Ariel," she said, smiling somewhat mischievously. "And now, my dear, I have to return to work. Break's probably been over for a while now. . . ."

And it was over as quickly and mystically as it had began. I took my cue to climb off her. She stood up to face me. She kissed me and was off, back toward the bar area, behind which her costume room likely lay. The taste of chlorine lingered in my mouth. As I stood in a daze, I could see Taylor approaching me. "Kiki! Oh wow, I made so many great contacts, this party was the *best*. Did you have fun?"

I blinked and looked at her. "Um, yeah. You can say that. Actually, I met that mermaid. You know, from the tank. Her name's Ariel. We fooled around a little."

Taylor burst out laughing. "*Ariel?!* As in *The Little Mermaid?* Yeah, right. Very funny, Kiki. She was hot and all, but can you imagine if she actually came out of the tank and hooked up with you? That would be, like, incredible. It would make a hot story, anyway."

I opened my mouth to respond but stopped. *Ariel.* Okay, so it was either a big coincidence or the girl had bullshitted me. But either way, it *had* happened. Hadn't it? It had been so surreal, but I knew I wasn't drunk, and I was certainly not crazy. Or was I?

"Hey, c'mere." Taylor impulsively pulled me to her and kissed me, slipping her tongue into my mouth. Distracted by "Ariel," I'd forgotten to capitalize upon her even more inebriated state. Maybe tonight had even more potential. I kissed her harder, thinking about leaving the bar with her, going back to my place, maybe having one last nightcap, and . . . Abruptly, she pulled away and looked at me in disbelief. "Kiki—is that . . . *chlorine?*"

I smiled.

The Dressing Room

Tara Alton

The planets had to be seriously out of alignment or there had to be some tropical, sticky fungus growing on the wheels of fate, because not once in all my twenty-five years have I had this much bad luck in one morning. To start the day off, I had gotten a low-calorie cornflake stuck up inside the back of my nasal passage for the most unpleasant five minutes of my life. I won't go into how the cornflake got up there in the first place, but not only did I wake up my neighbors trying to get it out, but also I woke up my roommate, Cheryl, the stewardess to the stars, or so she liked to call herself. Currently, she was dating a female Elvis impersonator in Vegas, which was an all-time personal high for her.

I wished I had that brilliant a career, but I worked as a receptionist at Michigan Brick and Panel, and unlike Cheryl, I wasn't dating anyone even remotely famous. I was dating Marla, a self-proclaimed tomboy in her early forties who owned a riding stable. We had met because she used Michigan Brick and Panel to remodel some of her buildings.

Marla had told me later she asked me out because I was so girlie and I was easy to talk to, but to me it seemed like we never talked about much. In the beginning, there were some sparks between us, but that was before she became so absorbed with her new stable that could accommodate twenty warm-blood horses for training. I used to

Published by The Haworth Press, Inc., 2006. All rights reserved.
doi:10.1300/5328_06

love her white T-shirts and Levi button-fly jeans. I was even more impressed with her aura of confidence and can-do attitude. Even though she never wore makeup and favored men's boxer shorts, she knew she was a woman. It was thrilling to know I could still be as feminine as I wanted to be and still be attracted to her. In addition, I loved the whole cowgirl rustic thing. As a young girl, I used to have vivid fantasies of old-west-type cowgirls rescuing me as a damsel-in-distress dance hall girl.

Lately though, there hadn't been much of anything between us. There were no lingering kisses, cuddles, or sweetly whispered words. I spent a lot of nights at home alone with my collection of sex toys. All of which I had given cute names like childhood stuffed animals, like Fluffy, Alice, and Muffin, which Marla said was extremely immature of me, so I just kept it to myself, and when she asked me what I had been up to, I just told her I had been waxing my legs or exfoliating.

The times I did see her, I felt like she was using me more like a perfect dress up doll during the day and a blow up doll at night than a real person. I wasn't sure if I would even be still dating her if I didn't owe her the money. Without my asking, she had paid off my Darcy Business School loan. I wished she hadn't done that. The power shift had become a sticky issue for me, and I wanted to get back to what we once had. I wanted to rekindle the romance if we were going to remain together. Tonight we were supposed to go out to dinner to talk, and I was even going to pick out the restaurant for a change.

That was why I wanted things to go well today, but right after I recovered from the cornflake, I chipped a nail and my manicurist, the only woman I trusted with my fragile nails, was on vacation in Jamaica.

Then I realized I didn't have any clean sexy underwear to wear tonight, and I didn't have enough time to do a load of laundry, drive to the mall to pay an overdue bill, and get to work on time. Therefore, I decided to stop by The Pink Bow in the mall to buy a new thong, because if things went well, I didn't think Marla would approve of the faded-cotton granny panties I was currently sporting.

I loved The Pink Bow. It carried everything from mild to wild, and the atmosphere was made for browsing with its rich velvet curtains, antiques in the corners, and the faux fireplace in the rear. I loved the deep maroon walls with the gold-framed paintings with scenes of Paris and pretty girls in bows. Not only did they sell silk corsets and peignoir sets, but they also offered chemises and gowns in every fabric and color of the rainbow.

This time though, I was actually trying on the underwear instead of just assuming it fit, because the last time I bought something expensive here, it didn't fit me. I know I wasn't supposed to be trying them on, but a girl only has so much money to spend.

As I was trying on a sassy mesh thong in oasis blue featuring a mesh back and a slightly scalloped front with a decorative bow at the center front, I turned and noticed something horrible in the mirror. There was a huge pimple on my ass! It was one of those blemishes you had no idea was there until you spotted it and then it hurt like hell because you acknowledged it. I had to get rid of it.

I spun around, trying to get a grip on the little white-headed monster, when suddenly I slipped. My right foot kicked my granny panties and my bias-cut miniskirt outside the dressing room. Damn slippery parquet floor! They slid across it as if it was ice. How was I supposed to get them? I couldn't parade into the middle of the store wearing only a thong and a fitted white cotton shirt could I? I couldn't cry for help either because I wasn't supposed to be trying on the thongs in the first place. Thank goodness, the sales clerks were out front, working on an amateur fashion show for tonight.

Peering out of the dressing room door, I scanned the store for maybe a sympathetic customer who might help me when I noticed a lone young woman near my age sitting in a chair, looking bored.

"Psst," I said.

She turned and focused on me. She had the most amazing doe-shaped eyes.

I pointed to my stuff on the floor.

"Can you get those for me?" I asked, sweetly with a smile.

Unfolding her legs, she got up, sauntered over to them and picked them up. She was tall with shoulder-length dark hair, perfectly arched eyebrows, rosy apple cheeks, and a distinguished nose. Although she was a little flat chested, her body moved with a languid grace. She wore a wispy shoulder-tie dress that looked to be made of silk and a pair of sexy high-heeled sandals. A tiny butterfly barrette pinned her bangs away from her face.

Please don't let this well-groomed girl unravel my underwear and see the granny panties, I prayed.

Slowly, she walked toward me, carrying them. Could she walk any slower? The moment she was within reach, I tried to grab them away from her, but she playfully didn't let go, so I grabbed her arm instead and pulled her inside the dressing room with me.

The door shut behind us. We looked at each other. Then her gaze traveled down the length of my body to the blue oasis thong, where it lingered. Titillated, I felt gooseflesh travel over my body. This was bad. I hated it when my body betrayed me. I had told myself a long time ago, I was going to stick with tomboys because they were less complicated. It was bad enough putting up with my own obsessions over makeup, shoes, and fashion magazines, but sometimes I couldn't deny that I liked it when I brushed up against a gorgeous woman in a flirty skirt.

I blushed furiously and tried to take back my stuff. She held on, her eyes twinkling.

"Don't you have anything better to do?" I asked.

She let go. My hand snapped back, my granny panties coming unfurled. Quickly, I rolled them back up, but she still saw them.

"Not really," she said. "I've been waiting for my friend for over an hour to finish setting up the fashion show out front, and it doesn't look like he's going to wrap it up any time soon."

"Oh," I said.

"It's always about work with him," she said. "There is never any time for me."

I nodded.

"That sounds like someone I know," I said. "She's a real workaholic control freak."

Her eyes gleamed as if I had hit the nail right on the head.

"Don't you hate that," she said. "It's like they can never have any fun, and then if you do something they don't like, you hear about it forever."

"I know," I said. "I once wore this really old disgusting pair of jeans to go horseback riding, and she nearly flipped. I heard about it afterward for weeks."

Suddenly, someone was outside the dressing rooms.

"Helen?" a woman called out.

Her body reacted as if she had been hit with a stun gun.

"She can't find me in here," she said.

To my surprise, she climbed up on the bench so her feet wouldn't be seen under the door. I tried to suppress a giggle. She glared at me and held a finger to her lips.

"Helen?"

The voice was taking on a shrill tone. You could hear her impatience by the way her heels were clicking on the floor. A moment later, her voice and footsteps faded. I looked outside to see if the coast was clear. It was. Helen climbed off the bench. She looked clearly shaken.

"Now this is an all-time low," she said. "I can't believe I did that. Things are so out of control. I'm not even sure if it's worth it anymore."

"I thought you said she was a he," I said.

Helen shrugged. "Sometimes it's easier to lie to people I don't know," she said. "I know it's not the right thing to do."

"I'm dating a woman, too," I said. "She's the control freak. That's why I'm trying on the thong. I'm trying to rekindle the romance."

Raising an eyebrow, she looked at me.

"Listen, I've tried it several times, and believe me, if the sparks are gone, the sparks are gone, no matter how many times you try to fan the fire."

"Then why do you stay?" I asked.

She looked thoughtful. "I don't know. Maybe it's just habit or the fear that no else would want me."

I swallowed at the lump in my throat. How many times had Marla said that no one else would want to put up with my quirks?

"Maybe I should try a different color thong," I said.

Helen glanced back down at the thong. Suddenly knowing she wasn't straight changed everything. I was standing practically undressed right in front of a very attractive woman who liked women.

"Well, that thong on you would definitely kindle something," she said. "You've got a great shape. You should try out for that fashion show tonight. You'd probably win."

I felt my cheeks redden, and I tucked my hair behind my ear. Gently, she pulled my hair free and looked at it.

"We could give you some golden highlights to brighten your features a little," she said. "I work at the salon downstairs as a colorist. It would be no trouble at all."

She twirled my hair around her finger. There was a nervous flutter in my stomach. Desire lurched inside of me. I wanted to peel off her dress and see what type of underwear she was wearing.

"You have a . . . ," she said, motioning toward my butt.

I looked down in horror at the white-headed offending monster.

"I know."

"May I?"

Taking my hips gently in her hands, she popped my zit.

I gasped in surprise and looked up at her. It had to be the most gallant thing a woman had ever done for me.

"Wow," I said. "I can't believe you did that."

Suddenly, I realized how close we were standing. She smelled fantastic. It was as if our auras were mingling or something. She was still touching me. The warmth coming from her was heavenly.

As her fingertips left my hips, she looked so disappointed, and I felt it, too, because while she had been touching me, I hadn't felt so heartbreakingly lonely.

I wanted to thank her for her gesture of kindness, so I went to kiss her on the cheek, but she tilted her head and our lips brushed together. The touch of her was so familiarly reassuring, the softest caress of lipstick against lipstick. It shook me to my core. Instead of pushing my tongue into her mouth, I drew the tip of her tongue between my lips and sucked it slowly, flicking my tongue against it.

I heard her gasp when we broke apart.

"Please, don't stop," she said.

Putting aside the thought that I was going to be late for work, I kept kissing her, along her cheeks, eyelids, forehead, nose, and then along her neck, where the skin was so warm and inviting. She smelled like soap and vanilla. Then I followed the line of her chin to the area behind her ears, exploring it with my lips and tongue. I was so impressed with her softness. Marla never felt like this. Everything about Helen was meltingly smooth. I blew lightly in her ear and felt her shiver.

Gently caressing the back of her neck, I felt the fine hair along her hairline and followed every nuance of her spine down to the small of her back where I traveled the contours of her narrow waist around to the front her ribcage. She sucked in her breath as I cupped her breasts from beneath. I never thought a woman with smaller breasts would be more sensitive, but maybe all the nerve endings were condensed.

Looking me in the eyes with a dreamy faraway look, she untied the bows on the shoulders of her dress. It fell to her waist. Her shoulders seemed so slight and vulnerable. She was wearing a strapless underwire bra with a soft lace overlay. Gently, I touched her stomach. She felt so much like me. Her belly button was deep enough to bury the tip of my pinky inside. I loved the spray of freckles across her ribs.

Under the hem of her dress, I slid my hands and pushed the fabric up until I found a pair of white cotton granny panties. I hesitated in surprise. She looked startled for a moment that I had discovered them, but suddenly she was pushing the fabric down her thighs and urging my hand between her legs. I had thought a girl like her would be waxed within an inch of her life, but she wasn't. For all her grooming on the outside, she was refreshingly natural down there.

Between her legs, I explored her folds and curves with my fingertips. It felt so good just to touch someone without being pinned down and being told what to do. I slid one finger inside her, cupping my palm over her fleshy mound over her pubic bone. My finger went in and out and the ball of my hand was pressed hard against her vulva. She pushed my palm down so it was grazing her clit and my finger went in further.

Seeing her so aroused and electrified by the feelings traveling through my hand, I felt myself flush, my body becoming unbearably warm beneath my white shirt, my bra feeling like it was strangling me. I had to be ruining the thong I was wearing because I was so wet and aching with desire. I wanted to be naked beside her in bed, exploring every inch of her, finding her G-spot, sharing all my deep, dark sexual secrets with her, and giving her the orgasm of a lifetime.

I was feeling so good about all this that I wanted to bring Penelope into the mix, a sweet little sex toy finger puppet that I always carried with me in case of emergency. She fit over your index finger and looked like a little cute devil. Fumbling in my purse, I found her and slid her on my finger. I brought her up to show Helen. Marla had hated Penelope so much that she nearly put her down the garbage disposal, so why I was showing this to Helen right now, I had no idea, but it seemed important.

"How utterly cute," Helen whispered. "Where are you going to put her?"

I smiled. Of course, I was going to put her between Helen's legs. I started with some traditional circles, throwing a few crisscrosses into the mix as I went along. She really seemed to like the bumps of the horns. I couldn't believe how quickly she and Penelope were being acquainted. In no time at all, my cute little plastic finger puppet was performing all sorts of tricks in an effort to please her. I once thought Penelope was a shy little thing. Not today. She was really getting aggressive as she skipped, danced, and glided across Helen's clit.

The sensation of Penelope inside Helen put her right over the edge. She started to come, her breathing changing, a pink flush spreading across her face and chest, a sprinkle of sweat on her shoulders, her pelvic muscles contracting, her toes curling in her high-heeled sandals, her nails digging into my skin, my hand cramping. The smile that broke out across her mouth made the entire morning of bad luck worth it.

As we straightened our clothes, she asked me to tie the shoulders of her dress. As I did it, I couldn't believe her beautiful lips had just been against mine. I had to buy the thong now, but not for the same reason as when I first came here.

When I came out of the store with Helen, a Pink Bow bag in my hand with my blue oasis thong tucked inside, I was still feeling a little dizzy and overheated from our dressing room games. A small pit of fear bloomed in my stomach as I saw Helen focus on a well-coifed woman near the fashion show runway. That had to be her girlfriend.

To my relief, Helen closed her narrow fingers around mine, and she didn't let go even when the woman looked over at us. I smiled. Good. There was a phone call to Marla ahead of me as well. I had to tell her that I'd learned something very surprising about myself today.

– 6 –

Zenda

Anna South

She had never been Dr. Austen's favorite student. Laura vogued into every class period late, flaunting a slutty, outrageous costume. Her black PVC dress made Anne Austen's most die-hard groupies forget creative writing and stare at the Goth girl's round ass. Laura would cringe when the professor glared at her, but sauntered in just as late the next week. She was a drama queen, too, filling Anne's e-mail inbox with dirgelike excuses: she *meant* to show up for class, but then her roommate's relationship crisis . . . She *planned* to write an insightful critique of a short story, something better than, "Hey, nice job—awesome characters!" but life forced her hand, again, as usual. Sometimes Anne caught herself thinking about it—what it would be like to make Laura stay after class and, just once, bend her over a student desk, pull up her skirt, and make her rethink this whole "bad girl" routine.

But Anne didn't let herself get too attached to that daydream. She knew such fantasies could lead professors to bad places, and after what happened to her two years ago, Anne felt nervous even *thinking* about this girl. Frankly, Laura reminded her too much of the male student who had falsely accused her of misconduct: they were both bright but flaky, majoring in theater, with youthful looks that belied their years, and earning Cs in Anne's undergraduate fiction course. His descriptions of kinky sex with his professor had made the English

Published by The Haworth Press, Inc., 2006. All rights reserved.
doi:10.1300/5328_07

department head blush, but how many of her colleagues had believed the lies? Most of them knew she was a lesbian, though she wasn't close to any of them. During her review, Anne had easily shown the sadistic exploits in his complaint were stolen word for word from her own best-selling novel, *The Velvet Scream*. Still, the damage to Anne's career had been done. Since the accusation, Anne felt even more distanced from her colleagues, which made her resentful. She had developed a crippling case of writer's block and for the past two years hadn't crafted a decent sentence.

Laura, however, *could* write; that is, whenever she actually managed to find paper, sleep, a working printer, and her own pretty head out of her ass. Her witty, angst-filled stories starred a character also named Laura: a pink-haired, perky-Goth teenager trapped in a Midwestern 'burg. The girl wasn't merely theatrical, she was sensitive— so Anne was not surprised when, late in May, Laura burst into tears during office hours. "What are you planning to do this summer?" had never brought a student to tears before, but Laura was obviously unique. *Or maybe,* Anne thought, *I just have a gift for making girls cry.*

"What's wrong, Laura?" From behind the mahogany desk, she held out a box of tissues, but felt uneasy at the student's display of intimate emotion. She was glad the office door stayed open.

The girl smeared some eye shadow across her thin cheek. "I couldn't find a summer job this year." Unlike Anne, who worked out regularly, Laura was skin and bones except that round ass. "I guess my references didn't pull through. I sort of have this little problem with lateness."

No kidding. Anne willed herself not to roll her eyes. It wasn't that she lacked concern for the student's welfare, but she remembered being twenty and overdramatic herself. At thirty-seven, Anne was a stunning blonde woman with long legs and a classic style of dressing, but lately being around hipster divas like Laura made her feel old and out of touch. Long ago, she'd traded in her cool prescription sunglasses—and the drinking habit that went with them—for a six-hundred-dollar pair of horn-rims and a yoga fetish. She kept her image conservative on purpose, but there came days like today when her blonde bob and camel-colored pencil skirt struck her as downright stuffy next to Laura's apple-red corset top and knee boots. *Where does she buy that silver eye shadow anyway?*

"I have all these dreams," Laura was saying. "I'd love to write something half as good as *Velvet*. I've read that book a dozen times. I even read all your reviews!"

Anne smiled. She had heard all this before. "That's very flattering." *But you're still getting a C.*

"I just wish there was some way I could get around it. I *dread* going back home—spending the summer in Zenda."

Zenda, Wisconsin, was the setting of Laura's stories, and while Anne was amused to confirm it existed, she found the remark ironic. Anne had grown up in a Central Valley farm town. She'd penned *Velvet* while staying with her folks, trading chores for rent, saving her waitressing stash, and choking in the thick air of her parents' shame at having raised a bookish spinster. When her "little book" became a best seller they had read it and disowned her. What did Laura have to compare to that—anything?

"Do they . . . torture you at home?" Anne tried to keep her voice clear of sarcasm.

"Well, there's Martha . . . my stepmother. She's kinda evil." Laura smiled through her tears. "But mostly it's just dull there. I'd *rather* be tortured. I could write about that, at least. I'm sure even *you* couldn't write a great novel in Zenda."

"What makes you say that?" Did her parents make her cover her thighs for church? Did they make her scrub her face? Boo hoo.

"It's not that kind of place." Laura said, and for a moment her voice sounded older—almost bitter. Actually it sounded a little bit like Anne's voice. "I don't know how to explain it. You can just tell— some towns you want to get into and explore. Some towns you need to get out of . . . before they kill your dreams."

Oh, cry me a river, kid, Anne thought, but despite herself she felt her chest tightening. Laura's words had plunged her memory back to one particular day at the old house—her mother sitting on the front porch, looking up disapprovingly as she walked out in short shorts and got on her bike to meet her girlfriend: "If you're not writing in your notebook you're locked in a room with that white-trash girl."

"Well," Anne coughed, "I'm sure you'll think of something, Laura. Maybe you could stay on in Berkeley as someone's nanny." She could have kicked herself. This is what her own parents had told her to do, and Laura was even less suited to it.

"Sure," Laura said politely. "I'll put an ad online." She wiped at her eyes with tattoo-ringed fingers. "Maybe I could be someone's personal assistant . . . or something. Oh, god, who am I kidding." She put her pink head down on the desk, banged it once, then started to cry again.

Most days Anne wished she had never become famous. She was tired of being eaten by writer's block and sexual guilt. Sick of being stereotyped as "a literary De Sade" as the *New York Times* had labeled her in a review that seemed to have been mailed to everyone she knew, and everyone she was destined to meet. Even so, she found herself flattered by Laura's admiration and more flattered still by her openness.

"My apartment has a guest bedroom," she heard herself say, "but I rarely have guests anymore." Why had she admitted this? What was she doing, inviting Laura to the penthouse? Some alarm in her head beeped over and over. Yes, Laura was a pretty good writer—so what? She was a hardcore pain in the ass. What kind of personal assistant would she make?

"I can cook!" Laura said, as if reading her mind. She beamed up at Anne through the black and silver mess of makeup. "I'll cook wonderful vegan food for you every day. I'll even bring you breakfast in bed!"

Anne felt the girl's thankfulness and it made her feel good—better than she had in awhile. "That won't be necessary," she said with a smile. "You can just serve it on the table."

Over the next few weeks, while she worked on grades, Anne began to agonize about her impending houseguest. She hardly knew Laura—what if Laura was a drug addict and trashed the apartment in a stupor? What if she invited strange, punk-rock boys to sleep over and *they* trashed the apartment? Even worse, what if Laura decided (no, what if she *discovered*) that Anne's lifestyle was sedate and monastic, another deadly Zenda to escape? The crowning irony of Anne's isolation was that readers constantly wrote her saying how close to her they felt. Over time, this had become her pet peeve. When an interviewer asked her what she loved the most about being a writer, she answered, "Let me tell you what I *hate* most—people who read my book saying they feel like they know me."

The weekend after school let out, Laura and a pretty white boy with dreads showed up with her two suitcases of clothes, a fishing tackle box filled with beauty products, a jasmine plant in a hand-painted pot, and an iBook. Laura French-kissed the boy good-bye. "My ex," she explained to Anne. Anne hadn't seen any of her exes in years. During the house tour, Laura noted the bland decor, feeding Anne's anxiety. In particular, she had commented on Anne's white bedroom walls. "I know *tons* of local artists," she'd said, "but, then again, their stuff is a little more . . . funky . . . than your furniture." On the plus side, she was impressed with Anne's wine collection, her chocolate brown Italian leather sofas, and the sleek chef's kitchen with its granite island.

At least Anne didn't have to worry about Laura falsely accusing her of anything. It wasn't just she lacked the level of organization required to file a complaint, it was also that Laura didn't play by school rules. She clearly didn't give a fuck about them if she noticed them at all, and for once this quirk would work out well for both of them.

What surprised Anne was how much she *enjoyed* coming home to the smell of wheat-berry biscuits or tofu fajitas, the buzz of National Public Radio news from the kitchen where Laura stood listening in a velvet bra and flour-dusted miniskirt. And Laura asked how her day was. They talked about their days, sitting at Anne's rarely used dining table, eating home-cooked food and drinking good wine (Anne could have a glass of wine now, though technically she wasn't supposed to even have it in the house). Anne had okay days teaching summer classes. Laura had really good days writing her novel. Sometimes they talked into the evening, about their dreams. Laura dreamed of writing a best seller with lots of sex in it. Anne dreamed of conquering writer's block, but that was a secret dream because she would never admit she had writer's block in the first place. Instead of opening up, she fed Laura some platitudes about making things happen for yourself through courage and careful preparation. They would sit close together on the couch, Laura leaning toward Anne, absorbing her wisdom, a wing of her bubblegum hair brushing Anne's knee. At first, Anne was jealous of Laura's writing success. But as the days passed, she felt a new book growing somewhere in her own brain, and the occasional pulsing of hope there made her eyes sting.

Then, after two blissful weeks, Laura abruptly kicked the cooking habit. Instead, Anne would return to find her wandering the rooms, absently running her burgundy manicured fingers along dusty surfaces. She would pick up a book, frown, and replace it. She would open a bottle of Anne's wine and wrap her lips around it. "I had a bad writing day," she would announce, and put her boots up on the ottoman. When she watched reality TV over a fast-food dinner, Anne retreated to her own bedroom or the gym.

As a personal assistant, Laura was a cheerful nightmare. Anne would request she stack the dishwasher, and Laura would nod and smile, but then not follow through. More complex requests were doomed to complex failures: "I need you to make copies of these and collate them." "No problem!" But she would get it wrong. "Oh, I didn't know what collate was." "You could have just asked." "But see, I *thought* I knew. I thought it meant make them two-sided." To Laura's credit, her failures pained her. "Oh, shit, I'm sorry, Anne!" she would say, rolling her eyes at her own mistakes. She had started calling Anne by her first name. They were getting to know each other. Anne couldn't help but feel it was the same old dance, now in a different building: she got excuses from Laura instead of results, and she responded, like any good teacher, by asking Laura what *she* could do for *her*.

By July, their dreams of symbiosis and novel writing lay comatose in the dirty kitchen sink. It now seemed clear that Laura was a glamorous airhead and Anne herself an elegant has-been. Their sharing an apartment might have made a decent sitcom, but it was certainly not productive. It was frustrating. Alone at night in her white-walled bedroom Anne's sadistic fantasies about Laura ran wild—sometimes she would give her a hairbrushing, pants pulled down, up against a wall, for drinking Anne's favorite wine without permission. Sometimes she made her clean the apartment naked except for her makeup and lace-up knee boots. Sometimes, after a firm lecture, she would simply flip Laura over her knee and administer a spanking with her bare hand. Laura just needed some direction.

On the last Friday in July, they were picking at yet another Chinese takeout dinner Anne had ordered, since Laura had not cooked or shopped. Anne sat ramrod straight in her chair, seething quietly. She was itching to give Laura a good scolding, but instead she kept taking swallows of ice water, waiting for the urge to pass. Laura chewed her hair and looked thoughtful. Finally Anne asked her, ceremonially at this point, if *she* could do anything to help Laura.

"Yeah, actually, I have an idea," Laura said. "I think it would work for both of us, too."

Laura had never offered a suggestion at this point in the ritual. Anne raised an eyebrow and waited.

"From now on, every time I fuck up as your assistant, I think it would be . . . most appropriate . . . for you to beat me."

Anne's face filled with nervous blood, and she nearly swallowed an ice cube. How did Laura know what she was thinking? She felt as transparent as if her brain were a movie screen. *I could lose my job,* she thought irrationally. With a shaking hand, she set the tumbler of ice water back on the table.

"You probably want to anyway," Laura continued, reaching for an egg roll, "and I hardly blame you. I'd probably want to bitch slap me too. I mean, you've been incredibly patient, but everyone has their limits, and besides, I've always wanted to get my ass kicked by the—"

"Laura, stop it!" Anne's heart was beating fast in her throat and she could feel a pulse in her nose. "I know you were just kidding, but people's jobs have been threatened over jokes like that."

Laura smiled. "One thing I really like about you? You are *way* too intense." She calmly bit into her egg roll, chewed, and swallowed. "It's not like anyone would find out. It's not like I'm some complete asshole, like that one guy from your workshop."

So everyone knew about that, even naive undergraduates. Anne felt humiliated, though she'd done nothing wrong.

"I'm not your student," Laura said, reading her mind again. "Grades posted a month ago. Forget work for a second." Her smile was coy. "I mean, I read your book. I know what you're all about."

"No, you don't." Anne rose from the table, annoyed at herself for sounding so mousy when she should have nipped this conversation minutes ago. Why didn't she? "No, you don't," she snapped. "And I'm still fifteen years older than you and I am still . . . your mentor."

"My mentor? Whatever." Laura snickered. It was a time-honored way to get someone to hit you, but Anne was not having it.

"Let's forget this ever happened." She needed to get back in control, of herself at least. For one moment she had considered taking Laura up on her offer. Exploiting the small-town girl, her former self really, who had come to her for help. Surely no matter what people said about her she was better than that.

In the hallway, Anne removed her brown suede pumps and lined them up on the floor, then grabbed her yoga mat off the shelf. Maybe it would help to do some stretches in her bedroom.

"Wait!" Laura zipped down the corridor. She was standing in the doorway between Anne and Anne's bedroom. "I'm sorry to block the door. Tell me the truth, am I ever going to write a great novel?"

"I don't know." She paused a moment. The honest answer was no. Laura had a way with words, but she lacked sufficient focus to write a haiku. "Probably not. But then again—"

"I knew it. You think I have no talent. Which proves you only invited me here because you want to fuck me." Laura said the word *fuck* in a throaty voice, holding the note out a little longer than necessary.

"That is *not* the case! First of all, you do have talent."

Laura ignored her. "So . . . do you like my ass?" She held out her arms, showcasing her body parts. "What do you like about me—my lips, my boobs? My cool outfits?"

Anne looked at the doorway. *I wish I'd never agreed to help her out.* She considered pushing Laura's slender body out of the way. It would take barely any effort. The thought made her sad. "I like you as a human being, and as a writer," she said to the beige yoga mat.

"But is *that* why you invited me here?" Laura smiled ferociously, hands on her hips.

Anne said no.

"Well, then . . . why are you not fucking me, Dr. Austen?"

"Because," Anne said softly, aware of her own hypocrisy, "because that would be unethical."

Laura was waiting for her, lying barefoot on the couch in what passed as lounging around clothes for her: a sleeveless black zip-up top and stretch-velvet miniskirt. "So?" she said. She was not drinking wine. A bottle of mineral water sat coasterless and nearly empty on the coffee table.

Anne's stretches had relaxed her greatly, but that didn't change anything. Things had gone too far with Laura—she'd been foolish to think they could ever go back to their platonic relationship. Neither of them would write anything good in this apartment, either, and she didn't want to get in the way of Laura's dreams. She felt guilty enough having used her as an acolyte slash fantasy object.

There was no good way to break it. "I'm sorry. You are released from your duties as my assistant."

"Yeah, I already packed."

That stopped Anne. "You did?" Laura was not usually a step ahead when it came to practical matters. "But I thought you . . . couldn't stand being at home."

"Can't stand it here either." She killed the bottle and set it firmly on Anne's IKEA end table, a relic from her student days that she kept forgetting to replace. "What I really can't stand, if you want to know the truth, is my plan didn't work. I couldn't even get my ass kicked by the literary De Sade."

"Wait a minute. Your plan? *That* was your dream?" Anne felt herself floating. The stretches had relaxed her as much as a glass of wine. "I thought you wanted to be a writer."

"Oh no. I've always had my heart set on being an actress."

"I see." Anne sank into the leather couch next to Laura. "When did you come up with . . . your plan?"

"A year ago, when I first read your book. I could tell what you were, and when I met you I knew for sure. I didn't want to mess it up by coming out and asking—you'd have turned me away. So I . . . I just wanted to create a fantasy you would get into." Laura looked nervous as she admitted all this, but Anne's own shoulders relaxed a little. "You always say to use archetypes in your stories, play to your audience. I guess I didn't pick quite the right fantasy though. You're probably wondering by now if Zenda is even a real place. I'll save you the Google search. It is real; I found it on Yahoo! maps."

"Did you really." Anne felt oddly glad to know she'd been deceived. It was flattering, like finding out someone planned a surprise party for you, only a little more twisted. Okay, a lot more twisted.

"I knew you were from a small town. Your reviews said you'd become bitter and isolated lately. I . . . wanted to get into your life. I wanted to play a minor part in it. What do you think? That I'm a psycho? That I'm pathetic?"

Anne realized it was happening again—she was being set up by a student. But this time she found herself interested and aroused rather than anxious. "You're definitely . . . quirky," she said. "So where are you actually from—New York? LA?"

"I'm from here." Laura kissed her. Her mouth tasted like mint, but her lipstick smelled like vanilla. "Good old Berkeley, where it's okay to be a freak." Anne pressed Laura's lips against her own, savoring their taste, wondering how much of the color had transferred to her mouth. Would she look like an aging poseur in violet lipstick or would she look exotic and alluring? She started to give herself permission to sink into the fantasy Laura had built. She prepared to flatten her identity into her role and found it wasn't as easy as she'd thought.

"I don't care how you do it," Laura moaned in her ear. "I just want it. Don't care if there's anger, or detachment, or if you just hate me for lying to you. You can hate me. I just want . . . I want something." Laura unzipped her tank top. She was trembling. Her skin was smooth, her bare breasts pale like the meat of an apple. Anne felt her clit swell tight with blood. "Will you touch me? Please. Hit me. I read your book so many times . . . *I feel like I know you.*"

Anne smiled. "Then you're a fool." She grabbed Laura by the back of the hair with her left hand and guided her down to the rug. "Let's get one thing clear. You're just new material to me. See, I've had writer's block for the past two years. I need something to shake it, and maybe it's you. A piece of meat for my memory." With her right hand, she slapped Laura hard across the mouth. It felt so good. If she lost her job this time, at least she would deserve it.

Laura melted all over the rug. She knelt with her head down, following Anne's fistful of her hair. "What can I do to help you?" she whimpered.

"You can start by admitting you have no idea who I am, like I have no idea who you are." Anne slapped her again, this time on the cheek. Laura flinched, then cried, "Ow!" when her own movement caused her hair to be pulled. Anne sat down on the couch and adjusted her grip on Laura's head. "Let's see. You read my book and flunked my class, now we're best friends? Let me suggest you are a touch naive."

"You're so right—I didn't see you trash everyone's writing in class. I didn't hear your sarcastic voice all the time. Or from that reviewer who called you bitter! You're not bitter at all!"

"Get your ass up higher." She pulled the elastic velvet skirt down to Laura's knees and set her red cotton string bikini briefs at mid-thigh. She spoke in a loud, slow voice, as if to an idiot: "Your job is very simple now: just keep your ass up high and *count*. If you don't understand how to perform those tasks, you better ask me *now*."

"Come on—no one knows what collate means!"

"Everyone knows." Anne took the opportunity to slap her face again. Then she unhooked her braided leather belt and doubled it. Laura let out a long sigh. "By the way, whether you were doing it on purpose or not—and I'm not sure which is worse—you're God's own most useless *fucking* personal assistant." She raised the belt and snapped it down across Laura's bare butt.

"One!" Laura squirmed but she couldn't move too far because Anne was gripping her hair. Her right ass cheek glowed pink. "Two! . . . Three! . . . Four! . . ." She started to whimper around five and was crying openly at fourteen. After twenty-two swats, Anne put the belt down and moved to Laura's right. "How do you like the life of an actress so far? I hear it doesn't pay."

Laura moaned and sniffed. Her ass was a burning red.

"I wonder if those tears are real, or if you're just *acting*."

"They're real!"

"Look at me, Laura."

Laura turned her wet, slapped right cheek to Anne and got another six spanks across the face. She cast her eyes down. "I'm sorry."

"I know you're sorry." Anne's voice was patronizing. "But it doesn't end just because you're sorry." She let go of Laura's hair and reached around to squeeze her nipples with both hands. "Did you really think anything you could say would have an effect?"

"I'm an optimist," Laura whispered.

"God, I'm tired of hearing your Pollyanna blather. Get your face down low. Spread your ass for me." Laura lost her balance trying to pull off her underwear, and Anne snapped her fingers. "Go, faster! Scramble!"

"I'm sorry!" Laura was completely naked now, balanced on her knees and face. Her red, round ass jutted out toward the belt. Moaning with shame and anticipation, she spread her ass cheeks apart, and the belt spanked her hard across the hole.

"Mmmm!" Laura's sounds of pain were turning wilder.

"What a shock to see your pussy's dripping all over my rug. How original, a bitch likes to be slapped around."

"Mmmmm!" Now Laura sounded hurt. Her nakedness made the pink hair on her head look natural somehow, as if she was some breed of elf rather than a person. A blue metal ring peeked from between her shaved labia.

"I see you've modified your body. You're pretty unique and special, to someone else I'm sure." She whipped her across the asshole again and Laura jumped. "Unfortunately, I've already met a lot of dirty sluts, most of them far more interesting than you." She reached forward and yanked on the ring. "Mm. Better writers too."

"Aughhh!" Laura cried out, then suddenly both her hands were connected to her soaking pussy. She writhed and balanced on her elbow, pushing her butt up higher, as she slid her fingers around swollen cunt lips.

"What do you think you're doing? You didn't learn a thing about pacing from me. You'll never write anything but shit if you keep rushing things."

"Oh, please, oh!" She was moaning and crying, thrashing madly on the floor. For all her talk about dirty sluts of the past, Anne had never seen anyone lose control quite this much. It was inspiring. "Please hit me until I come!" Laura growled.

This is the point, Anne thought, *where it becomes clear who's serving whom.* She obeyed, of course, delivering rhythmic strokes to the soft, inner part of each ass cheek. It occurred to her that Laura might be wondering if the status of things had changed since they were sexually involved. That maybe she would be invited to stay after all. Anne felt conflicted about it. She liked Laura but missed having the apartment to herself. And wasn't it better to end things on a good note, honestly, before they ran out of conversation and the weirdness of their age difference set in? And Laura would probably dump her anyway—maybe she would hate Anne's *next* book. *"You're not bitter at all." Not at all.*

Laura fell quiet, shuddering, and Anne was shaken from her thoughts. For a moment she sat staring at Laura's beautiful smooth body in ecstasy. Then she set the belt on the couch, bent forward, and slid two fingers into Laura's warm cunt. She was still coming in soft spasms, like drumbeats under water. *It's been so long, so long since I met someone I liked who called herself an optimist.*

"Please don't take your fingers out of me yet," Laura murmured, and Anne again obeyed. Time slowed down again. *I'm going to ask her to stay,* Anne realized, and felt shocked at her own courage. She wasn't even drunk.

"That was amazing," Laura said from the floor. She lifted her head, then stood, shaky on her legs. *"You're* amazing." She wiped her face on her shirt and kissed Anne briefly on the lips. "Hey . . . thanks for making my dream come true."

Anne smiled, feeling dreamy. "Hey . . ." It wasn't a word she used often, and it showed. "No problem." She watched Laura dress and disappear into the guest bedroom. But then Laura came back with two suitcases. Anne realized then that if she didn't speak the moment would pass forever, and Laura would leave. She followed her into the guest bathroom, where Laura was collecting stray bits of makeup. "You don't have to go now," she said.

"Oh, but I don't want to do the lingering thing." Laura ran cold water on her face. "I'm going to grab my stuff now, before things get weird."

"I'd like to see you again."

"Oh . . . yeah." She looked down. "My schedule gets pretty hectic during the school year—you know, shows and everything—but maybe we could get together sometime."

"I understand," Anne said, and she did. She would be upset later, alone. "Leave this for me, okay?" She pointed to the tube of purple lipstick, which had rolled behind the jasmine plant.

"You want that?" Anne could feel Laura's hesitation as she performed cost-benefit analysis. It never would have worked, dating someone as calculating as herself. Still, she felt something—a deep sadness and longing. "Sure thing," Laura said after a pause. "That'll look great on you."

When she was gone Anne spent half an hour in front of the mirror with a lip brush. She stared at herself from every angle. Something about her had changed, or something about the apartment had changed. She looked down at the lipstick tube and read its label in swirly calligraphy. The color was called Martha's Wine.

− 7 −

Schooled by a Straight Girl

Khadijah Caturani

I needed cash. Bad. Now. At least that was the excuse I gave myself. They paid me $300 a day, under the table, three days a week. I started to forget to ask my mom to borrow money.

The first few times were weird. Me and a bunch of other Everest-high femmes—hair teased, lips glossed, pubic/leg/armpit hair waxed, eyebrows tweezed, nipples rouged, nails manicured, vaginas lubed—all trying to be the prettiest, most alluring porn princesses we could be for the camera while trying to ignore the girl fingering/licking/fucking us, eyes screwed up tight half the time trying to imagine it's our butch top/husband/girlfriend/mistress/daddy/slave/boss/boyfriend/ lover fucking and sucking us, anyone but this limp, lifeless, dead fish Barbie doll between our legs. I still got off on it, don't get me wrong. I'm great at fantasizing, and subsequently had the loudest, juiciest, most real orgasms in the history of lesbian porn for straight men. And I'd go home after a long day's work and let my butch give it to me every which way she wanted, just like she had in my fantasies, thanking God she wasn't a femme.

But then there was Linda. Linda was straight. Forty or so. Fake tits. Fake blonde hair. Fake laugh. Fake orgasms. Had three kids and a deadbeat abusive husband to support, so she came on board ready to work like a dog. She'd do pee scenes; she'd do poop scenes; she'd do anything. She always had on the same plastic smile when listening to the

Published by The Haworth Press, Inc., 2006. All rights reserved.
doi:10.1300/5328_08

director, and the same depressing, vacant stare when she'd get ready. She cleaned her "twat," as she so lovingly called it, like she was scrubbing a stove. She was fully shaved and had a beaver tattooed above her . . . Well, you know. I hated being around her. Her palpable apathy and exhaustion reminded me of my days spent with my mom in line for welfare cheese, my nights spent covering my ears to ignore the vicious sounds of fighting in the other room, my experience as a fifteen-year-old dominatrix when I had no money for rent.

I didn't see Linda as a sexual being in any way. She seemed to treat sex like . . . well, like work, but it really did something for the director, so I presumed I must have been missing something when they closed the door to do the scenes. She was pretty, in a Midwestern, wide-eyed, corn-fed kind of way. Her honey-blonde hair, pulled back in an austere ponytail when she arrived in the morning, tumbled gorgeously across her breasts and shoulders after she had showered and blow-dried. Her childlike, full pout looked honestly illegal when coated in red lipstick, and her long, leanly muscled legs were adolescently gangly and awkward and graceful and gorgeous. I envied every part of her ageless body except her stomach, which she kept carefully covered in every scene—a leathery, puckered topography of stretch marks. In a camisole, though, she was divine. Your mother, your daughter, your sister, your cipher, ready to receive the imprint of whatever fantasy you wanted. The one time I had peeked over the editor's shoulder to check out her dailies, her languorous gaze shot through the screen into mine; she was the sexiest thing I had ever seen. I was terrified of her.

I got to work early on the day of reckoning. So did she. My heart was palpitating, but she looked calm and sweet as always. We had already shot the build-up scene where her daughters tie me up and ravage me, and the director said I was appropriately flushed as he secured my final cuff. Linda sat on the edge of the bed and stroked my hair as she asked me what my limits were. With her big eyes locked on me, I forgot I had any, let alone what they were. "Ummm . . . no scat," I managed to stammer out, and then she waved and was gone, off to the hallway to shoot her big entrance. As she walked away, I got queasy realizing that, for the first time since I started doing porn, there'd been a moment where my girlfriend had been nowhere on my mind. I still couldn't recall her face as I stared at this overgrown cheerleader's ass, at her hair swinging from side to side, a perfect metronome to the deep drumbeat of her hips. I wished, for a moment, that I was her big beefy husband, that I could pick her up by those hips and ram that softness around my cock, watching that hair sway in time with my thrusts.

It was then I realized my mission. I would make her forget that shithead husband, wipe every thought of him from her mind, like she had wiped thoughts of my (very sweet) girlfriend (God, I hoped she'd forgive me) from mine. I would fuck the straight right out of her, the kink right into her. I'd make her forget she was at work. When they finished in the hallway and set up for our scene, she shot me the sweetest of straight girl smiles. I memorized it, with full confidence it would be the last one I'd see, and shot her my cheesiest smile back just before the director called "Action!"

Linda's face morphed from little-girl sweet to mistress hard in an instant. She entered the room slowly, menacingly, sizing me up like a predatory cat, sending goose bumps up the backs of my legs, across my stomach, down my arms, all the way to the top of my skull. I had memorized the script, but her words still made me jump.

"Do you know what you've been called to my chambers for?"

The line was cheesy and grammatically incorrect, but its delivery was chilling. "No, madam. I . . . I don't."

I gulped as I delivered the line, trying desperately to provoke some saliva to comfort my parched throat. With that, she slowly, seductively presented a gigantic strap-on black dildo from behind her back, and unceremoniously pulled it on while speaking.

"I've been watching you enjoy the fruits of my labor, in every sense. You have done nothing but consume since you got here: consume my food, consume my daughters, and consume my attention." With that, she slapped me hard across the face and stood over me, fuming.

"I am successful because I work hard. Working hard takes focus. But you would know nothing about that, would you?"

She grabbed my face in her hands, squeezing my cheeks. I forgot my name. I forgot where I was. I knew nothing but my role as her servant. How could I answer that would please her?

The director fed me my line when it hit him that I was paralyzed with fear. "My only focus is pleasuring you. C'mon, ladies, breathe."

I delivered the line with complete sincerity. It had the desired effect. She leaned in and kissed raw heat through me, grabbing my hair, grabbing my breasts, groping my stomach and thighs.

"I. Can't. Focus. On. Anything. But. Fucking. You."

With that, she climbed on top of me and rammed her rubber cock into my already-hungry cavity.

My juices spewed around her, streaming onto my thighs, as she shoved in all the way to the hilt, driving in my G-spot and squeezing my urethral sponge dry. Her eyes went wide and she grinned, teeth gleaming, as I came. A wave of satisfaction and pride washed over her, energizing her to pound me over and over again until I pulled her into me, shaking, the universal femme-bottom sign to please stop. With this, she started kissing her way down my body and gently pulled out of me, making her way down to my cootchie, where she lapped lovingly at my overwhelmed labia. I relaxed into her mouth and rested my full weight against the cuffs. I was almost asleep when I felt a soft flicking on my ass.

My eyes widened for a moment at the electricity shooting upward from my anus into my clitoris, and then I eased back into it, enticing her finger to go deeper, as my eyes rolled into the back of my head. I had been fucked up the ass plenty of times, but never with a full-size dildo, only those little pencil-like things. My girlfriend "didn't want to hurt me." I relaxed all of those muscles I knew I had and focused on my breathing as she worked into me, first one finger, then two, then three, then I don't remember because I couldn't think. All I knew anymore was rhythm and opening, rhythm and opening, as I rocked her deeper and deeper inside of me.

We had missed at least eight lines of dialogue, but my director wasn't dumb enough to interrupt; he knew a good thing when he saw it and the only sounds that entered my consciousness occasionally were those of the camera assistant changing tapes as we rolled. Then her hand was on my heart and her mouth was off my cunt and she implored me to "breathe." I took a massive breath in, and as I exhaled, all I thought was "open, open, open." I felt like my newborn baby had decided the world was too cruel and was crawling back inside of me as her knuckles edged deeper and deeper into me. Unlike when I was fisted vaginally, though, there were no pesky bones to contend with, and I just kept on unfolding for her. She began rubbing my clitoris wildly with the hand that had held my heart, and, as my clit pulsed its way toward orgasm, she let out a warrior's cry and pushed all the way into me, taking me past the wrist. I felt her come with me, I don't know how, but she bucked and jolted it through me like a man.

I felt the strange heterosexual urge to suck the come off her cock, so I pulled her around and on top of me, flicking her bobbing cock with my tongue as I probed her deliciously wet vagina with two fingers. Before I knew it, I was fisting her back, my middle knuckle almost pressing through her cervix. We were a perfect circle of sexual energy, and I wished it would never end.

As I had that thought, the director reminded Linda to "switch positions, we only have so much tape." She gently rocked her arm out of me, at which point I noticed the elbow-length rubber glove (where had that come from?), which she peeled off as she pulled away from my fist, kissing me and repositioning herself.

"What can I say? You are a black hole. You were born to consume. I guess that my only choice is to fulfill your need."

With that, she clapped her hands twice and in came her "daughters"—the two girls I had worked with prior to now. One blindfolded me as the other removed my leg restraints. All the while, Linda remained over me, kissing me, whispering sweet words, and massaging my body. Her nails felt incredible against my skin. Her sweet perfume, clean hair, and the smell of her sex combined to form the most deliciously intoxicating aroma I'd ever experienced. Her huge soft lips made me hungry, and she loved when I'd bit them. I didn't know whether I felt like a bigger lesbian than ever before, a straight man, a straight woman, or a narcissist. I think it was a little of each. I just knew that I felt relief and excitement when I heard the girls undoing the buckles on her harness. And that suddenly, at some silent command, all three of my orifices were filled at once—my cootchie, my ass, and my mouth.

An even huger dildo than before was now shoved up my ass from below; a different, incredibly textured, smaller dildo was twirling in and out of me from behind; and the wettest, largest, most delicious punani engulfed my face from above. I knew it was Linda's immediately, and I channeled all of my energy into becoming a cunnilingus machine, sucking and plunging and vibrating and humming in a perfect dance with her gyrating hips, pulling forth the climax of her life that I knew it was my destiny to have.

I opened my eyes to see the ultimate vision of femininity—Venus rocking on the waves, Salome dancing through the palace; my lover, my mirror, my goddess, my self. I saw in her eyes the openness and power that made my girlfriend cry when she saw it in mine; I felt through her body the rippling energy of life channeling through her, into me, and into the earth. She looked down at me and smiled lovingly right before she entered the final trance that sent her eyes fluttering back in her head; that sent her fingers clawing through her hair, my hair, my skin, the sheets, the air, trying to grasp her soul and keep it here on Earth, to no avail. I was the perfect lover, she knew she was safe to completely let go, and so she had no choice. Her orgasm built for at least five minutes (could've been twenty, though, for all of the time awareness I possessed)—a slowly winding spiral moving upward and outward and filling the room. It even possessed the dead fish sisters, whose usually lackluster thrusts now fell into perfect sync with Linda's gyrations and filled me with the verve I needed to really push through to the other side of sex, that place where the machinations no longer matter. By the time she was ready to actually come, she was doubled over, her head rolling in circles around and around her neck, her nails drawing blood as she grasped my outstretched arms to stabilize herself, and her breath, slow and powerful, warming my face as she exhaled the fire building inside of her.

Her orgasm was the opposite of what I could have ever expected after a buildup of such intensity. It was like tinkling light rain, like fairies dancing, like sparkling crystals. She started laughing like a tiny child and stretched her arms out as if to bask in a rainbow. She shook so lightly, and her cootchie pulsed so gently, I wished I could escape the restraints and put my arms around her to encase her fragility. The laughter slowly, gently unfurled into tears that dropped onto my face only to have her lick them off, laughing again, as she pulled herself off my face and curled up on my bosom. I nuzzled her like a cat and drifted off to sleep.

I vaguely remember the other two girls coming out of me and my hands being freed. When I awoke my arms were entwining Linda's body and we were alone. I stroked her hair for a long while before she woke up, pondering the bizarre feelings I had experienced over the course of my "day at work." As turned on as I had been by Linda's exploration of her dom persona, I was completely unhinged by her softness, her femininity, her beauty. I felt as though I had fallen in love with her—a feeling I knew would likely pass once she woke up and we had to return to reality, but what if it didn't? And what would it mean to me, to my identity, to be able to mesh so well with she who was supposed to be my sister, my competitor, another yin, someone to share lip gloss with?

When Linda woke up, her wide eyes looked straight into mine and she let loose a wide cheerleader smile. She laughed and jumped off of the bed. "God, I'm starving! Let's go get something to eat!" She brusquely swept her hair back up into its trademark ponytail and pulled on a robe before sauntering off to the kitchen to attack the cold cut tray. I shook my head and laughed in disbelief. I guessed big philosophical questions would have to wait for a different time—this was just another day at work.

– 8 –

Dressing Desire

Tenille Brown

Ivy was unlike any other I had ever dressed. Where other women hesitated and fidgeted when I asked them to disrobe, Ivy slipped out of her flowery sundress in one fluid movement, letting it slide down her legs and settle in a crumpled heap on the floor. There was no ducking inside the bathroom, no hiding behind a screen; she stood squarely in front of me—a tall, sleek wonder in red bra and matching high-cut panties.

She would be a young bride, just over twenty-three when she walked down the aisle, and although I was only thirty, I felt ancient crouching beside her as I fixed her hem or did whatever little thing that called for my attention. It only mattered because the woman entranced me, and although I knew I wasn't bad looking by any means, I knew Ivy would never look at me *that* way.

Just from looking at her, where her meager breasts sank into her bra, where her waist and hips formed a deep curve, I could tell there would be more altering. I pulled the gown from the torso that stood in the corner of my sewing room, gathering the train and tossing it over my arm so that it didn't drag on the floor.

The satin was cool and the lace tickled my skin. I had gone clear to Charlotte for the fabric, spent twice what I normally would have, and charged Ivy thirty percent less. I had shaped it to match the curve of

Published by The Haworth Press, Inc., 2006. All rights reserved.
doi:10.1300/5328_09

her bosom, placed the lace where the brown of her skin would show through beautifully.

I handed Ivy her gown, though I longed for her to stand there just as she was.

"You've lost more weight, haven't you?" I asked, though the answer shone on her thin frame.

She lowered her eyes, her high cheekbones dented with dimples, her girlish smile all the answer I needed. "Yeah. But I didn't mean to." She pulled at the small bow at the center of her bra. "It's just been all the stress of the wedding. I can hardly keep anything down lately."

"I understand the stress, but you can't keep doing that to yourself," I said, bending in front of her and lifting the skirt of the dress and nodding for her to step into it. "You'll be too weak to walk down the aisle if you keep this up."

"I know, I know," Ivy said. "But you know how it is . . . easier said than done."

She stepped into the gown, placing a hand on my shoulder to steady herself. My shoulder became warm where she touched it, and I briefly studied her skin against mine, where hers was colored honey and mine a deep dark chocolate. I helped her gather the heap of satin and lace and pull it over her long gleaming legs. With both feet firmly on the floor, she bent to pull the gown over her thighs and the lace of her bra grazed my face.

Ivy pulled the gown over her chest, over her shoulders. She pressed the sagging bodice against her chest, pulled at the half sleeves. I stepped behind her to fasten the fifteen satin-covered buttons, and when the low-lying neckline sufficiently covered her breasts, I slipped the bra straps over her shoulders and she pulled it down underneath her breasts. She turned and stood in front of me with her hands extended at her sides, an apologetic pout on her face.

Anxious to fill the silence that allowed my thoughts to go to her bare breasts, her slender waist, her curvy hips, I said, "Do you have a strapless bra to wear underneath or will you wear a corset?"

"Actually, I won't be wearing anything underneath. I figure it'll be tight enough not to need anything. Besides, I think it's kind of sexy not having anything on underneath, don't you?"

The answer sent a sharp bolt of heat between my legs and I fought to steady myself. "Oh, yes, definitely," I managed.

I stepped back for a better look. I shook my head at the way the dress hung on her.

"It'll have to come in three more inches in the waist." I tugged at the loose material at the outside of her soft bosom. "And about an inch and a half here." And where it was loose at her buttocks, "and two inches here." I took several pins from the cushion on my desk and stuck them in to mark my place. "You lose any more, you'll disappear. Promise me you'll keep the remaining meat on those bones, will you, Ivy?"

"I'll try." Ivy giggled.

"Good." I motioned for her to turn around and I undid the buttons that trailed her back, taking my time so that my fingers grazed her skin ever so lightly. I pulled the gown over her shoulders, my breath quickening at the sight of her bare back. "You can step out now."

She complied, pulled her bra up from her waist, and replaced the straps. She bent down to retrieve her discarded sundress, her legs, her lace-covered buttocks inches away from my face.

I turned away from the painfully beautiful sight of her, hung the dress back on its torso, and jotted down the new measurements on my notepad.

"So I'll just come back in a few days, then?" Ivy queried.

"Yes," I said to her without turning. "It'll be ready then."

"Okay."

I heard the rattle of her keys, her purse bump against her thighs, and the heels of her sandals on my hardwood floor as she walked down the hall to the front door, and as it snapped shut, I exhaled and collapsed at the train of the gown.

The dress hung on the outside of my closet door, the final alterations having been done in my bedroom over the course of a rainy Friday night. I ran my fingers along the fabric, against the narrow waist and full bodice. I imagined how elegant she would look when she wore it. I imagined the minimal loveliness she would wear underneath.

I pressed the pearl-kissed waist against my face. I imagined it against her skin, hugging her curves. I imagined the pearl-kissed veil covering her head of thick, dark hair. I imagined it sliding from her shoulders, over her breasts, down her waist on her wedding night.

I stood in my robe in front of it, pulled it against my body. My own unruly mass of curls grazed the satin and lace. The stark whiteness of the gown was a deep contrast to my dark skin.

I imagined Ivy in the gown, in front of me, her breasts pressed against mine. I rocked from side to side, imagined us dancing.

I imagined it was *I* in the honeymoon suite on her wedding night, waiting in bed for her to emerge from the bathroom in a graceful white gown. I imagined laying on top of the covers in my own white nightie, waiting to be undressed.

I let the gown fall against the closet door, walked weak-kneed to my bed, and sank onto the mattress. I lay back against the soft cushion with the completed dress draped over me. I reached down between my legs, slipped my fingers beneath the fabric of my panties. I pulled my fingers along where I was already wet, imagined my hands were her hands and massaged myself so softly and sweetly that I moaned and shivered and whispered her name.

☙❧

When I buttoned the final button, smoothed the full skirt, and stepped back, I prayed for a loose waist, a fallen stitch, anything to bring her back for another fitting, but it clung to her frame perfectly.

"Well, what do you know, you kept your word," I said, stepping back for a better look. "It fits you perfectly."

"Oh, it does."

She twirled in front of me, practically floated to the mirror, and twirled again.

"You did wonderful work."

It was my best work. It was for Ivy.

"You look beautiful in it."

She gathered my hands in hers, kissed me on both cheeks. I wondered if she noticed the new scent I had splashed behind my ears and along my neck just before she arrived. I wondered if she noticed I had straightened my hair.

I helped Ivy with the parts of the gown that she couldn't get to, but saved myself the agony of watching her slip back into her slacks and sweater. I mixed myself a gin and tonic instead, my mouth too full of the pungent liquid to say good-bye when she left.

༒

I cursed the double stitch required to hold together the wide waist of the gown of my newest client. My eyes strained at the sewing machine, heavy and tired from another sleepless night.

The gown was bulky and unflattering, the fabric bland and outdated. It had been the girl's taste—she called it classic, I called it old-fashioned and ugly. It would fit her like a tent, nothing like the way Ivy's gown fit her. It wouldn't hug her curves or . . .

When the doorbell rang it was a welcome interruption. I tied the sash on my robe, sufficiently covering my short nightgown. I pulled open the door without peeking through the window and there a portrait stood.

Ivy was a vision in her wedding gown. The white stretch limo was just behind her, taking up most of my driveway, the driver standing obediently at its open door awaiting her return.

"Ivy . . ."

"I think I have a button loose." The words tumbled from her mouth. She turned slightly, pulling at the waist of the gown. "Down here, near the bottom."

I gently pulled her shoulder and peeked down the slope of her back. "Yes, I see it. Come inside for a minute."

She followed me inside the corridor and stood idle while I went to fetch my sewing kit.

"This one is interesting," she said when I returned, her fingers on the fabric that hung over the sides of the sewing machine and into my chair.

"Interesting indeed." I pulled gently at the shoulder of her gown. "I'll just have to undo all these others to get to it, but it won't take but a minute.

I held the threaded needle between my tightly pressed lips. She turned and I lifted her veil, draping it over her shoulder so that it lay against her chest. Her neck glistened with powder and scented soft lilac. I fumbled clumsily with the buttons, my fingers brushing her exposed skin. When they were all undone, the one in need of repair barely held the dress over her hips and a hint of her white lace panties peeked above the dress.

It was clearly torn loose, whether intentionally or by nervous, unsteady hands but I didn't inquire.

"I can't get to it with the dress on," I said. "I'll need you to step out of it a minute."

"Okay."

Ivy turned to face me instead of letting the gown fall where she stood so that I could see the front of her. The dress slipped from her shoulders, lingered over her bare breasts, then fell to her waist, the front hem brushing the floor. "Can you help me? I don't want to dirty the hem."

"Of course, just grab on here." I put her hands on my shoulders and maneuvered the dress over her hips. Her underwear was fitted with white garters that clung to silvery white stockings.

I pulled the dress down her thighs, and losing her balance, she fell onto me, her breasts cradling my cheeks, her belly pressed against my chin. Her fingers gently gripped my hair as she struggled to regain her balance.

"I'm sorry. I've been such a klutz all day."

I forced a chuckle. "Oh, it's perfectly fine. I've seen my share of nervous brides. Did I tell you about the one who vomited all over me *and* the dress the morning of her wedding?" I began my mending as she stood bare-chested and beautiful.

"No, I don't think so."

I mended the button with shaky fingers as she stood uncovered, retelling the tale that interested neither of us until I was done.

"There," I said, "absolutely perfect."

"It is," she said. "You've done wonderful work."

"I'm only doing what I love to do."

It was my *best* work, but only because she made it that way.

Her hands rested on my shoulders again as I helped her step back into the dress. I bent my head this time so as not to come in contact again with her breasts and run the risk of brushing my lips against them. Her soft, flat belly grazed my forehead and nose. Her belly button contained the scent of baby powder.

She giggled.

I paused, holding the bodice of the dress just beneath her buttocks. "What?" I backed away, afraid that I was pressing too hard, or even worse, too soft, giving myself away.

"Oh no, it's just your hair. It tickles."

"Oh, I'm sorry," I laughed nervously. I pulled my head away.

"No," Ivy said pulling me back toward her. "It's nice. Your skin is warm."

I pulled the dress up over her hips, fumbled for the bottom button. She pressed my face deeper into her and suddenly I was overcome by the overwhelming need to kiss her belly. My lips moistened the smooth, brown space between her navel and the top of her panties.

I glanced up at her face for her reaction, and her head was thrown back, her eyes closed, and her lips spread into a smile. She exhaled, her breasts brushing my forehead with the exertion of her breath. Her legs now unsteady, she fell to her knees, her face, her eyes and lips even with mine.

"Would it be terrible if I kissed you?" she asked.

"You're getting married, Ivy. Today is your wedding day."

She placed a slender finger against my lips. "All that aside. Would it be terrible if I kissed you?"

Still silenced by her finger, I shook my head, unable to find my voice even if I was free to speak.

Her lips dropped onto mine. I closed my eyes as she parted my lips with her fingers and tongue. Her tongue tasted and moved like molasses, exploring my own tongue, my teeth, the roof and sides of my mouth.

I reached up and gently pulled at the soft, dark ringlets that escaped her veil and rested on her cheeks. My own hair touched her neck and draped over her shoulders. Our tangled hair lay upon us, a dark mane like a blanket over our shoulders.

The dress surrounded us, a white satin pool around our knees. Her fingers searched my throat, massaged my shoulders, trailed my back as she gently sucked my tongue and rubbed her breasts against mine.

I held her waist, pressed gently at her sides with my thumbs. My fingers pulled at the band of her panties, her heat searing my fingers.

She reached for my hand and held it in her own, guiding me away from her panties. She pressed two final ruby kisses onto my lips.

"I shouldn't keep the driver waiting."

I found my voice again. "Yes, the driver."

I pulled the gown up, buttoned each button, and straightened the bodice. "There. You're all set."

Ivy shrugged. "I guess I am."

She grabbed my hands in one last glorious moment and kissed my fingers. She reached for the doorknob, her eyes still on me, the train of her dress still at my feet. I pulled my pair of snips out of the pocket of my robe and clipped a stray string that dangled on her chest. "Now, go on and get married."

She nodded, smiling. She said, "You don't do only wedding gowns, do you? I could bring by some patterns for my summer dresses and things, couldn't I? And maybe some pantsuits for you to alter?"

"Yes, of course. Bring by all your patterns and alterations. I'll take care of them."

I pulled the door open for her and nodded for her walk down the driveway. I watched the driver assist her into the backseat.

I have left the window before she pulls away.

– 9 –

Looking, Really Looking, at a Painting

Jessica Melusine

1. Observation

I pause, standing in the gallery, my red Indian skirt swishing around my ankles, my boots thunk-squeaking their rubber soles across the floor. The guard in the corner moves on to the next room, leaving me in silence, looking, admiring, lusting.

As befits any fine courtesan, she is painted as Venus, although she started as an actress, smearing on greasepaint rather than preening with doves. She looks out at me, a forward, come-hither, come-hotter glance, brown curls cascading over her shoulders, sloe eyes gleaming and her body lush, exquisite; she is in copper silk, gleaming, clinging tightly to her flesh, luxuriant, her waist cinched with a corset, showing her full, curvy hips, breasts swelling out from the busk, one bare, the other barely covered with a wrap of the silk, letting the curves peek through. And her jewels! She has ropes of pearls, wound in her hair, draped around her neck, twining along her skin, like a come-splashed tribute to her fleshy splendor. An old joke, but *oh god* she wears it well. There is so much to touch, so much to taste, and the painted blushes at her throat make me hunger. Seeing the valley between her breasts, I think about burying my face between them, tonguing along the soft skin heavy with sweat, musk, the heat of the unending painted summer afternoon.

Published by The Haworth Press, Inc., 2006. All rights reserved.
doi:10.1300/5328_10

I am suddenly, shamelessly wet at the thought of this, of tonguing the nipples that a merry monarch compared to rubies, corals, flames of love alight; I think of the apocryphal tales of his sport in bed with his favorites, her and two others at once. Perhaps they are the two in the background dressed as allegorical figures Grace and Temperance (O painterly irony!), draped in gauze with strings of emeralds and rubies wrapped around their throats, hair sausage curled in red and gold ringlets, hips ample under the sheer gauze, hint of round, soft bellies and delicious breasts hanging heavy like ripe fruit. *Three Goddesses, Three Graces.* I think and think of how many men had spent themselves thinking of the ladies sporting in the royal bedchamber, how many art historians had surreptitiously retired to the men's room to squirt themselves into an ironed handkerchief, thinking about their face buried between musky thighs, imagined rubbing themselves to hardness against the milky spheres of the slut Venus' grabable, fuckable ass, *oh jeezus* and I think of the kind of picture we would paint together, the Three Graces and I.

II. Banquet

Her flesh is white and reddens like cherries and cream when I bite, sinking my teeth into her shoulder, soothing it with my tongue, taking one breast in my hand, overflowing, heavy, more than a handful is beyond, so far beyond all right, rolling the pink nipple between my thumb and forefinger until she moans, rolling up her skirt to show white stockings gartered at the knee, heavy, white, solid sweet thighs and the finest cunt in Christendom, all coral fringes and wet silk under the full swell of belly and coarse, dark curls. I feel her body quiver and shake as she slides her fingers in, frigging herself as I lick the back of her neck, biting and biting, grinding my own wet cunt against her, an unrepentant tribadist.

I am licking further and further down, along the roundness of her breasts, the lace marks left from the corset, flesh too much to stay contained and I tongue furiously, wetting her skin, my face, diving to lick at the juncture of her thighs, burying my face in her dark curls, head clasped between her legs, the taste of flesh and salt, lapping at her fingers as she fucks herself again and again, screaming and moaning, seeing her body shake and quiver, the flesh on her belly ripple with every move, every shuddering sigh.

She tastes of salt and musk and honey and I could drink her dry, moving in long full strokes, covering my face with her fluids. Above me, her cries are drowned in kisses; Temperance is kissing, golden hair grown curled and wet from exertion, grinding and grinding and as I lick, I feel Grace's breasts at my back, nipples growing hot and hard, as my cunt drips. I am drunk on flesh and the taste of women known for pleasure; but now no men spend, now the finest courtesans play alone, away from prying eyes, and I am richer than any wastrel king. My tongue is entrenched in Venus' cunt. Closing my eyes, I lick and lick as if my life depended on it, working her clit with my tongue and teeth, flicking the rosy flesh until her legs scissor around my head and my face is bathed with moisture, filling my mouth, my nostrils till all I taste and breathe is her, her now sticky fingers twined in my long black hair.

It is then, with my eyes closed, face dripping, that I feel hands on my breasts, squeezing, pinching, Temperance's light fingers running over the full swelling of my belly to reach my cunt, pinching it again and again between her fingers, as I moan my pleasure back into the mass of flesh before me; Venus' legs are wider and I am licking from clit to cunt to asshole, sliding and slipping back and forth, lips vibrating as Temperance tweaks my clit, electrifying me.

It is then that I feel cruel Grace, hear her chuckle behind me, feeling a pair of hands spread me open, feel a wet, slippery tongue licking around my asshole, making me scream into the wet, fleshy thighs, buck against Temperance's heavy arms and breasts in pleasure and sob as one by one, I am violated, pearl by pearl by the necklace that Grace is sliding into my asshole, wiggling it back and forth. Then I am full and all is tongues and flesh and lips around me; I lick earlobes and wrists, toes, cunt, with fervor, enthusiasm, worshiping at the altar of graces and harlots, licking the rich curves of bellies and breasts, the sweet S of back and ass, drunk on flesh, on softness beneath and above me twisting and twisting. I hump thighs, calves, arms, still full of the necklace, feeling my head pushed back to Venus' gates, the king's favorite grotto, my shrine of lust, my site of hungry worship. And it is with my face buried in her cunt, her fingers scraping the back of my neck, Temperance's hungry fingers at my clit and Grace tugging the pearls from my ass that I come, a deep shudder, screaming into the flesh of harlots, dripping fluids growling, screaming smothered by breasts and hips and hot white thighs, the electricity building and building until I burst and burst at another caress, a final hip twitch, the last squeeze of my asshole as it releases the last two pearls. . . .

I squeeze my thighs together, discreetly still admiring the painting. The guard passes through, ambling slowly in blue, and I exit, breath still heavy, cunt still slick, still sweetly drunk on flesh.

– 10 –

Betty Came

M. Christian

She remembered the first time that Betty came. Sitting in her tiny kitchen, beams of warm sunlight painting it with brilliant yellow stripes, it was so easy to think of Betty as being there, next to her. It had been one of Audrey's all-night parties. Another of the ex-boy's "No other reason" Friday night dancing and drinking bashes. June had gotten pretty toasted early on—washing down the stubborn truth that she and Wendy had broken up the month before—and was quite satisfied to sit in a corner of the hideously cluttered apartment and get lost in the Pussy Tourrette album blasting from Audrey's Frankensteined sound system.

Didn't know the tiny black girl's name, didn't even see who she'd come with. One second June was belting back her fifth Red Rock and the next the room exploded with a billion flashbulbs when she had walked in. But Wendy was still a dull ache and the one thing you don't think about when you have that "no one loves me anymore" pang is that someone, suddenly, would.

Somehow, intros were made and June found herself fighting that fifth Red Rock to be on her best behavior. Chat. Joke. Smile. Flirt. Smile some more. Bat those eyelashes. Flirt. Chat.

While the sexy heat of the sparkling little girl was something that made all of June's clouds blow away, the beers (and a bitchy week at work) had started to take their toll. Even against the searchlight bril-

Published by The Haworth Press, Inc., 2006. All rights reserved.
doi:10.1300/5328_11

liance of the girl's smile, incredible cheekbones, and humming eyes, June's own face started to feel haggard, drawn, and—yawn!

She remembered saying something like: "Sorry. Luckily I live right around the corner."

"I'll walk you," the dream had said, smiling a sunrise at her.

Her place was a mess, of course. Isn't it always? Some kind of universal law: bring trick (or love of your life) home and the first thing they see when they walk in the door is a pair of stained panties tossed on the floor.

"Wouldn't want you to be too clean," the lovely charcoal sketch had said, leaning in close so June could slip an arm around her.

A cup of coffee had sounded good. June prattled some kind of empty dialogue, pretty much to herself, as she ground the beans and tried to find the sugar. She was pretty sure she had said something about what she did for a living (messenger), what she liked to do (theater), what she liked (pecan pie and sleeping in), and what she wanted (someone special). Now, sitting in the same kitchen, June wasn't sure if she'd mentioned Wendy. She hoped she hadn't.

Sometime during the beans, the milk, the water, and all the talk, talk, talk (that mostly June did), she found herself next to Betty again, found herself with one arm stroking her T-shirt–covered back, feeling the strong planes of her shoulders and the thick warmth of her dark skin. She remembered, strongly, perfectly, the girl looking up at her and smiling a glowing smile. June had kissed her.

It seemed to last forever, that first kiss (well, don't most first kisses? Another universal law). June felt herself catch fire from head to toe. To the background sounds of the percolator, she had felt her hands fall to the girl's shoulders, arms, and then her perfectly shaped tits.

The T-shirt came off quickly as Betty stood up. Holding her close, June had stroked and kneaded her arms, sides, and even her tiny pot belly. They had sighed, moaned, and groaned together as they touched (Betty's hands on June's own big biceps and almost nonexistent tits) and kissed. Somewhere, June lost her flannel shirt and the black girl her jeans and shoes.

Betty had circled June's big nipples with hot kisses as she squeezed June's cunt through her own jeans like a trick fondling a john. June couldn't keep the hissing moan in, so she had let it out into the girl's mouth—feeling it echo through her as her hand cupped a shaved and slippery cunt.

With Wendy it had been walking on eggs. Her first real lover, June had treated Wendy like she was priceless, fragile—even though Wendy was five years older than June's twenty-six. June had barricaded them in June's tiny place against her being alone again and tried to do whatever it would take to keep Wendy there. If Wendy liked something, June did it. If Wendy didn't like it . . . it never happened again

After a point, June followed Wendy everywhere. Never led. Tried not to want, desire, anything.

But in June's kitchen that night, something different was happening—it was just June and Betty. No top, no bottom, no give, no take. Just kissing, tits, cunts, and heat.

Betty had sat down in one of June's battered old wooden chairs and spread her legs as if to let some of the heat escape. June had sat down herself, surprised and almost squealing at how cold the linoleum floor was on her bare ass (lost her own pants and shoes somewhere). Since she was down there already (yeah, right) she kissed the girl's thighs; that delicious, all-but-invisible belly; and then rummaged in her hot slit with her nose: playful rooting and tickling like a frisky puppy.

Betty had sighed and spread her legs wider.

June gently brought one hand up and pulled the girl's cunt lips apart, spying with almost childish delight a pink clit the size of a marble in a sculpture of black and pink lips, almost smoking in the cool air of the kitchen. Of course she had licked. Of course she sucked, kissed, and stroked it with her tongue.

June had forgotten her name almost the instant it had been told her. She called her Betty because she looked like a black Betty Page.

In the same, now empty, kitchen: Betty came.

Now empty. June got up and wandered back into the rest of her apartment. Not the same, but the same kind of slightly yellowed panties on the hardwood floor next to her stack of *Bay Times* newspapers. The same old, barely working, Mac Classic her father had bought her. Same futon on the floor. Same Pier One rattan blinds.

Same sketch Fish had done of her at the Folsom Street Fair. Same tiny stack of playbills for shows she had helped with.

It scared June when people reminded her that they were only together for two months. It seemed longer. Lots longer. Betty was the kind of girlfriend she thought she always needed. Looking at the futon, with its discolorations, stains, and lumps, it was too easy to feel her again. Standing, as she always seemed to, so that she was just touching June's hip or arm.

June sat and absently flashed through the newspapers, trying not to think about the bed. Betty.

Lots of luck.

One night—oh, boy—that night: it was their second week together so naturally Betty had hauled over most of her stuff. They had gone long into the night prowling through her records, books, tapes, clothes, sharing stories about them or June's similars—when this thing of plastic and nylon webbing came out of one box.

"Haven't you ever?" Betty had said, digging in another box for the main part of it.

June hadn't. Wendy had been an old-world dyke. Plastic or meat, it was still a cock and she wouldn't have had any part of it. June had actually been interested for a long time but never had the opportunity—and after Wendy had left she pretty much lost interest in much of anything.

Betty found her cock—a pretty, stylized blue thing that looked more like a gizmo from a science fiction movie than a penis. Maybe that's what made it easier for June. As Wendy protested in the back of June's mind, she kept telling the phantom: have you seen a cock like this? Buckle, snap, cinch. Condom, lube. "Bend over, dear."

"Wait a minute," June had said, feeling out of control. "Who wears the pants around here?"

"You do," Betty had said, stroking her penis, "but I have the cock. Now bend over, or do I have to call you a bitch?"

"No, sir!" June snapped in sarcasm, but added in a much smaller voice: "Take it easy with that thing: I'm a virgin."

"Then this is going to be a novel experience," Betty had said, all smiles and enthusiasm. "I've never deflowered a virgin before."

June had suddenly been aware of a different part of her: a part that wanted the cock and Betty behind it. A surprising desire to feel the plastic penis in her cunt. It wasn't just horniness. It was love. She wanted to be wanted by her.

It almost made her cry. It was something she thought she'd lost when Wendy had left to find someone even more subservient. Having it back was almost too much for her to handle: that, and the fear that it could go again.

Slowly, June had stood up on the lumpy futon, unbuttoned her jeans, and then, teasingly, dropped her panties. She did it slowly because while it seemed that all she and Betty did was fuck, the magic of their bodies hadn't rubbed off yet. She had loved to get naked in front of Betty, watching her eyes dance and hunger for her.

It was a little chilly in the apartment, so June left her T-shirt on.

"Make like a doggie, love," Betty had said. "It's easier that way."

Slowly, kind of scared, June had: she got down on the futon, first on her hands and knees and then—because her arms started to ache—leaning down on a pillow.

"So pretty," Betty said from behind her.

The kiss was kind of a shock. June had been so psyched to receive the brilliantly blue silicone dildo that the one thing she hadn't expected was the sister kiss of Betty's lips on her cunt lips.

Slowly, worshipfully, Betty kissed her again and again: on the cheeks of her ass, on the little knot of her asshole, on her puffy outer lips, and then, with a little skillful positioning, on the little dent where her cunt lips started and where her clit lay hidden.

"So very pretty," Betty had said, massaging June's cunt with a smooth, slightly cool hand—rubbing her mons and lips and thus her clit in its folds and valleys of very warm skin (and getting warmer). It was the kind of touch that June loved. It was a kind of gentle, worshipping touch that was almost unfamiliar. Wendy had done it, very early on in their relationship, then tossed it aside as she got bored.

June had missed it.

Betty had been so gentle, so tender with her touches and kisses that June almost didn't realize that the cock was entering her. It was warm, not too big, and definitely not persistent. It had felt, in fact, like Betty had just sort of parked its condom-covered plastic head just outside her cunt and was just sort of letting it be there as Betty stroked and gingerly touched June's back, thighs, and ass.

June had been so caught up in the gentleness of something she had always considered harsh and probably painful . . . fucking . . . she almost didn't notice, didn't pick up, that Betty was talking.

"Such a beautiful woman. Such a gorgeous woman. Oh, god, I look at you and I get all wet. Yeah, my pussy, too, but me, inside, too. I get all warm and squishy when I look at you and touch you and . . . god . . . I get all gold inside, all sunlight and hot and tingly—"

The cock had slowly started to ease inside of June, to make its way very slowly and very sedately into her cunt. In some way it reminded June of taking a dump—backward: the sense of being filled, or being stretched by something warm and slightly resident. It wasn't an uncomfortable feeling but it was . . . different: sex had always been quick and flickering things like tongues and fingers—not big solid things like plastic cocks.

It was very unique, but something, June knew, there on her lumpy old futon, that she could grow to like. A lot.

She was filled, she was empty, she was filled, she was empty—the transition from just being occupied by Betty's cock to being fucked by Betty's cock was so smooth that, at first, June really didn't know what was going on. The sensation was warm and rhythmic, like her whole ass and cunt was breathing with the dildo—like she was expanding and contracting with each thrust. Heavy, warm surges ran through her and she found herself panting into the pillow she was resting on. Her legs had started to ache.

She must have said something, because Betty had taken a few careful moments to adjust her—putting a bigger pillow under her tummy and moving her legs so she was more flat out—before easing her cock back into June's cunt.

It was like floating in a boat, June decided as Betty had fucked her. Gentle, warm waves on a lightly moving sea. She liked it. She wasn't going to come—no way—but it was like an internal massage.

"Try rubbing your cunt," Betty had said in a voice laced with an aerobics pant.

Thoroughly committed, June had done exactly that. She had snaked her right hand down to her clit and found it delightfully hard and wonderfully wet from the juice and lube that was dripping from her slurping cunt. Since she loved it usually when she jerked off, her left also went to her left nipple where she found it, also, incredibly hard. As Betty fucked her she started to really get down and nasty with her clit as she rubbed and pulled at her nipple.

Oh, boy, she remembered thinking as the first of five deep and rumbling comes surged through her. She also remembered the leg cramps and the huge wet mark on the pillow where she had been drooling in excitement.

Slowly, cautiously, because of her raging leg cramps, she had turned over and hugged Betty. A delightful surprise awaited her as she did so: in her arms, Betty had her own hand down between the harness and the plastic cock, and was furiously working her own clit.

June held her, feeling her fiery heat. Then Betty came.

That was then. Now, June got up from the futon and her old newspapers and tried to think without thinking of Betty. Even though the tiny black girl had been pretty thorough about taking everything of hers, it was still painfully hard not to try and think of her. Every room brought back flashes of wonderful times: tea and talk, tears and hugs, and comes . . . lots and lots of comes.

Even the fucking bathroom, June thought with a sudden flash of anger, remembering that one morning: cold tiles under her back as Betty lowered herself onto June's face. It was an odd scene, one she would never have thought of. She remembered that they hadn't talked. It had just sort of happened the same way that first time in the kitchen had happened. June had been taking a piss. Betty had just stepped out of the shower. Betty had walked over to her and asked June to towel her off. June had, then kissed her lips and then the younger girl's nipples. There was such joy in Betty—like life was just a game of come and come again. She didn't seem to worry like Wendy had, about right and wrong things to do and enjoy. Betty had just drifted from one fun thing to another.

The fun, for instance, in hauling June down to the cold tiles and carefully lowering her sweet little cunt down onto June's face. It was kind of scary—to have someone, no matter how tiny, hovering over your eyes and nose and mouth and tongue. But then it started to kick in for June, and she felt an explosion of pure, crazed horniness: Betty was using her, shoving herself down onto June's tongue in eagerness.

In the hall, looking into the now-dark bathroom, June didn't even have to close her eyes to experience the taste of Betty's cunt—the heady perfume of her excitement. She remembered waking up many mornings to that smell on her lips and fingers, permeating even the time she spent away from her.

She remembered the bathroom, the gentle weight of Betty on her face. She recalled the giggles and the sighs that eased and surged out of the little dark-haired black girl as June licked and nibbled and sucked at her cunt and clit.

Sweet music—

Betty's hands, always busy, always hunting for June's tits, ass, or cunt, had fluttered on the tight skin of June's thighs, forced them apart with the crazed energy of the very, very excited, and then had started to work on June's pussy. Betty had been surprisingly deft, considering the feverish licking June had been giving her, and soon June was staring down into the white light of a brilliant come.

Together, they went there. June came from Betty's fingers.

Above her, Betty came.

June found herself in the hall. Down the stairs was the front door. Probably the one place where they hadn't played, where Betty hadn't come. She'd gone, though.

What she said, what Betty said, was pretty well gone. All June could remember was a bad week—bad work, bad parents, bad city— and a fight about . . . something. Maybe she had talked about Wendy. She hoped not. Betty had gone.

Now, five days later: The little apartment was cold and empty. It was dark and quiet. June, and June alone, slept on the lumpy futon, made coffee in the morning, and read her newspapers. No calls came in, and she didn't feel like making any.

Except one. Now, in the quiet dark.

June's fingers felt numb. It was hard to admit that she wanted Betty, wanted her back. It was hard to say she wanted anything. It was a scary place—as dark as the apartment was: What if she said no?

But could it be any worse?

Audrey answered on the second ring, her surprisingly deep voice: "Speak your peace."

"Is Betty there, Audrey?"

"Just a minute, you heartbreaker—"

"Yes?"

"Come. Please come. I want you."

Betty came.

− 11 −

Cinderella's Shoes

Kate Dominic

I was certain Cinderella never had to wait in her room for her ugly stepmother to come upstairs with a spanking strap. Not that Deirdre was really ugly. Even when I was mad at her and feeling more than a little scared, I appreciated that the potential trophy wife my father had briefly dated was a beautiful dark-haired woman in her mid-forties with a slender, curvy figure and flashing brown eyes. She'd built her own multimillion-dollar security consulting company from the ground up. She gave me good advice about boys—and when she realized I wasn't interested, better advice about girls. She even taught me to drive her Porsche, much to my father's dismay. After she and Daddy's totally amicable breakup, I was ecstatic when she gave in to my begging and agreed to let me live with her while I attended classes at the university a half mile down the street from her house.

My only complaint about Deirdre was that she was convinced the only way to get the attention of an undisciplined young college girl was through her bottom. That meant every time I was in trouble, I found myself over Deirdre's lap with my panties around my ankles, her arm tight around my waist, and my butt high in the air. She whipped the bejeezus out of me with a nasty leather hand strap that packed a world of hurtin' into twelve short inches of supple, black cowhide.

Published by The Haworth Press, Inc., 2006. All rights reserved.
doi:10.1300/5328_12

Fortunately, my crimes were paid for as soon as my bottom was on fire and I was crying on the corner. If I needed to make restitution or had to apologize to someone else, her company's chief investigator, a rude macho dyke named Amanda who was also Deirdre's ex-lover, used state-of-the-art surveillance systems to verify that I'd done what I'd said I was going to do. I got a double dose of Deirdre's strap if I didn't. I learned to follow up quickly, partly to stay off Amanda's radar, but mostly because I'd realized how much I liked kissing and making up with Deirdre.

It had taken me a while to realize I was in love with her. She was so different from the women to whom I usually was attracted. I liked young, mouthy butches who wore masculine clothes and comfortable shoes. Deirdre was older and sophisticated—a total clotheshorse femme, just like me. We went shoe shopping together at least once a month and stood in line at the crack of dawn for the semiannual clearance sales at our favorite department stores. We even got our nails done on Saturday mornings. She kept hers long and painted in subtle, classy colors. I couldn't figure out how she'd never once poked me when we were panting on our Egyptian cotton sheets. I kept my nails typical dyke short, though lately I'd been getting a clear gloss finish rather than just buffing. We had so much fun together. When she held me close and told me she loved me, her kisses made me quiver.

Her fucking strap also made my bottom hurt so bad. I was fairly certain how she was going to react to my having gone 800 minutes over my cell phone limit this month, in addition to the horrendous long distance and roaming charges I'd forgotten to mention. When she'd specifically asked me if I'd incurred any during my outlet trips with my friends, I'd told her "no." I figured I could brush off a few. But then I'd gotten so busy, I'd forgotten to keep track of how many extras I was adding. If the additional charges had been an emergency or even if I'd made arrangements ahead of time, and most especially if I hadn't lied, Deirdre wouldn't have minded.

She was going to mind this, in a real big way. Right on time, I heard her car pull into the driveway. I tried not to bite my nails any more than I already had. I knew better than to not tell her now. But

I'd taken the coward's way out and just left the open bill waiting on the table with the rest of the mail.

Five minutes later, Deirdre marched into my room. She was still in her pastel pink power suit. She held the bill in one hand and her strap in the other. Staring directly into my eyes, she dropped the damning evidence on the bed next to me.

"Is there anything you'd like to say in your defense, or should we get right to spanking your bottom?"

I looked sullenly at the floor. It seemed like there should have been some other options for someone my age. Okay, so there were. Any time I wanted, I could take over paying for my entire phone bill, rather than just paying the additional charges the way I was going to be now. Well, as soon as I earned enough money to pay that and my overdrawn credit card bill, which Deirdre had strapped me for last week. I sighed heavily and muttered, "No, ma'am."

"Very well." She took off her jacket and draped it over the back of my desk chair. She was wearing a cream-colored silk blouse and pale pink pearls and the buttery soft Italian designer heels we'd picked up last weekend. I was still nervously admiring her outfit when she sat down on the edge of the bed and patted her thigh.

"Take off your shorts and panties and get over my lap, Melissa."

I looked up at her in surprise. "Take them off?"

"Yes, young lady," she said firmly. "Your behavior has been in a downward spiral for the past few weeks. It's time to nip this in the bud." She smacked the strap loudly against her hand. "Strip from the waist down and put your clothes in your hamper. You won't be needing them any more tonight."

Deirdre's look told me there was no point in arguing. My face flamed as I unbuttoned my shorts and hooked my fingers in the waistband of my panties. I skimmed them down together and quickly stuffed them in the top of the hamper, hoping Deirdre hadn't noticed that I still hadn't done my laundry.

"I see you'll be doing your laundry as soon as you're done with your corner time," she said firmly.

"Yes, ma'am." I blushed. I took a deep breath and marched stoically over to the bed. With each step, the edge of my T-shirt brushed the top of my behind, making me even more aware of the nervous tingle in my skin. Deirdre took me firmly by the elbow and guided me over her lap.

I scooted forward, wrapping my arms firmly around my pillow. I got extra on the backs of my thighs if I reached back to cover my bottom. I usually didn't do it. But sometimes I did. Deirdre always got me really crying when she strapped me. With it being summer, I didn't want to have to wear long pants or skirts to cover the marks on my legs. If I was honest, Deirdre had never given me a spanking I didn't richly deserve, but I was still embarrassed enough over getting strapped that I really wanted to keep my punishments private between us. Deirdre resituated my bottom so it was right up over her leg. Then she lifted my shirt up over my waist and wrapped her arm tightly around me.

"You're going to get a good sound spanking, Melissa. Cry all you want to, but don't cover your bottom or try to move off my lap."

"Yes, ma'am," I squeaked, pressing my thighs together. I was determined to keep my mouth shut. I'd never succeeded, but once again, I promised myself that this time, I'd stay quiet.

The first crack tore the breath from my lungs. I lurched up against her arm, gasping as fire screamed across my right cheek. I gasped again as the next crack burned across my left. Two strokes later, I was yelping, hugging my pillow as hard as I could and squirming wildly over her lap.

"Ow. Ow. OW!" I arched forward, tightening my butt as much as I could, trying to squeeze the pain away. It didn't do any good. Each crack was hard and hot and it burned deep into my tender bottom flesh. Before long, I was yelling and twisting, frantically kicking my legs as Deirdre strapped me with the same thorough effectiveness she used each and every time. I shivered hard when she reached down and pulled my outer leg to the side.

"Deirdre! Pleeeeease!!!!" I howled. Her grip was like a steel band, exposing my poor sore bottom even more.

"You know you deserve this, young lady," she snapped. Then that nasty fucking strap cracked into the tender flesh of my wide open sit spot and way up between my cheeks. I wailed, lurching and thrashing like a wild woman as she strapped me until my bottom hurt so much I knew it had to be on fire for sure.

When she finally stopped, I collapsed over her lap, sobbing and apologizing profusely for being so irresponsible. I promised I'd never do it again, not ever. I was so sore I almost meant it. In fact, I meant it so much I knew I was really going to try to behave for a good long while. The sound of the door opening in back of me barely registered.

"Your apology is accepted, Melissa. But at this point, I need to be certain your irresponsibility is going to cease. Thank you, Amanda."

I looked up, astonished to see the chief investigator standing next to me. "Deirdre?" I gasped. She had never spanked me in front of anyone before. I tried to reach back to cover my bottom, but she held my hands firmly away.

"Come now, Melissa. You didn't think your little escapades had escaped surveillance, did you?"

I gave Amanda my dirtiest look, but she just glanced at my butt and whistled sympathetically. "You're getting one heck of a strapping, young lady. Your bottom looks almost as sore as mine used to feel after a good session over Deirdre's knee."

I was stunned almost to silence. "You?" I gawked. I could not imagine the big, strong, suit-clad dyke standing in front of me hanging over anybody's knee, especially with her pants down, getting a spanking.

"Yes, indeedy," she said seriously. "You better believe that as long as I lived under her roof, I ended up with a blazing sore bottom whenever I misbehaved. She didn't use a strap on me, though." For the first time, I realized Amanda was holding a long, slender stick in her hand. "She used a willow switch, just like this."

I gasped as Deirdre swatted my blazing bottom. "Since the strap isn't getting through to you well enough, I've decided you should have a good sound switching as well today, so you know just how serious I am about your behavior changing."

As I stared at them, too shocked to speak, Amanda sat down at the head of my bed and took my hands in hers. "I know we haven't gotten along well before, honey, but you better hold on, now. A willow

switching really burns, and Deirdre is going to light your butt on fire
by the time she's done."

I stiffened as Deirdre held my leg out and open again. But before I
could say anything, the air whistled and a lightning flash of pure,
white hot pain slashed across my bottom. I screamed and Amanda
winced, but she held on tight to my hands, murmuring "There, there,
dear," as I shrieked and bucked over Deirdre's lap. Deirdre lashed four
more horrifically painful strokes from the top of my backside to the
bottom, then she added two more to my already blazing sit spot. I was
still wailing at the top of my lungs when she whipped the last one
down diagonally, igniting my whole backside into a solid wall of
flames all over again. When I collapsed over her lap this time, I was
crying so hard I could hardly breathe.

I was certain my bottom would never stop hurting again, not ever
in my whole life. Amanda patted my hands before she left. Then it
was just Deirdre and me again. When I'd finally settled to hiccupping
sniffles, she stood us both up and pulled me into her arms. I cried out
when my shirt brushed over my scalded skin. Then I clung to her for
dear life, soaking her silk blouse with my tears as she petted me and
told me I was a good girl, and she knew I'd do better from now on.
Oooh, my bottom burned. I told her I was sorry. I promised I'd be
more responsible, I really would. Then I cried some more because my
behind hurt so bad.

Eventually, I'd calmed enough for Deirdre to lead me to the corner.
As I pressed my face to the juncture in the walls, she leaned over and
gently kissed the side of my neck.

"Would you like to be alone now, dear? Or do you want some additional comforting?"

I clenched my bottom involuntarily, wincing at the pain of my
well-whipped cheeks pressing against each other. Even though I was
really sorry for what I'd done, my backside was sending waves of electric heat surging into my pussy. Each time I tightened, the feelings
got more intense. Deirdre's kisses were making me shiver so hard the
hair on the back of my neck was standing up.

"More comforting, please," I sniffled, swiping my hands over my
tear-filled eyes.

"Very well," she said quietly. Her next kiss was so wet and soft and tender I moaned into my fingers. "Compose yourself a bit more, darling. I'll be back when I've changed and your corner time is up." She set the timer on the dresser for ten minutes and closed the door, leaving me alone with my thoughts.

The wait seemed like an eternity. As the timer ticked loudly into the quiet evening air, I thought about how sore my bottom was and how mad I was at Deirdre for spanking me, and about how mad I was at myself for being so naughty, and how embarrassed I'd been to have Amanda see me get switched. It was so unfair, even though I'd pretty much asked for it. When I reached back to gingerly touch my bottom, my skin felt so hot and I was so tender even my own hand hurt. I sniffled as more tears leaked out of my eyes. The switch had left a crisscross of horrifically sore thin, raised welts. And I was so horny that just thinking about Deirdre's kisses made my pussy throb. I pressed my thighs together hard, ignoring the pain in my bottom as I squeezed pressure on my clit.

I was wiping my eyes again when she walked back in the room. I heard her pull out my desk chair and move it over near the nightstand. She rummaged around in the drawers, then quietly said, "Come here, darling."

I turned around and my breath caught. Deirdre still wore her pearls and her fancy Italian shoes and the gold bracelets that usually adorned her wrists, but she'd peeled off her skirt and slip and blouse. Her luminescent silk stockings were held up by a lacy garter belt with butterflies embroidered around the edges. She wore a matching satin demi-bra, and she wasn't wearing panties. In her hand, she held a black leather thigh harness with a large purple latex dildo secured into the ring. My bottom tingled at the sight. Deirdre sat down on the chair and buckled the harness on her right thigh, just above the top of her stocking. The nightstand drawer was open, the one where we keep all our supplies. She reached in the drawer and took out an accordion-shaped lube applicator. As I stepped in front of her, she peeled off the cap, then patted the tip with her long, polished nail.

"Turn around and bend over, dear."

Tears stung my eyes before I even put my hands on my bottom. I slowly turned my back to her and spread my legs. Then I leaned forward, hissing as I gripped my sore cheeks and pulled them open for her.

"A little more, sweetheart." She patted my bottom gently. I yelped. I was so sore, even her fingertips burned.

"It hurts," I whispered, tears falling down my cheeks as I dutifully pulled my burning cheeks as far apart as I could. I shivered as the cool evening air tickled over my anus.

"Little girls who need spankings end up with very sore bottoms," she said tenderly. "Your bottom's bright red and very hot."

I moaned as her finger traced lightly over an excruciatingly sore line. I knew it had to be a switch mark. Then the tip of the applicator touched my anus. I jumped as a cool smear of lube glided over me.

"Keep your bottom open and bear down for me, darling."

I hated that part. It was so embarrassing, yet it felt so good, even though my bottom hurt so bad. The slippery nozzle teased until my ass lips fluttered against it. As I pushed back, straining to kiss my anus over that hard plastic tip, my sphincter opened just enough for the nozzle to slide through.

"Oooh!" I trembled as it slid up into me. Deirdre laughed softly.

"Good girl."

I shook as she squeezed the cool dose of lube up into my bottom. She pulled the applicator slowly out and I stood there, holding my bottom cheeks open as my anus squirmed and clenched and squished on the cool, viscous lube filling my rectum. Deirdre set the applicator on the nightstand.

"Stand up and turn around, dear. Take off your shirt and bra, and when you're naked, you may straddle me."

I peeled off my shirt and unhooked the back of my bra. Deirdre had picked it out for me, a simple cotton uplift style with a chaste white ribbon between the cups. It made me feel so innocent and sexy—and hers. As I undressed for her, she took the big lube bottle from the drawer and slathered her huge purple cock until it was dripping. I moved my legs over her thigh, spreading them wide and bracing my hands on her warm, feminine shoulders. Then I squatted slowly, until just the tip of the dildo brushed against my anus. Deirdre reached in back of me, her bracelets jingling softly as she cupped my bottom, pulling me open. I gasped hard. Her hands hurt so badly, and her latex cockhead felt so good. It pressed against me, just enough to gently kiss my anal lips.

"Ow," I moaned. Deirdre's hands stilled instantly.

"Does the dildo hurt you, Melissa?"

"Nooooo," I sobbed, leaning down more in spite of myself, reaching for the delicious slippery stretching. "My bottom hurts. You spanked me so hard, Deirdre!"

"Yes, I did." She licked tenderly over my nipple. I shivered as it hardened. She licked again, and I lowered myself further onto the plug. The tip slid in.

"Ooooh! It feels so good!" I gasped.

Deirdre laughed softly, pulling my bottom cheeks further apart. I yelled at the pain, shuddering as the slippery cockhead slid further into my lube-stuffed bottom. Then the head popped in.

"Deirdre!" I wailed her name, shivering as she held me quietly, letting me adjust to the huge, relentless stretch in my hungry sphincter. Eventually, I slid lower, taking her cock gradually into me. Deirdre raised and lowered me, kneading my pain-filled bottom as she fucked me over her cock. I cried out at the pain, my ass lips trembling at the exquisite sensation of sliding over her huge latex toy. Each time I descended, she slid further in. I was so close to coming. Her cock always got me so close. It got me craving the touch that would push me over the edge.

"I expect you'll be remembering for a good long time what happens to little girls who need their bottoms punished." She licked soothingly from one breast to the other. "And to little girls who take their punishments and are forgiven." As she started to suck, her fingers gripped right into my sit spot, right where the strap and switch had burned in so hard into the sensitive tender skin. She squeezed, very, very hard.

"I'll remember, ma'am." I sobbed. The fullest part suddenly stretched me wide and slid in. My tender bottom landed hard against her thigh. As I cried out, Deirdre slid her hands up to my waist, holding me tightly onto her leg as she sucked hard on my nipples. Finally I lifted my legs, shifting my weight so my sore, spanked bottom rested almost entirely on her, letting the pain wash over me the way I knew she wanted me to. As tears streamed down my face, I clutched her shoulders, ignoring the pearls trapped in my fingers as my anus trembled over her dick in a frenzy that had me so horny I could hardly stand it. Deirdre rocked me back and forth on my bottom and the dildo until I was shaking.

"Deirdre!" I wailed. "I'm sorry! I want to come so bad!"

"I know you do, darling." She lifted her head and kissed me. "Milk your nipples now." The well-sucked tips were so sensitive that when I took them between my fingers and pulled out, my bottom clenched hard. I cried out, squirming hard over her thigh.

"You're so beautiful, darling."

I moaned in relief as Deirdre's fingers slid from my waist. She poured lube into her spanking hand until it glistened. With the other hand, she peeled my slippery labia open, baring my clit. Then her cool, lube-slicked fingers slid down and rubbed tenderly over my quivering nub. I cried out, grinding against her thigh as my anus clenched hard around her cock.

"Rock on my thigh, love, while I give you your orgasm."

Her beautiful fingernails moved in slow, deliberate circles over my throbbing clit. I ground against her, frantically tugging my nipples. The sensation vibrated deep down into my pussy and my wide-stretched asshole and my screaming sore behind. I let the pain and the heat and the glorious pleasure of her thigh cock press deep into me while Deirdre slowly and relentlessly drew the orgasm from me.

"I'm gonna come," I blurted out. Deirdre laughed softly. She didn't let up on her circling, not even once. The orgasm washed over me, and I threw back my head and howled. My legs quaked as I rocked against her and her fingers, her fucking wonderful fingers, made me come so hard I thought I'd quit breathing.

"Please stop," I whispered, my hands falling free as I leaned forward and rested my head on hers. I was shaking so hard I knew I'd fall if I weren't held firmly in place by the dildo embedded deep up my ass. Deirdre tenderly slid her hands back around my waist and held me until I'd stopped shaking.

I cried again when she squeezed my bottom cheeks wide open so I could rise up off of the plug. I pulled free and squatted over her, my hands holding tightly onto her shoulders as the tears again streamed down my face.

"Stroke your anus, darling," she said softly. I groaned. She always made me do it, and it was always so embarrassing. But it felt so fucking good. I gingerly reached in back of myself, working my arm past hers as I slid my fingers down my crack. I shivered at my own touch. My anus was puffy and still slightly opened.

"Stroke your fingers in and out."

I did, whimpering as she squeezed my burning cheeks and I finger fucked myself. Touching my slippery, open sphincter felt almost as good on my fingers as my own touch did on my anus.

"This is what happens to naughty girls who need their bottoms strapped and switched. Have you learned your lesson, dear?" She squeezed my bottom very, very hard.

"Yes, ma'am," I shivered, sliding my fingers in and out of my open hole. A small wave of pleasure once more washed over me. "I've learned. I promise."

"Good girl," she smiled, letting my bottom cheeks close. I lifted my glistening fingers back to her shoulder. "You may now lick my pussy and give me an orgasm, darling. But you may only use your tongue. Your fingers have been in your bottom. While you're licking, remember that if you want to put your fingers in Deirdre's pussy, you have to be a good girl."

"Yes, ma'am." I dove between her legs. Oooh, her pussy tasted good. It was sweet and sticky. Her stockings and the strap from her harness and finally her leather-clad heels rubbed against my arms and shoulders as she wrapped her legs around me and held my face to her pussy. She let me eat her to three orgasms. Then she gave me a deep soft kiss and told me she loved me forever and ever.

We went downstairs, with me naked and Deirdre in her underwear and heels. After I'd started my laundry, she let me serve us homemade European salads and she even let me take a sip of her Chardonnay.

Three nights later, I looked in the mirror, gingerly touching the last of the deep red marks and the long thin switch bruises still crisscrossing my bottom. I was thinking if I wore nice soft panties, maybe I'd be able to sit still in the car long enough to go across town with Deirdre. As always, my spanking had been the end of the matter. We'd worked out a loan plan to pay my outstanding bills, and I was making damn sure that fucking Amanda wouldn't have anything bad to report about me. Well, maybe she wasn't all bad. But I still wasn't going to give her any ammunition for narking to Deirdre. I pulled on a pair of loose silk tap pants, another gift from my sweetie, and went downstairs to go shoe shopping with her. There was a moonlight madness sale at the mall, and we wanted to be first in line.

– 12 –

Practice Makes Perfect

Zoe Bishop

My roommate and I were sunbathing at Baker Beach in San Francisco when it happened. Vanessa is my roommate and best friend. And . . . I'm not sure what else. But after what happened at Baker Beach, I'm starting to get a pretty good idea.

Baker is an interesting place. If you've ever lived in the Bay Area, you've probably heard of it—even though it's technically not a nude beach, nudity is "tolerated," which means some people get naked and others don't. Of course, most of the time in San Francisco you don't *want* to be nude, because it's foggy and cold as often as not.

But this was one of those rare summer days when the mercury hits a hundred degrees in the city, and everybody in town, so unaccustomed to that kind of heat, goes crazy and strips down to their skivvies. My friend Vanessa and I decided to hit the beach, and found a crowded strip of sand with plenty of pasty-white, oiled-up bodies sprawled everywhere. I guess because of Baker's reputation as a gay beach, there wasn't a kid in sight—no screeching brats howling about with sand in their swimsuits, no daddies throwing beach balls; just the other kind of daddy, the fortyish guy who brings another guy my age. And even they looked at us.

Vanessa and I weren't pasty white at all. We had been planning a trip to southern Cal, so we had already been visiting the tanning booth. For the first time in my life I had a rich, sexy, golden-brown

Published by The Haworth Press, Inc., 2006. All rights reserved.
doi:10.1300/5328_13

tan, and as Vanessa and I laid out our beach blanket and stripped out of our shorts and tank tops, I felt a glow of pride at my firm and tanned body. I also felt a little embarrassed; this was the first time I'd worn my new string bikini in public, and I could feel the eyes of all the male beachgoers roving over me. It was amazing to me how blatantly the guys on the beach looked at us, not even trying to disguise their admiration, their attraction, their hunger. It felt good to be looked at like that. Even though it made me a little nervous, I liked it.

But what was strange was that there was a line of guys up on the cliffs overlooking the beach, looking down at the beach with binoculars, camcorders, and digital cameras. They were far enough away that I couldn't be absolutely sure, but I felt confident that Vanessa and I were the focus of many of those instruments and the rapt attention of the dirty old men up there looking at us.

The back of Vanessa's bikini was nothing more than a string, but that wasn't enough for Vanessa. As soon as she sat on the blanket, she started unfastening her bikini top.

I looked at her with my eyes wide. "Van-*nessa!*" I said, shocked.

"What?" she answered, shrugging as she slipped off her bikini top and tucked it in her beach bag. Her breasts glistened, sweaty and tawny, in the sun. "It's a nude beach."

Vanessa has great tits. Like me, she didn't have the faintest hint of tan lines. Thank God for technology. "But all those guys are watching."

She smiled. "Let 'em look. It's not like they'd dare touch. I've got my pepper spray." That made me laugh.

"They've got cameras," I said. "You'll probably be on the Web by tonight."

"Guess I'll have to give up my career in public office." Vanessa up-ended the bottle of sunscreen and smeared it over her breasts, paying special attention to the nipples. I tried not to watch too closely, but something kind of intrigued me about the way she rubbed the oil all over her nipples, making them swell until they were glistening and hard. How the hell did a girl get so shameless? Vanessa had always been like this, much more daring than me. I glanced up toward the ridge; many of those cameras and binoculars were now quite clearly focused on Vanessa.

I loved that Vanessa was so edgy, but I didn't follow her lead. I brushed suntan lotion over my body, smearing my belly, my legs, my cleavage. Vanessa looked at me and smirked.

"Tit for tat," she said. "Come on, let's see 'em."

"What are you talking about? I'm not taking off my top."

"You take off your top or I'm going to take off my bottoms."

I laughed. "Go ahead."

Without a moment's hesitation, Vanessa slipped her thumbs under the waist of her bikini bottoms and began to tug them down, squirming as she lifted her ass off the blanket.

"Stop!" I said, glancing toward the ridge. "Everyone's watching."

"Your tits or my bush," laughed Vanessa. "Flash or gash, Zoe."

Vanessa loves to push me like this; she kids me about being too conservative. She'd even talked me into "practicing" our makeout skills with each other, which had quickly turned into something I wasn't quite sure if I should like as much as I did. I knew I definitely wasn't bisexual, but Vanessa and I did things it still made me wet to think about. And whenever I saw her body revealed like this, I remembered them vividly, wondering if we were going to try them again.

"This hot weather has made you crazy," I said nastily.

"It always does. All right, Zoe, I'm taking them off on three," smiled Vanessa. "It's snatch and patch, or tits and nips. One, two—"

"All right, all right!" I snapped. I unhitched my top and peeled it away from my tanned breasts, trying to hide the fact that my hands were shaking. I felt a weird rush of adrenaline as I exposed my tits, and I couldn't keep myself from crossing my arms across my chest, hiding them from the shameless onlookers.

Vanessa made a "no-no-no" gesture with her index finger. "That's cheating."

"All right," I said, putting down my arms. The second I revealed my tits to the guys on the ridge, the guys playing Frisbee on the beach, the guys doing nothing but laying there on their beach towels looking at us, I felt a flush of excitement. I couldn't believe I was doing this.

"Here," said Vanessa, tipping the bottle of lotion. "We don't want those pretty things getting sunburned."

I blushed deeper than my tan as Vanessa poured sunscreen onto my tits and began to rub it in. I felt her palms stroking my nipples and got even more embarrassed. I remembered how it felt when she'd done that with her mouth plastered to mine, her tongue exploring, and her thigh tucked between my legs, rubbing against my clit through my jeans. I remembered what it had felt like when I'd come, moaning against Vanessa's parted lips.

I don't know why I did it. As Vanessa stroked sunscreen onto my tits—plainly taking more time and care with them than she needed to—I bent forward and kissed her. On the lips. Not a quick one, either. It was the first time I'd kissed her; she'd always kissed me. I made up for lost time, though; my tongue eased into Vanessa's mouth and teased hers as she caressed my tits more firmly, the sunscreen forming a slick, greasy pillow that made my nipples tingle.

When my mouth left hers, I was breathing hard. My thighs were pressed tightly together, because I was afraid the guys on the ridge could somehow see the heat building between them. Did they have infrared cameras? I was sure my pussy would show up as a blazing-hot sun, ignited by the feel of Vanessa's fingers on my breasts.

Vanessa smiled. "Now they're *really* watching."

And they were. Guys all over the beach were pausing to look at us. When I glanced up toward the ridge, I was damn sure that every lens was focused on us. We would be all over the beachfront lezzies Web site by tomorrow.

"Maybe I don't care," I said.

"Oh, you do," smiled Vanessa, leaning closer to me. "That's what makes it so hot."

She squirted more sunscreen onto her breasts and kissed me. "Rub it in," she said, even though she'd already done an admirable job of oiling herself up. I hesitated, blushing even hotter than the merciless sun was making me, but when our lips touched and her tongue grazed mine, I couldn't say no to her. I pressed my legs together very, very tightly, instinctively thinking I could hide the blazing heat from the imaginary infrared cameras studying us and recording our every move. I put my hands gingerly on Vanessa's tits and began to smear lotion everywhere as we kissed.

My clit felt like it was throbbing. I wanted Vanessa down there, the way she'd been when we were "practicing," when she showed me how it felt to get fingerfucked. I had come so hard I was afraid someone would call the campus cops. No amount of biting my pillow could muffle the moans as I climaxed on Vanessa's fingers. That had been right after Christmas break, and she hadn't done it since; now we just cuddled occasionally. It had been our last practice session, and I only now was realizing how much I longed for a replay.

"You're a great kisser," said Vanessa, breathing hard when our lips parted. "You're going to make some very lucky guy a wonderful girlfriend."

I kissed her again as I pinched her nipples. I had all but forgotten that we were in public, our kiss being recorded on a dozen sleazoid's Web cams. I wanted her and I felt bad about it; this was supposed to be practice, wasn't it? But practice for what?

I glanced around and saw a bunch of guys trying hard not to look like they were looking. The guys on the ridge had no such compunctions.

"Why do guys like to watch girls make out?" I asked nervously.

"They like to watch them do more, too," said Vanessa, her hand forcing its way between my firmly closed thighs.

"Oh, no you don't," I squeaked, aware even as I was saying it that I didn't sound very convincing.

"Oh, come on," she said. "Just a little practice? Some day your boyfriend is going to want to fingerfuck you on a nude beach." Her smile looked wicked, vicious, like she was in total control of me and she loved it. I let her push my thighs open and felt her fingers trailing up the inside of my sunscreen-greased thigh. I couldn't believe I was doing this. I just couldn't believe it. Her hand slid down the front of my string bikini bottoms and I felt her fingers pushing into my Brazilian-waxed crotch. She entered me with two fingers, her hand stretching my bikini as her thumb worked my clit. I opened my mouth to beg her to stop, but I couldn't. I was too close to coming.

All that came out of my mouth were little squeaks and tiny moans of pleasure, as I felt the cameras clicking and whirring away, capturing my ordeal forever. I wanted to tell her "Don't." I wanted to tell her "Stop." But I didn't, because I couldn't, because stopping was the very last thing in the world I wanted her to do. I wanted her to keep fucking me until I came.

I finally managed to whimper out a sentence, though I have no idea why I picked this one to say. "This isn't practice," I said.

"No, it's not," Vanessa said. "No guy'll ever fuck you like this."

I would have thought I could never come in public—the stress and discomfort of it all would prevent me from reaching the peak. But nothing could stop me now. Knowing they were watching turned me on. But what really did it was knowing that the private little games I had shared in my dorm room with Vanessa were now public for everyone to see. I was eternally branding myself as a lezzie.

I buried my face between Vanessa's breasts and moaned wildly as I came. I tried to keep it quiet because all those guys were watching—many of them within earshot—but there wasn't a chance of that. I pressed my mouth, open wide, against Vanessa's tits and tasted sunscreen as my orgasm exploded through me. Vanessa kept fucking me and rubbing my clit until I started to twitch and squirm, too sensitive to receive any more pleasure. And still I lay there spread, letting her do whatever she wanted to me, content to let her use me until she was done.

"Oh, God," I whimpered when she finally eased her fingers out of my pussy. "They're all watching."

"Yes, they are," she said. "We'd better get going, or we're going to have an awful lot of guys coming over wanting to give us their phone numbers."

Vanessa had to help me back into my clothes. I didn't bother with the bikini top, instead slipping my tank top on with nothing underneath, the sticky sunscreen making it mold to every contour of my skin. I put on my flip-flops and followed Vanessa up the beach, painfully aware of every guy looking at me. More than a few of them were smiling.

When we got back to the car, Vanessa grabbed me by the back of my head and kissed me, hard, tenderly. This wasn't practice, either.

"Take me home," I told her.

That night was the first time we spent the whole night in one bed. We didn't get much sleep, though. I still don't know if I should like it as much as I do, but I don't care, because I do. I like it more than anything else in the world. Vanessa and I are going to be roommates next year, too, in an off-campus apartment. And even with one bedroom, we'll have plenty of places where we can "practice" till we get it right—and then some—and no one but Vanessa and me can watch.

13

The Crush Party

Michelle C.

I put the finishing touches on my eyeliner and stood back from the mirror to survey my work. I had tried to achieve a classic "fallen-woman" look, like Belle, the madam in *Gone with the Wind,* with makeup a little darker than natural, but not *Rocky Horror* garish. I finished by smoothing the curls in my hair a bit and adding an additional dab of lip gloss—over my kiss-proof lipstick—to the center of my lower lip for that hungry look. My first rule when I have a party is that I get to kiss everyone at the party. No need to leave clues as to where I've been, though.

My second rule when I have a party is that I never wear panties, but I wore a black lace slip to conceal this fact from the thirty other girls in the bathroom, all of whom were doing their makeup in similar states of undress. Thongs, boy-cut lace panties, and demi-cut bras were the rule, and the final result wouldn't cover much more than that.

Our sorority's annual "crush party" would start in one hour, and this year's oh-so-classy theme, as chosen by the Social Committee and as approved by me, the Social Chair, was "Pimps n' Hos." This generally meant that I would dress as the "madam" of the house, and all of the other girls in the house, and especially the party committee, would be dressed in the short, tight, low-cut outfits typical of hip-hop videos, and the low-cut, slit-to-the waist "cocktail dresses" preferred

Published by The Haworth Press, Inc., 2006. All rights reserved.
doi:10.1300/5328_14

by the dancers on "G-String Divas." We figured it would be like *Girls Gone Wild*, but with the girls in charge.

A crush party is a special type of sorority party in which all the girls in a sorority anonymously invite a fraternity boy that they have a "crush" on. Written invitations are issued, and no party crashers are allowed. I, of course, had invited my friend Eric, a good-looking architecture student with a fraternity-boy fetish. All my sisters seemed to always crush on the same boy anyway, so I was sure that there would be extra for him. What's more, inviting him ensured that I could spend my time at the party cruising my real crush. But we'll get to that in a second.

All the girls in the ladies' room seemed to be making good progress in their transformation from "mildly slutty" to "complete whore," so I went back to my room, tossed on a black silk kimono and some Chinese velvet slippers, and went downstairs to check the progress of the social committee's preparations.

The ballroom looked amazing. What had once been an uptight Greek Revival ballroom could now be easily mistaken for any Astoria, Queens, gentleman's club, complete with rental stripper poles at either end of the dance floor. One of my resourceful committee members had rented red velvet drapes to cover the walls and red velvet slipcovers for the couches in the adjoining lounge. A neon COCKTAILS sign over the bar completed the trashy look. Two scantily clad committee members stood behind the bar, premixing pitchers of the night's theme cocktails—Thug Passion (Alize and cheap champagne) and Nice Melons (Midori, Absolut Vanilia, and pineapple juice), sweet drinks that would get everyone sloppy drunk before they knew what hit them. Of course, some kegs of beer were hidden under the bar as backup.

"Christy, I think I should taste those nice melons of yours, just to make sure they're ready for the party, what do you think?" I teased. Christy looked up and poured me a generous glass, bending toward me so that I could see her luscious cleavage spilling over her black velvet corset, which she was wearing over red ruffle-bottomed boy shorts. As she dropped a maraschino cherry into the green drink, I smiled. "Looks great, Chris, really good."

"Thanks, boss," she smirked. "Jamie and I have been taste testing all afternoon," she confided, jamming a thumb over her shoulder at Jamie, her "big sister," and, I suspected, her secret crush as well. I had assigned them to bartend together for a reason. Jamie was tall, blonde, and athletic, and I thought that she and the dark, voluptuous Christy would make a great match. Tonight Jamie had her hair in high pigtails and wore a white button-down shirt tied at the waist over a black lace bra, the shortest plaid skirt I had ever seen, and white go-go boots. Amazing. Like most of the girls in my sorority, she had a tattoo in the small of her back. Unlike most of the girls, it looked like this tattoo was of a brunette Vargas girl bending over. This was a hint of Jamie's darker side that I figured was attractive to Christy. "I'll be back down when I'm dressed," I said, taking my drink, with a wave to my slightly tipsy staff.

My clothes were waiting for me on the small loveseat in my room. I sat down and eased on a pair of silky black thigh-high stockings and a heavily padded black strapless bra. I stood up and looked at myself in the full-length mirror. Yum. I reached into the lower drawer of my vanity and pulled out my red sparkle harness and a very big black-and-red sparkle cock. I stepped into the harness and tightened the straps around my waist, then put the dildo through the hole in the harness, upside down so it wouldn't attract attention until I wanted it to. I stepped into my skirt, purple-black iridescent taffeta over a black tulle crinoline, and smiled. All the layers shielded my considerable bulge from public view. My black lace corset went on easily over my padded chest—I had replaced the back lacing with black elastic cord so that I could put it on myself and breathe a bit. Shoulder-length lace gloves finished the look. I filled a small beaded purse with cigarettes, lighter, lip gloss, and mints. As I slid on black patent leather pumps, I felt my body jut forward, and my cock with it, and remembered condoms and a few small packets of lube at the last minute. I checked myself in the mirror one last time. I looked slutty, but classy, and my tits looked amazing. I checked that my nipples weren't going to pop out of my dress just yet and, satisfied, shut the door behind me.

As I walked down the hallway to the staircase, I heard the doorbell ring. Frat guys dressed as pimps were beginning to arrive, each with a

key with their name on it that had been sent with their invitation. After checking their coats and checking in at the door, they were led to a
table full of padlocks. Each padlock had a girl's name on it, and when
the boy found the lock that fit the key, he would know who had invited him. I got another drink and sat down in the lounge with some
of the other girls, watching the guys come in. The DJ was playing excellent house music that made me giddy and relaxed at the same time.
I tapped my feet and tried to act like what I was excited about was the
party. Fortunately, Eric showed up, wearing black slacks, a purple
velvet jacket, and huge sunglasses, just as I was getting bored of my
sisters' chitchat about their crushes. He pretended to try to open a few
locks before opening mine. When I saw it open I made eye contact
and waved him over to me.

"Hey, sweetie, how you doing?" I murmured in his ear.

"Just fine, sugar, let's get us a drink." He helped me off the couch
and put his hand in the small of my back to help me to the bar, the
perfect fake date. Drinks in hand, we slipped out to the porch just off
the ballroom to have a cigarette. "Someday I must get a cigarette
holder," I told Eric as I slipped off my right glove so as to avoid getting it all smoky.

"Me too," he smiled. "Someday we'll leave this shithole town for
New York City. We'll sit in piano bars and smoke long cigarettes out
of long cigarette holders."

"Ha!" I laughed. "If we go to New York, your hands and mouth
will be too busy to smoke."

"That's true," he laughed with a wry smile as he finished his cigarette. "You know me too well." As we got up to go inside, I excused
myself to make my rounds and make sure that everything was going
smoothly, and to allow Eric to begin his cruising of the frat boys.

"Make me proud, honey. Don't get into too much trouble." I was
sure I wouldn't see Eric for the rest of the night, as he'd probably be
making out with frat boys in dark corners until the wee hours.

The party was going great. The room had filled up while we were
outside, and frat guys in outlandish pimp outfits danced with girls in
PVC bikinis and platform boots. I checked with the girls working the
front and they told me that only a few guys had not shown up yet.

"Great," I said. "You can go off duty in half an hour or when they show up, whichever comes first."

"Will do," said the girls, both busty brunettes in lace tops over black bras with short black skirts.

"Nice uniforms," I commented wryly, knowing that they wouldn't get it.

"Thanks, Michelle!" they chirped as I walked away.

Since the party appeared to be under control, I decided to retreat to the lounge, give my feet a rest, and people watch a little bit. Girls were getting pretty drunk and trying to do pole tricks on the stripper poles, and the guys were loving it. I was loving it. I sipped on my drink and imagined that I was really at a strip club as I watched one of the more talented girls shimmy gracefully down the pole. I crossed my ankles in front of me and was instantly reminded of the presence of the cock buckled tightly against my clit. I smiled to myself, enjoying the feeling for a second but shook it off. Too much, too soon. I was about to ease myself off the couch when I saw Rebecca, the sorority president and my crush, coming toward me. I gulped.

"Great party, sis!" she said, putting her arm around my shoulder and joining me on the couch. "It is so fucking sleazy in here, it almost makes me want to start giving lap dances!" With that I envisioned her lithe body straddling me on the couch, leaning her perfect small tits into my face while she ground her pussy onto my lap, just grazing my cock . . . gulp again. I needed some fresh air.

"Thanks. I was just about to go out for a smoke. Want to join me?"

"Sure, but let's go up to the balcony instead."

"Excellent." I followed her up the back staircase, and I spied Eric under the staircase with a frat boy's hand down his pants. Lovely. I held my skirts so I wouldn't trip on them on the way up, and watched Rebecca walk up the stairs. She had opted for a 1970s' style ankle-length black jersey halter dress with an extremely low back, a cut-out front, and rhinestones directly under the bustline. Were it not for the hint of butt cleavage, she would have looked like she was dressed for any other party we held. "Nice tattoo," I said snidely, referring to the garish tattoo of a hibiscus on her tailbone which she had doubtless gotten freshman year.

"Yeah, whatever." She smiled. "Now I can see why you don't have any tattoos. I'm trying to figure out how to get this covered up by a Celtic cross or something now. It's such a pain."

We walked through the sleeping room, full of bunk beds, over to the balcony. The second floor is off-limits to boys, so we were pretty sure that the sleeping room was empty.

It was my favorite kind of spring night. The air was still crisp but not cold, and I could feel that muggy summer days were just around the corner. I leaned over the balcony with Rebecca while we lit our cigarettes, taking my glove off once again and draping it over the rail. Rebecca seemed nervous and kept repeating that it was a great party. I was confused. I mean, I knew that she was my crush, but did she know? With two weeks left of school, two weeks before she would graduate and I would never see her again, I knew that I would have to take my chance tonight. I exhaled and leaned in. "So, Bex, who's your crush?"

"Don't you know? You are in charge of this party and all!"

I instantly kicked myself for being such a good delegator. "Sorry, Bex, the committee handled the crushes themselves; I just did the party."

"Well, that's the thing. There's been something I've been wanting to do since you rushed this sorority, and I haven't gotten up the nerve to do it yet."

"What, kick me out?"

"Do you always have to be silly? No, this." And then, out of the blue, I swear to God, she leaned in, put her hand on the back of my neck, and kissed me. Hard. Oh my god. I could not believe this was happening.

"You know that you have to keep this quiet, right?" she whispered, still leaning in close so I could smell her perfume and sweat. My decision-making processes were already completely fucked up by this unexpected turn of events, so I just nodded and went in for another kiss. "Not out here." She motioned for us to go back inside.

I walked with her to her bed in the sleeping room. I eased her onto the bed, my hand on her tattoo, then unhooked the neck of her halter top. I could not believe I was actually getting to touch the tits I had been checking out in the showers week after week for three years. I tried not to hurry. I kissed her mouth, her neck, her shoulder, and finally her breasts. I could feel my heart beating all the way into my ears. She began to make small moaning sounds and I returned to her mouth. "Quiet, baby, we don't need anybody to know we're up here," I warned her. "Okay," she murmured, but the second I returned to kissing her neck she started making noise again. "Bex! We have to be quiet!" "Okay, I have an idea," she said, getting up from the bed and throwing the straps of the halter over her shoulder. She led me to the side of the room and a door on the far wall of the sleeping room. "The formal closet," she whispered. "Ohh . . ." I moaned.

The formal closet is a huge walk-in closet where all the girls' formal dresses are kept so that they don't wrinkle and so that they don't take up space in our regular closets. Rebecca opened the door and walked in, motioning for me to follow her. Once I closed the door behind me it was completely dark. "Over here," she whispered through a cloud of lace, satin, taffeta, and tulle. I got down onto the carpeted floor and slid back to where I heard her voice. "Oh, there you are," I said as I bumped into her shoulder. "Silly again," she breathed into my ear, and began sucking on my earlobe. I laid down next to her on the closet floor, and I could feel the fabric of the dresses brushing my skin wherever Rebecca wasn't. Velvet and taffeta winter dresses caressed my chest, satin spring dresses draped on my arms, and tulle crinolines tickled my nose. I was in absolute heaven. Bex slid her finger down my collarbone to my sternum, then began unhooking my corset in the front. She giggled when she felt the pads on my bra. "I knew you were cheating, but I do have to say that your tits almost looked real!"

"Thanks," I smiled, then drew her on top of me for a kiss. She instantly felt my cock between her legs. "Would you call that cheating?" I whispered in her ear as I grazed her earlobe with my teeth.

"N-noo, I would call that . . . great," she moaned as she slid her hand down between her legs to make sure she was feeling what she thought she was feeling.

By this time in college, I had fucked enough straight girls that I knew that chances are it was going to be all about them, but in Bex's case, I really didn't care. If all she wanted me to do was go down on her for three hours before she fell asleep after giving me only a kiss, well, fine. I would have gotten to sleep with Bex, and that would be almost enough.

But as I slid my hand down between her legs, intending to put my fingers down her panties and slowly turn her over, she held my hands down to my sides. "Not so fast, girly. I didn't become sorority president by putting my heels in the air. This is about what I want to do. And didn't I say something about lap dances earlier?" She let my hands go and leaned in, placing her elbows on either side of my head. She moved her pelvis in small circles and brushed her nipples lightly over my lips, too quickly for my tongue to leave my mouth but slowly enough for my lips to enjoy the feeling. She slid down and brushed her breasts against my chest and my belly, and I could feel dresses and her hair tickling me as her mouth reached my tits. Sensory overload was nearly complete. "Oh, Bex," I moaned.

She eased herself down my body and spread my legs. "I know who your crush is." And with that, she pulled my skirt up to reveal my cock. "No panties, nice." She adjusted my cock so that it was in its full and upright position, and fumbled in her purse for lube and condoms. She found a Magnum XL and some lube and began expertly applying both to my cock, which felt as if it was actually throbbing in her hand. "What?" I gasped, just as her hand left my cock and dropped down to my slit. I could feel that my wetness had dripped all the way down to my asshole. Her finger on my inner labia was insistent, and I raised my pelvis up to meet it. Her hand suddenly left my pussy, and she pushed her wet, lube- and come-soaked fingers, into my mouth.

She straddled my torso and looked down at me. "I said, I know who your crush is."

I really did not feel like talking at this moment. But I was curious. "How?"

"Not how, who. I want you to tell me." Her voice was warm but urgent. She moved her cunt down so it was teasing the head of my thick cock. "Tell me who." She kissed my mouth. I wanted her so badly I would tell her anything.

"You're my crush, Bex, you know that." As I said it, she slid her cunt slowly onto my cock and leaned deeply into me. My cock was thick, but she was very wet. I moved my hands to her waist and whispered in her ear as she moved up and down on my cock, "You're my crush, Bex, Bex, you're my crush," until we were both so caught up in the rhythm of fucking, and our own cunts and sweat, that even breathing was a challenge. As she gained momentum she raised herself up so that her body was perpendicular to mine. She grabbed at my tits, my neck, my chest, and finally settled on grabbing onto my shoulders to keep herself up. Dresses rubbed against all our available skin, and the tulle and satin of my own dress rustled between us. She moved on me quickly, bumping my cock against my clit at just the right pressure and speed. She leaned into me, and I took her nipple into my mouth. I bit it slowly, intending more pressure than pain and it was just enough to send us both over the edge. I would come at any second.

"Shelle?" she gasped.

"Yes?" I somehow was able to ask.

"Shelle, you're my crush, baby, baby, you're my crush," she screamed into the closetful of dresses. I couldn't hold back anymore and grabbed her ass tight, slamming my cock deep into her pussy, squeezing my eyelids tight, torn between paying attention to the amazing feeling in my cunt and the amazing feelings of fabric and girl all over the rest of my body. My cunt won and I writhed beneath her, tensing every muscle in my body to force my cock deeper into her, and my clit with it. I could feel her body tensing and relaxing as she came, riding my cock and finally pushing the dildo out of her with a flood of ejaculate. She leaned down to kiss me and slid off of me, settling in on her side next to me. "Oh my god," she sighed.

I reached down and unbuckled my cock from my waist. She reached down to rest her hand on my belly. "You know, Shelle, you've got a nice dick for a girl."

"Thanks," I murmured, my mind racing. How long had we been up here? Had anyone heard us? "Listen, Bex, I don't want to be abrupt, but we should probably get out of here," I whispered.

"Yeah, you're probably right," she replied, and we kissed as we attempted to find our clothes. I realized that I would have to put my dick back on under my dress so that I could exit with it undetected. As we approached the closet door, I took her arm. "Bex?" She turned to me in the dark. "So, um, next year, alumni weekends?" She giggled.

"Of course. Also, Mom's weekend, Rush, everything. I'm the sorority's Alumni Director next year, so I'll be visiting a lot. Oh, and also? I'll be staying off campus."

"Awesome."

I smiled into the darkness as we left the closet and moved back into the real world. We tiptoed back through the sleeping room and went back to our rooms, acting like we had just been up smoking. I thought I heard Christy and Jamie up there giggling, but I was too dazed to care. I went back to my room and exchanged my wet clothes and dick for fishnet thigh-highs and a floor-length velvet dress. I smoothed my hair in the mirror and added some gloss to my still-perfect lipstick, tissuing off some of Bex's. I went back to the balcony to recover my glove and had a cigarette by myself, before returning to the biggest party of the year. Perfect.

14

The G-String

Jen Collins

For Kathleen

Once outside of the Bedrock, Monique twisted out of Cherry's grasp and slammed her fist into the bar's solid oak door.

"That goddamn bitch!" Monique screamed, as she began sobbing anew. The young woman turned, cradling her fist in her other hand, and fell back against the brick wall that quietly announced the name of the only dyke bar in town. Howling with pain and humiliation, Monique slid down the wall. Her spandex shirt top caught on the brick, the fabric raising to expose a pierced navel and the hint of intricate tattoos weaving their way below the waist of her skirt and down toward her nether regions.

Cherry watched the girl's display, furious with Bobby, the butch who'd just torn Monique's heart in two—the butch who was forever tearing young femmes' hearts in two. It had become almost a rite of passage: femme dykes in this part of town exchanged their Bobby war stories and laughed at her, and for themselves.

Bobby didn't know this, never noticed the looks all the femmes in the room gave one another when she strutted through the bar with a new young innocent. The femmes knew that Bobby paraded for the other butches, though they shaded this knowledge behind brightly

Published by The Haworth Press, Inc., 2006. All rights reserved.
doi:10.1300/5328_15

painted fingertips and smoothly downturned smiles. Let her figure it out for herself, the sexist bitch.

Cherry shook off the smirk—she had other things to focus on. She dropped down to a half squat, balancing on her four-inch casual heels, and ran soft fingertips across the girl's forehead. She brushed away the hair that had fallen into Monique's eyes, and waited for Monique to make eye contact before she spoke.

"Oh, honey—you poor thing," Cherry said softly. "Didn't anybody warn you about Bobby?"

Monique snuffled and flushed anew, shaking her head. "I met her at work, you know? She came in to buy shoes and had me back behind the curtain in the storeroom before I was even a hundred percent sure she was a woman!" Monique sighed, rolled her eyes up toward the bright street lamp glaring overhead, and continued.

"She did such amazing stuff to me, Cherry. I never knew my body could feel that way."

Cherry stood and offered a well-manicured hand to Monique. "Don't call me that, honey. Call me Cherise. And listen—" Exhaling a bit while heaving Monique up to her feet, Cherise said, "I taught Bobby most of what she fucking knows. Come on."

Cherise started walking, but Monique stayed put. "Where are we going?" Monique called after Cherise, arms folded across her chest and a pout scrawled across her face.

Where, indeed? thought Cherise. She took in this club-queen femme, her black top threaded through with silver lamé and swollen with the young woman's round breasts. The shirt hung loosely around her midriff, stopping just at the top of her loose-pleated plaid purple skirt, which fell only a handful of inches down Monique's thighs. It swayed in the evening city breeze and threatened to expose the girl's glory if a sharp wind blew just the right way. Her bare legs sunk into the black leather boots laced clear up her calves. Long dark hair fell in loose curls to her shoulder blades. Cherise could just imagine the fun Bobby had with this girl. But she also knew that Bobby hadn't tapped even half of this young femme's sexual desire: Bobby only brought them out as far as *she* wanted them—and that was never really far enough.

Cherise cocked her head at Monique and offered her hand again. "Let's get you a drink, honey. You can drown your sorrows."

Monique hesitated, searching the face of her ex-lover's ex-lover for something, but all she found was concern. With a halfhearted smile, Monique accepted Cherise's hand, and they walked away from the Bedrock.

After a number of blocks, and a shared cigarette, Cherise stopped abruptly at a door that lead into what Monique had always assumed were some abandoned warehouses. She noticed fine script etched into the door: THE G-STRING.

Cherise flung open the metal door, and music flooded out over them. "Hey, Cherry! Good to see you, baby! Who's your friend?"

"This is Moxie, Jack. She's new around here." Cherise glanced back over her shoulder, winked at Monique, then offered a salacious grin to the bouncer. "Thought I'd show her a few things," she said and nodded her head toward a runway deep inside the smoky darkness of the room, where a naked woman did remarkably dirty things to an innocent fireman's pole.

Monique blanched at this development in her evening but recovered quickly enough to smirk at the bouncer's comeback (which she didn't quite catch) as he waved them in.

She trailed into the smoky darkness behind Cherise, who leaned back and said, "Never give 'em your real name, baby. You never know when they'll want something from you. Moxie fits you, I think." Cherise slipped an arm around Monique's waist and briefly fingered the girl's navel ring. Before releasing her, she felt the shudder run down Monique's back. Cherise smiled to herself, then said, "Let's go get your drink."

Monique stumbled after the powerful woman. What was going on? Her cunt tingled in response to Cherise's handling, just as it had when Bobby used to stroke her hair and whisper nasty things to her over dinner. But hadn't Bobby told her the way things were, explained that a femme needed a butch if she wanted the world to see who she really was? Monique considered Cherise in her tight-bodiced but loose-flowing dress and smooth leather jacket, firm legs encased in straight-seamed stockings, brown hair caught up in a loose bun and falling out in wisps around her face, catching in her huge hoop earrings. *She* certainly didn't seem to need anything else—or anyone—to complete her. Monique's confusion mingled with arousal as she glanced around: from Cherise, who was making rounds down the bar, to the newest dancer, a tall, round, and large-breasted amazon, throwing a prop chair around like it was a Nerf ball.

She closed her eyes to clear her head, and she opened them to Cherise holding out a drink. Monique accepted the amber-filled rocks glass. Before she could ask what they were drinking, Cherise turned away.

"Come on, honey. Let's go sit down." They found an empty table against the back wall, farthest from the runway, where they could converse without hollering. Cherise raised her own glass, smiled broadly, and said "Let's toast, honey. To us."

Monique met the toast. "To us," she said, then took a drink. Given the expression into which Monique's face immediately contorted, Cherise was impressed that Monique hadn't sprayed the empty side of the booth. She chuckled and sipped from her own drink.

Monique wiped her mouth with the back of her hand and demanded, "What's in this?"

"Scotch and soda," said Cherise with a grin. "Well, mostly scotch. If you're gonna be drinking alcohol, you ought to know it's there, honey. Get into less trouble that way—my grandfather taught me that."

Monique raised the glass to her nose, already wrinkled in anticipated distaste, but her brow smoothed after a second. She took another sip, then another, and then a third. Cherise smiled, nursing her Glenlivet. Monique closed her eyes, and Cherise figured she was savoring the burn.

"I usually go for sweeter drinks than this, you know? But this—I've never had anything like it."

Cherise smiled and watched Monique toss back the tail of her first drink. "You want sweet? Go up and ask Jocelyn for a rusty nail—get a little honey-sweet Drambuie with your scotch. They're dangerous, but they're good."

Monique hesitated. "Go on, honey. She'll love you." Cherise sipped her drink and watched Monique flirt with the bartender, who poured the strongest drink of her career for the girl, before stumbling back to where Monique stood leaning over the bar and offering more to the bartender than she'd ever give.

Fucking butches, Cherise thought. You gotta love 'em, but they're so goddamned easy.

Monique sauntered back a few minutes later, sipping her drink and appearing much happier. She slid her ass into the booth, bumping into Cherise, and giggled.

"Thanks, Cherise. This is much better than those stupid foofy drinks Bobby was always getting for me."

"A girl should always know what she's drinking—" Cherise began, before abruptly cutting herself off. Monique followed Cherise's focused gaze to the runway, its dusty length lit up red and purple.

"What is it?"

Cherise put a finger to her lips. Indeed, Monique noticed, the whole bar had fallen hushed.

After a moment, Cherise said only, finger still across her lips, "Bailey."

So quiet was the club that Monique started when the announcer's voice rose over them. In a deep, rich voice, he intoned, "*Ladies* and gentleman, we have a *special* treat tonight. A *surprise* performance by one of *the G-String's all-time favorites*. She has asked me to inform you that tonight's dance is in honor of a *friend*." The voice paused as a wash of whispers and glances traveled through the room. "Please *welcome*— Babette!"

Through a burst of applause, a woman appeared on the stage as though she'd materialized there. She wore a belly dancer's filmy blue-and-yellow silk, although without the usual opaque undergarments. The golden skin visible on her legs, arms, and face glowed in the soft light, and her dark hair hung thick about her face.

Cherise whispered under her breath, to herself, "Fucking Jocelyn must have told her." She knocked back the rest of her drink and set the glass firmly onto the table (with some concentration, to avoid throwing it against the wall), leaned back into the booth, and watched Bailey move.

The dance was like nothing Monique had ever seen: a kind of strip belly dance. The deep, ethereal music, dense with bass, sounded on its surface akin to the music her Saudi grandmother would listen to when she thought all the kids had gone outside to play during the summer months that Monique and her sisters had been sent to her house outside London. But this music was sexier, a techno backdrop weighty behind the main melody that snared her body.

The woman on the stage undulated her body like a snake driven by a charmer—or the charmer herself. Slowly, and with exquisite timing, the woman removed bits of flimsy material, which she dropped past her strongly built and well-muscled calves and let fall to her bare feet. Monique wondered what the dancer's belly would feel like if she could rest her hands upon its sonorous and never-quite-still surface. She wanted to join Babette and learn all those slow and sensual moves.

Babette seemed suddenly to look directly at Monique, who felt herself go hot all over in response. She smiled a bit, though she knew that the dancer couldn't possibly see such a slight change in expression all the way across the dim and smoky room. And then: "Oh my god," Monique gasped. "What's she doing?"

Cherise's expression combined lust with irritation as her cunt blossomed fully to life watching Bailey perform her crowd-pleasing climax. With just one piece of material clinging around Babette's hips, the dancer curved her body backward. Back, back, back—Monique was certain the dancer would fall. Instead, Babette dropped into a backbend, her thighs open and exposing the woman's dark fur and the glistening lips of her cunt. Monique's mouth fell open and went dry.

Money appeared on the runway while Monique gaped. She realized Cherise was digging around in her little bag. "Here." Cherise nudged Monique rather brusquely and handed her something—a twenty. "Go take that up to her."

Monique began to protest, frustrated as much with being ordered around as with the perplexing lust rushing through her body. She caught the edge of something raw in Cherise's eyes, though, and decided not to argue. She stood and walked, somewhat unsteadily at first, to the runway. As she approached, she watched in awe as the dancer righted herself with grace and strength. Babette didn't appear to use her arms to shove herself up—rather her thigh and stomach muscles seemed to pull her body back to standing.

Monique came to a halt at the end of the runway and waited, awkwardly, for Babette to notice her. She felt uncomfortable, and altogether too turned on, standing where everyone in the bar could see her seeking the attention of an all-but-naked and glistening woman. Monique reached her arm out to drop the bill on the runway just as strong thighs appeared directly before her. The dancer dropped down into a demure squat, a last bit of material only the barest sheath over the swell of her sex. Monique smelled the perfume of the woman's cunt and sweat, and she swayed, unsteady again.

Before she could stumble backward, however, the dancer caught Monique by the back of her head, then leaned her face down over the edge of the stage. They kissed, and Monique felt her cunt flood, while the crowd applauded and hooted around her. When Babette broke the kiss, she deftly plucked the bill from Monique's limp fingers and whispered, with an accent Monique couldn't quite place, "Tell her thank you." A sharp smile broke across the dancer's full, lush mouth, although it didn't quite reach those almond eyes. Then she was up again, moving away from Monique and her quivering body.

Dismissed, Monique strode slowly back to her table. Cherise, who appeared just the slightest bit envious (Pissed off? Turned on? Monique couldn't tell), asked, "What did she say?"

Monique managed, "She said to tell you thank you," before slumping down into the seat and bursting into tears.

Cherise allowed Monique to cry a minute or two, understanding the need for that kind of release. She watched the tail of Bailey's dance, following the roll of the woman's ass and shoulders. Cherise wanted to kiss Monique, to catch a trace of Bailey's essence and perfume. But now the girl was crying. *Oh well.* The stage lights intensified around Bailey just as she snatched that last bit of material away and revealed her strong, radiant self in all her power. How well

Cherise had known that body once. She took a long drink, first with her eyes, then of Monique's rusty nail. The lights fell black to a crescendo of music and applause.

The girl next to her began to settle down, and Cherise absently handed her a napkin. "Here you go, honey. I'll explain later, okay?"

But Monique didn't take the thing. She reached over and grabbed Cherise the way Babette had caught her, and kissed the woman.

Caught off guard, Cherise snapped to attention fast. Monique kissed with arduous need, nipping at Cherise's lips and suckling hard on her tongue. Cherise thought that maybe—*there*—she could still taste Bailey, and found herself light-headed with the lust that slight remnant inflamed.

Cherise had just got her hands into Monique's thick, curly hair when she heard, "Are you busy?"

The two women abruptly broke their kiss and looked up. There stood Bailey, dressed in not the belly-dancing outfit (which had been left strewn around the runway after her performance, to be collected by the barbacks-*cum*-stagehands, along with empty glasses and wet napkins), but tight blue jeans with those goddamn red Converse, and a tightly fitted, cap-sleeved T-shirt, under which her breasts reigned unrestrained. The face of Ram decorating her shirt had been shorn in half, exposing the dancer's smooth skin and well-developed abdominal muscles.

Bailey cleared her throat as Cherise straightened herself out, then offered Cherise one of the two glasses she carried. "Here, Cherise. I thought maybe you were . . . dry." She placed the drink next to Cherise's empty glass and sat on the empty side of the booth. She kept the second glass for herself.

Nobody said anything for a moment. Monique stared at Babette, then felt Cherise nudging her again. With money, again. "Monique, honey. Your glass is empty. Go flirt with Jocelyn for a few minutes, okay?" That same edge in Cherise's voice caught Monique's attention, and her frustration with Cherise's dismissiveness clenched her stomach. She rose from the booth and stomped toward the bar, intending to make Jocelyn disintegrate completely this time. *Send me away, will you?* She thought. *Well, watch this.*

Jocelyn did, in fact, fall flat on her face, tripping over her own feet while creating a buttered nipple for Monique. But Cherise took no notice, too ensnared was she by her former lover.

"What are you doing, Bailey? I thought you weren't dancing anymore . . ."

"Jocelyn got the word to me that you were here—it's been a long time since you've been in, Cher." Cherise cursed Jocelyn one more time, under her breath. "And I thought it'd be nice to get back out there again. I miss it sometimes. And then there are the brave girls who bring me big tips." Bailey smiled and indicated toward the bar with her glass. "How old is she, Cher? What are *you* doing?"

Cherise shrugged and said, "Bobby dumped her tonight." She laughed gently into Bailey's understanding look. "I thought I'd try to get her mind off it, you know?"

Bailey nodded, the barest look of disapproval crossing behind the smile. "Well—she certainly appeared to have her mind off of Bobby when I walked over here."

Cherise flushed, then pulled herself together with a grin. "She kissed *me*, Bail. I was just finishing what *you* started."

"Uh-huh," Bailey said, unconvinced. They both took long drinks, each glancing away from the face of a woman who knew her too well.

"How are you, Bailey?" Cherise asked, finally.

"You know, things are going all right these days. The club's doing great. Have you seen our dancers? I can't believe some of the talent we've got here." She broke off to sip her drink, then said, "I miss you, Cher."

Cherise let that sit between them for a moment or two, just longer than politeness would dictate. Then she raised her drink and offered the old toast. "To your G-String, Bailey."

Bailey laughed and returned, "And to *your* G-string." Each woman emptied her glass.

Monique returned to the table a little drunk. She could see that the two women were rapt in serious conversation, in spite of the clinking glasses, and was surprised by the vehemence of her jealousy. Why *shouldn't* Cherise be talking to someone else—and why should Monique care? After all, they were all femmes here. Hadn't Bobby told her the old joke about what femmes did in bed together—that is, their nails? Why on earth should she find herself wanting all of Cherise's attention for herself?

Monique slid back into the booth, ensuring that her hip bumped into and remained firmly pressed against Cherise's. She giggled and met each woman's eyes in turn, choosing to ignore their annoyed expressions. She could write off her behavior to tipsiness. She was the young, cute one here, after all, and was unused to having to compete for anyone's attention.

Almost reflexively, Cherise found her hand caught up in Monique's curly hair, needing something to fidget with. She ran her nails along the back of the girl's scalp, and smiled at the shiver that was Monique's response.

"Things look pretty serious back here," Monique teased the older women. "What're we talking about?"

A grin splashed across Bailey's face. "Why, we were just discussing your future, honey."

Cherise's confused but quiet "Oh, were we?" got engulfed up by Monique's squealing, "You were?"

"We sure were, baby." Had that New Orleans accent thickened while Monique had been away from the table, or was it just the alcohol? Cherise placed a delicate fist against her mouth and bit down to keep from laughing. When Babette went French Quarter, somebody better watch out.

Bailey slid out from the booth and held her hand out to Monique, as Cherise had earlier in the evening. "C'mon, honey. Let's get you ready."

As they walked off, Monique tottering at a near trot to keep up with the taller woman's stride, Cherise heard the girl's "Ready? For what?" and allowed herself to laugh right out loud, now that Monique was out of earshot.

Then she turned and caught Jocelyn's eye at the bar, raising her empty glass and eyebrows simultaneously. Jocelyn nodded and, after a moment, appeared at Cherise's table with a fresh scotch. Trading the new drink for the empty glass, she noted, "Dangerous one you got there tonight, Cherry."

Cherise nodded, thoughtfully. "Yeah. Reminds me of myself once, actually."

Jocelyn winked. "Once?" Cherise's smile went sly for the bartender's benefit but slipped back to sad as soon as Jocelyn left.

"Once," she repeated to the empty booth. Sipping the scotch, she thought back over the years to when she'd been new to the city herself, to those first hot months with Bobby, when she believed herself gorgeous, invincible, and able to withstand the worst the johns could dish out as long as she had a good woman to come home to. She'd learned otherwise the hard way. She remembered, too, the several ensuing years with Bailey—how good it was to get off the streets, the excitement of dancing and then setting up their own club. And then the drugs, and the incessant, ever-escalating arguments. *Why did the hottest sex have to happen with the people one was utterly otherwise incompatible with?* Cherise wondered for the umpteenth time.

The DJ's voice boomed across Cherise's memorial landscape, calling her back to the present. "*Well,* ladies and gentlepersons, we *do* have a *treat* for you *tonight.* Not one but *two* performances from our own *Babette*—" He paused for effect and the scattered applause. "*And now* she brings with her to the stage, for her *G-String debut,* the very fine—*Mox-ie.*"

Several folks moved from tables to seats up around the catwalk. Newcomers were always big moneymakers and Bailey knew it. Cherise leaned back into the soft velvet of the booth, stretching out to enjoy the show.

The lights dimmed to near-black. When they came back up, the two women stood with their backs to the audience, each clad in micromini latex dresses and precariously high heels. Monique had allowed Bailey to pull her hair up into long pigtails, while Bailey had knotted her own hair into a loose twist atop her head. The song Bailey chose was a rather recent redux of Simon and Garfunkel's "Mrs. Robinson," so cliché that Cherise found it almost painful.

But the crowd ate up the performance. Babette acted the role of the seductive older woman inducing a young girl into a life of sex and crime. The women stalked the stage, unbuttoning themselves for the audience. Whenever they met up, they pulled up each other's skirts (thereby flashing the audience with glimpses of mostly bare ass), loosened hair, or simply kissed and writhed one against the other. When the two climbed the pole together and hung upside down by their strong thighs alone, stripping off those shiny dresses, the little crowd went crazy. The women wore matching latex G-strings, which they couldn't keep their hands out of for the rest of the number.

Cherise had to admit that Monique was a great performer—her moves and rhythm kept the crowd engaged. Toward the end of the song, the two women made out while humping the pole, and Cherise crossed her legs tight, squeezing her cunt in an attempt to alleviate some of the ache swelling there. She downed her drink, then wandered off backstage while Babette and Moxie collected the money tossed on stage and worked the crowd for any last singles tucked into their G-strings.

Back in the dancers' dressing room, Cherise was met with squeals of delight from the other dancers. She smiled, trying to keep her energy light, although she was thoroughly weighted with desire and history. Shortly thereafter, before Cherise was completely inundated with questions, Monique and Bailey came offstage in their G-strings and heels, sweaty and laughing. Monique could not stop talking— "Oh my god that was *so fun* can we do it again Babette you were *wonderful* did you see that one guy I thought he was going to *pass out* how'd I do *oh* it was *so* fun"—nor would she release her grip on Bailey's arm. Bailey managed to turn the girl toward the waiting and similarly manic attention of the younger dancers, who were unusually excited to have a new girl on the scene, someone with whom to share stage time and precious tips. Perhaps it was due to her obvious connection with both Cherise and Bailey, but the other dancers couldn't wait to fawn over Monique, offering compliments, towels, water, and uppers. Bailey, quietly drying off, made eye contact with Cherise in the mirror. Raising her eyebrows, she spared a glance at the girl, then returned to Cherise's gaze.

Cherise, still leaning against the wall with arms crossed under her breasts, hoped she looked calmer than she felt. Adrenaline and lust raced through her like a caffeine high or a three-day speed binge. It had been so long since they'd brought in a new girl together. She simply gave Bailey that old little smile; not even a nod was necessary.

෫ঌৣ

Eventually, the other girls left Monique, now somewhat dazed, on the couch, returning to their own preparations, heading out to the stage or lap dance rounds. Bailey, redressed in her street clothes, helped the girl out of her little piece of latex and back into the gear in which she'd arrived, whispering to her all the while. Cherise knew exactly what Bailey was saying to the girl: how gorgeous Monique was, how much the crowd had loved her and what a natural she was. Monique, for her part and without quite understanding what was happening, was agreeing to show up for a shift the next night—and the night after.

Once the girl was dressed and somewhat reanimated, the three walked out the back door of the G-String together, arm in arm in arm, like coconspirators in a big plan. Monique strode between the two older women like she knew what she was in for. They rode in Bailey's dark blue Mercedes back to Bailey's house. As ever, Cherise caught her breath when they arrived, again admiring what Bailey had done with her share of the money made off the club. The house, a medium-sized two-story Victorian, had impeccably maintained hedging and rose bushes out front, which invited visitors to imagine they'd stepped out of the urban neighborhood and into an English country garden.

Cherise, sitting across from Bailey in the passenger seat, glanced behind her and confirmed that Monique, in the fifteen minutes it had taken them to reach Bailey's house, had fallen fast asleep.

"I think we lost one, Bail."

Bailey chuckled that deep-throated laugh that always caught in Cherise's cunt. "Not for long, we haven't, I bet."

The garage door opened automatically in response to the car's approach, and the Mercedes purred inside. "We'll leave her here for a minute or two, get things going inside," said Bailey, killing the engine and stepping out of the car.

The garage led into the kitchen, and the women left the door open, in case the girl woke up and got spooked. Bailey removed her coat and tossed it onto the kitchen table.

"You want some coffee, Cher?" she asked, flicking on lights and switching on the radio to get some jazz into the room.

Cherise settled onto one of the stools that rested under the island between the dining area and the kitchen proper. "Sure, thanks. You mind if I smoke?"

Bailey slid a saucer over to her friend, moving into the kitchen to get the coffee going. "Never did, honey." They each went about their routines in a comfortable silence, as though they did this every night—as though it hadn't been several years since they'd sat in Bailey's quiet, nighttime kitchen, decompressing after a night at the club.

Once she'd poured the chicory-laced coffee, Bailey handed Cherise a mugful, along with the sugar bowl and a plate of sliced pear and Swiss cheese. "So. What'd you think?"

"Of the show?" asked Cherise, through a bite of fruit. "Fantastic. The crowd loved it."

"And you?" Bailey raised her eyebrows over her coffee mug.

"I thought you were incendiary," Cherise replied, holding Bailey's gaze for a hot second before dropping into a laugh. "I also thought you were gonna have to chain her to the pole just to get her off of you. Someone's gotta teach that girl that a stage kiss isn't a real kiss—she's gotta save something for backstage." She inhaled deeply on her cigarette.

Bailey nodded, also laughing. "I tried to tell her. But she was so tipsy, I think she wasn't quite getting all of what I was saying."

"Who was tipsy?" came a drowsily indignant voice from the garage doorway. Both women turned to see Monique, hair disheveled and clothing mussed, wiping her left eye with a fist and looking both very sleepy and very horny.

"You, honey," Cherise said with a small smile, waving Monique over to her with the hand holding her cigarette and creating a trail of smoke for the girl to follow. Monique joined her at the island, forgoing her own stool in favor of leaning up against Cherise like a still-sleepy child. She took the coffee Bailey offered, dumped in several spoonfuls of sugar and enough milk to turn the black to tan, then downed most of the coffee in several gulps. She then attacked the fruit plate, apparently too hungry or stoned to care how she appeared to anyone.

The other women doted on her, refilling her coffee mug and the plate of food. When the girl had got through the second plateful of pear and cheese, Bailey brought out tiny glasses of peppermint schnapps, which she suggested they take into the living room.

Holding the little glass surprisingly daintily given her altered state, Monique managed to get from the kitchen to the living room without spilling any of her drink. She trailed after Cherise, who was busy lighting candles, and Bailey, who had flicked on the gas fireplace, was fussing with the stereo. Monique looked around the room, taking in Bailey's sparse but fine furnishings, and gazed for a long moment at the Mapplethorpe over the woman's fireplace: a black-and-white shot of a woman's breasts and belly, the composition of which left Monique wondering if she was contemplating some strange fleshy plant. By the time the girl decided to sit down, the two plush, overstuffed club chairs in front of the fireplace were already filled. Not having a place to sit brought a pout to Monique's lips, but just as she was about to plop her firm rump into Cherise's lap, Bailey took a sip of her schnapps and declared, "Okay, Miss Moxie—let's practice."

"What?" Monique stopped moving and stared at Bailey.

"Your moves, honey. Let's see those moves. Soon's I know what you've got natural, I can help you shape it for the stage. We gotta have only the best at the G-String, baby," Bailey finished with a wink and a smirk, which Monique took for flirtation. She tossed her head back, inhaled the syrupy sharp liqueur, then set the glass atop Bailey's mantle.

Cherise was glad she'd crossed her legs *before* the girl started dancing—it would surely have caught Bailey's attention otherwise. Bailey, the bitch, had loaded Nina Simone into the CD player, and "Sugar in My Bowl," Cherise's old signature song, was just beginning. For a wonder, Monique knew the lyrics—leave it to Bobby to introduce the girl to the classics—and Monique worked the truth of the words as hard as she could.

"I want a little sugar in my bowl—" and she bent over, facing away from Cherise, ass hidden behind that tiny skirt. She raked her nails up from the tops of her boots and along the backs of her denuded calves and thighs, before tossing her hair back over her shoulders and looking back at Cherise with that smoldering pout.

"I want a little sweetness down in my soul—" She stood and gazed down at Bailey, switching her hips slowly in time with the song, and running her hands flat down over her breasts and just-bared belly until they cupped her cunt.

She went on this way for the short duration of the song, shifting her attention back and forth between the women. Like a pro, she sometimes worked them both at once: rotating her ass for Bailey while baring those full tits for Cherise. The women's eyes met across the girl's bent or writhing body more than once, pleased to have found such a talented dancer—and more than a little turned on.

During the brief saxophone interlude, Monique practiced her lap dancing, writhing her ass up and down Cherise's crossed legs, leaving Cherise all the more wet, as well as impressed with the strength of those young thigh muscles. Monique then crossed to Bailey, where she parted the woman's legs and ground so thoroughly against the woman's lap that Bailey expected to find a stain in the shape of her cunt marking the spot when Monique had finished.

For the end of the song, the girl unbuttoned her shirt, revealing her lace-clad breasts, then bent over and removed her panties from underneath her skirt, using the middle finger of each hand to slide them down her thighs and over her boots. She tossed them at Bailey, who left them where they fell on her arm. The girl flipped up the back of her skirt and finished the song bent over that way, mouthing the lyrics upside down between her legs while opening, with her fingers, the very bowl in need of a little sugar.

Cherise and Bailey found themselves short of breath as they applauded Monique's performance. She righted herself and beamed at them, clearly pleased with their appreciation, and asked, "Was I really good?"

"Oh, you're a natural," said Cherise throatily. Bailey just smiled, breaking into a little chuckle at Cherise's apparent desire for some sugar of her own.

The music changed. With Eartha's growl as a backdrop, Cherise stretched out her hand to the dancing girl, who continued to wiggle and writhe even while being pulled into Cherise's lap. Cherise expertly slipped her fingers around the edges of Monique's trimmed cunt, smoothing across soaked labia with her first and ring fingers. After a moment or two of this, she began to tease at pushing inside with her middle finger—all the while catching the girl's resonant, overstimulated groans into her own mouth.

Bailey, unwilling to be left out, came up behind Monique and ran her nails firmly along the young woman's exposed neckline. While suckling on Monique's earlobe, Bailey reached down and lifted out of their lace encasements those round breasts with their tiny dark nipples. She rolled the hardened nubs between the second finger and thumb of each hand, while Cherise gave the girl what her thrusting hips begged for, stabbing firmly into her cunt with just one finger. Monique clenched into a hard, volatile orgasm, jerking back against Bailey and exhaling sharp, high-pitched squeals into Cherise's mouth.

After a moment, as the girl's body relaxed, the women released her from their experienced hands. Bailey leaned down, easing her torso between Monique's body and Cherise, and kissed her former lover with such intensity that it was difficult for Cherise to keep herself from tossing Monique to the floor and giving herself over to all the anguish that always followed from the lust she felt in those moments. Bailey's kiss, as ever, was hot and musky, and completely filled Cherise's mouth.

Both women sighed before making any other sound, as if this were the thing they'd been holding out for all night—for years, maybe. Cherise lifted her cunt-slicked hand and thrust her fingers into Bailey's hair, clutching tight enough that Bailey bit down sharply on Cherise's tongue to get her to loosen her grip. Cherise complied, if only slightly.

Monique knew when she was in danger of being replaced. When she could move, she slipped off Cherise's lap and knelt on the floor in front of the woman. Pressing her hands to Cherise's calves, she fingered for a moment the silk of the woman's stockings and wondered where she might find a pair like them. She reached for the cool fabric of Cherise's dress, which she pushed up and onto Cherise's thighs, while also applying pressure to the insides of Cherise's legs until they fell away from each other. She caught her breath at the view: black lace banding each solid thigh, and between, a small swatch of dampening cloth.

Bobby didn't know about this particular talent of Monique's—the butch never allowed any of her lovers to touch her cunt. But it wasn't for nothing that every girl in Monique's old neighborhood had invited her to sleepovers clear through into high school. It was, as a matter of fact, what got her driven to the bus station in the middle of the night and left to fend for herself in the world.

While Cherise was preoccupied with Bailey, Monique shoved her hands under Cherise's ass and agilely removed the woman's panties, pulling them down her thighs and legs and off one ankle. And then she went to work.

Cherise was astounded: this young femme knew more about eating pussy than most butches she'd been with. She rapidly abandoned Bailey's kisses in favor of attending more closely to Monique's ministrations. Cherise eased down in the chair so Monique was better able to get at every nook and cranny, every tiny hidden fold of her cunt.

"Oh my god, Bail," Cherise gasped. "Talk about a natural." Bailey laughed, stroking Cherise's face while Monique worked the woman's labia hard and fast. Bailey drank in the scent of her friend's pussy, remembering how the juices used to flow like a fully opened faucet— and how she used to swim in them for hours.

The only time that Monique was unconcerned about her appearance was when she was eating pussy. She put her whole face into it, using not just her mouth, her lips, tongue and teeth, but her chin, cheeks, and nose. She adored everything about having her whole self engulfed between a woman's thighs, and worked painstakingly to get as far as she could into a woman's cunt while doing so. She ran her tongue along first outer, then inner, labia on either side, cooling the center of Cherise's cunt before returning with a hot, hard stroke up the middle, from oily center to clit, that left Cherise squealing. She suckled at the throbbing clit, snatching it into her mouth and vibrating her tongue across its round head for just a moment, then circling the little shaft several times.

An attentive pussy licker, Monique focused on gasps and quiet moments, undulations of hips and the point at which they stopped. She remembered what got good reactions from a woman and returned to those strokes later. With Cherise, it was those long, wet strokes up the middle of her cunt, the ones that started out agonizingly slow and got progressively faster, until Monique lapped at Cherise's cunt like a dog at a waterbowl. This resulted in Cherise's hands twisted into the girl's hair, pulling at her with deep groans of need.

Bailey decided to draw this scene out a bit by distracting the muff diver. She refilled her schnapps glass, then returned to stand next to the entwined women. Pulling up on Monique's head resulted in angry complaints from both of them, which Bailey ignored. She took Monique's slick face in her hands and kissed the girl, suckling at the tongue that'd been doing such hard, sweet work, and savoring the taste of Cherise's pussy. She pulled away from Monique's lips and sipped her schnapps, which she quickly passed to the girl.

"Hold it," she murmured, taking the girl by the hair and directing her back to Cherise's cunt. Bailey delighted in both women's gasps, as Monique savored the pleasure of commingled flavors and Cherise ground into the cold heat of schnapps glazing her cunt.

While they were experimenting with the newly induced sensations, Bailey stepped back and reached down for Monique's hips, lifting up until the girl's legs formed an A-frame. Monique's face pitched forward into her workspace due to the platforms on her boots, and she pressed her hands against the insides of Cherise's thighs to steady herself. Bailey flipped up that little purple skirt again and ran her hands over the round ass that had so taunted her during the girl's lap dance. Her hot hands met cool skin, and an appreciative moan rose up from between Cherise's legs.

Bailey very much liked the way the flesh moved when Monique wiggled her ass, and she slapped the girl's right cheek lightly to gauge the response. Monique, apparently delighted, gave a bright little moan and switched her hips deliciously. So Bailey continued with the spanking, starting out gently and adding progressively more force to the smacks, which she alternated between cheeks. The room soon filled with the sounds of flesh striking flesh, Monique's dampened yelps, and Cherise's desperate gasps, the latter of which become all the more frustrated as Bailey continued to distract Monique from her ministrations.

Bailey glanced up at Cherise, as she gave Monique two final spanks that left the girl breathless and certainly no longer at work. Cherise's eyes were cloudy with thwarted desire, her lips parted and teeth clenched. Bailey wanted nothing more than to shove the girl aside and fuck her friend just the way she needed to be fucked. They both wanted it, in fact—but they also knew where it led.

Smoothing the palms of her hands over Monique's tender and reddened ass, Bailey growled, "Good girl. Now follow my lead—" and ran her thumbs down over Monique's asshole to her cunt, splitting open the lips and bringing a sharp gasp from the girl. Cherise's own groan affirmed for Bailey that Monique was following directions. Pressing through the smooth, slick flesh, Bailey sunk one thumb into the girl's cunt while leaving the other to dally over her clit. She paid no attention to the girls' begging groans and her writhing hips—her gaze was steadily trained on Cherise's face.

Shifting her thumb in and out of Monique's cunt a few times, Bailey replaced it soon enough with the first two fingers of her right hand, pumping in deep and slow. The muscles inside the girl's cunt clenched hard to the digits.

Monique's squeals became muffled, informing Bailey that she'd gone back to work with her mouth. Cherise closed her eyes and panted shallowly, offering up a small, groaning "Ohyes" or "Ohgod" now and then. Bailey returned her attention back to the cunt she was actually fucking. She added a third finger and fucked Monique in time with the backward thrust of her hips while moving the middle finger of her other hand rapidly over the girl's clit. Bailey stabbed hard into Monique's pussy and then yanked her fingers all the way out, reopening her cunt on each inward thrust. She fucked Monique faster and harder, and barely had she added a fourth finger in response to the girl's smothered "More!" before a second orgasm wracked through Monique's tensed body.

Bailey pounded the girl through the waves of her orgasm, then caught her as her knees gave way, gently easing the girl back to a kneeling position on the floor. She was thoroughly impressed with Monique's focus; the girl hadn't moved her face from Cherise's cunt once while she came. Monique fucked Cherise hard while sucking on her clit and flicking her tongue over its tip. Bailey leaned against Monique's hardworking back, then ran her hand up over Cherise's tits, which Cherise herself had loosed from the confines of her dress. Bailey pinched first one, then the other nipple, which brought Cherise's eyes flying open. She opened her mouth, muscles tensing, and Bailey slid her middle finger into Cherise's waiting mouth. At this, Cherise clamped down, tightened her thighs around Monique's head, and came hard enough to rock both other women up off the floor.

It took Monique's renewed sobbing to remind Cherise to let her go. The girl fell back into Bailey's arms, gulping air and hiccuping through her tears. Bailey wrapped her free arm around Monique and took the hand on which Cherise had been suckling from her friend's mouth in favor of clutching the spent woman's hand. For a moment, all they could do was rest against one another and try to catch a bit of breath. Nina Simone sang for them once again, and each managed to catch her pronouncement, "My baby just cares for me—"

When Cherise loosened her grip on Bailey's hand, and Monique's breathing returned to something like normal, Bailey stood and, after leaning Monique's limp body into Cherise's legs once again, she tottered on her own unsteady legs for some water. Turning on the faucet, she leaned against the counter and tore open the zipper of her tight jeans, digging several fingers into her pants. She bit her lower lip to keep from issuing an open-throated groan, and thrust her fingers into her cunt while twisting one of her nipples. The orgasm came on fast and hard, and rocked her away from, then back into, the Formica countertop, which rattled the dishes piled next to the sink.

"You okay in there, Bail?" came Cherise's knowing call in response to the sounds of shaking glassware. Bailey unclenched her teeth from her lower lip and cleared her throat.

"You betcha, Cher," she croaked, washing her hands. Grabbing three tumblers, Bailey filled them with cold water and carried the refreshment to the other room. Cherise, legs sprawled and top yanked open, played idly with Monique's hair. The girl was folded up half asleep, her face again just inches from the place she'd had it buried for so long, as though hesitant to get too far away.

Bailey set the glasses down on a small table next to Cherise's chair, offering first the girl and then her friend some water. Monique clutched the big glass with two hands and chugged, while Cherise took long, parched draughts. Each emptied her glass, while Bailey, after a couple of sips, found she wasn't all that thirsty—shaky, but not thirsty. She strolled around the room, flipping off the fire and stereo, then pinching out the candles. Then she roused the two women from where they threatened to melt into her furniture. Wrapping an arm around each, and allowing the balance of their weight to hold her steady, she led the party upstairs to her bedroom.

"Goddamn," Monique all but drawled, nuzzling her still-moist cheek against Bailey's neck. "Bobby doesn't know shit, does she?"

The two older women laughed almost in spite of themselves. Soon enough, the girl joined in.

– 15 –

Action

Ana Slutsky Peril

By the time the key turned in the lock, I was half asleep on the futon, dried blood caked on the nail marks on my palms, shirt twisted up past my bare nipples, probably raccoon eyes, and dead cell phone in the crook of my arm. I'd called my girl's new lover while they were in the thick of it; I'd wanted to hear them, to tell them what bitches they were for letting me get drunk, jealous, vicious, fearful alone. While I was at it, I told the boss that if she stuck so much as a finger inside my girl I'd report her for fucking her assistant, for sexual harassment, whatever power-hungry dykes lose their jobs for. I imagined her bending my girl over her desk, pinching her tits, slapping her ass. I imagined my stone femme, my top, loving it and crying for more. When she'd first told me about the affair, I told her I thought it was hot—fucking the boss. I thought she'd get promoted, fuck some intern in her own turn. Soon she was staying late every day, going out on weekends too. "You have nothing to be jealous about," she'd whisper, hooking the lacy pink bra I'd gotten myself for her birthday, stepping into my little-girl skirt, applying the raspberry lip gloss I've used for years, cheeks flushed. As a photographer, I could wear what I wanted, and as a Jewish girl who'd dated only Catholic schoolgirls until the age of eighteen, my fashion sense ran deep. By day, my girl went for tight sweaters, knee-length skirts, platforms, minimal makeup—all set for career climbing—but she'd always borrowed my

Published by The Haworth Press, Inc., 2006. All rights reserved.
doi:10.1300/5328_16

clothes, just a little too small for her, to fuck me in. It drove me crazy to be tied down by her, force-fed her pussy in my own lace panties under my own plaid skirt—like high school all over again. She'd never yet worn them with anyone else.

I didn't mind lending her those clothes—not really. But at 2 a.m. tonight, after checking the drawer and finding missing the dildo she used on me, I'd lost it, called them screaming and crying, threatened. "I gotta go," my honey said when the boss passed her the phone. I'd slumped on the futon and lain there for hours, images flashing through my mind—the first time we kissed, in college, under the stained glass in the chapel; the girls I'd cheated on her with, a long time—it felt like a long time ago; my hands clenching her shoulders as she slid her whole hand in me; and finally, always, her and the boss, doing shit she didn't do with me, laughing, ignoring the phone ringing. I touched myself—my bare tits, my cunt—furtively, ashamed, aroused, humiliated.

Now I heard the deadbolt slam, the bottom lock turn, and then— "I think she's sleeping," hissed my girl, and a laugh answered her. "Don't wake her." I crooked my head forward and saw my girl, hair disheveled and bra showing under the falling straps of a black camisole, clinging to the boss's arm. The woman looked just as rich as I'd imagined—tall, shapely, in a million-dollar blouse with too many buttons undone. I turned, miserable, guilty, forlorn, away. Did she have to bring *her* to watch her leave me?

Instead of heading straight for the dresser, as I'd imagined they would—the boss sliding open the zipper on a piece of my girl's leather luggage, my girl throwing bras, underwear, long skirts, blouses inside—they edged toward me. My girl leaned down to kiss me, and I shrank away. "Come on," she coaxed, and turned my shoulders firmly, gently toward her. Her lips tasted like that raspberry stuff, not like her usual, slightly bitter good lipstick. She was giddy, turned on, her hair coming out of its pigtails. She sucked on my lower lip and pried my mouth open, gently, with her tongue. I kissed her back. I couldn't help it. This was the last, the most, I'd get. I arched my back, pushed my tits into hers. Her nipples were hard. "Shouldn't you be packing?" I hissed bitterly.

She laughed. "I'm not fucking leaving you. And you know what? I like fucking who I want, and you are not going to make me choose, and you are not going to punish her just because you're jealous."

"I'm sorry," I whispered.

"That's not enough. You have to learn." I waited for her to slap me, the way she sometimes did when I disobeyed her in bed, that fucking made me so wet. Hands gripped my wrists firmly, suddenly. They weren't hers. What the fuck? As the boss silently, expertly wrapped my wrists, securing them to the futon frame slats, and as I struggled against her, my girl pinched my nipples with sharp nails and dove in to kiss me again. I squirmed, aroused and confused. She bit my lip.

"You can say your safe word at any time," she said perfunctorily, as the boss deftly bound my ankles to the futon frame. "But honestly, there's nothing you can really do about what's gonna happen. You might as well enjoy it."

She pinched my tit again, and then the boss was behind her, kissing the bare nape of her neck, slipping two fingers in her glossy mouth. Giggling, they dropped to the mattress beside me, and I craned my neck, ashamed, to watch them show off.

Pain throbbed in my gut as they climbed all over, clung to each other, kissing sloppily and laughing—not even at me anymore. The boss slid the straps of the camisole all the way down my girl's shoulders, kissing her neck and the cleavage that popped out of that lacy, see-through pink bra. I'd done the same when she first put it on. My girl let out a long moan, let the boss roll on top of her, and arched up to her, just as I'd done a few moments before, before they'd forgotten I was here. The boss pulled the shirt off, roughly, in one quick motion. I bit my lip. The pain pounded in my chest. "Finger me, finger me," my darling pleaded, and I watched the boss slip her hand under the lace that covered my girl's pussy. My girl kissed her, clung with her fingernails, begged, screamed, all the usual stuff I did with her, but never her with me. I thought of her long nails circling my clit, pressing hard under the hood. "Please, please!" she screamed, but the boss pulled her hand away and took off her own blouse and skirt, crouched over my girl, and pushed her braless tits into my girl's mouth. She rocked back and forth, pantyless, on my girl's thigh, as I'd done so many times. My girl whimpered. My neck hurt from watching, my chest ached from jealousy, and my pussy stung with desire. "Do it, please. Do it."

I watched, horrified, as the boss slung my girl's harness and dildo around her hips, tightened the belt, and stroked the dick lovingly. She turned my girl over and, to my shock, up to her knees. "Fuck you," I whimpered, through teeth determinedly closed.

My girl leaned over and kissed my mouth again, then slapped my pussy, hard. I moaned but didn't say the word. "I thought you'd like this," she said, maliciously. "I'm going to show you all the things I let her do. You can fucking cry right now, but I don't want to hear you give me shit about it ever again." For a moment, she sounded more like herself, the femme top who let almost nothing inside her, who preferred to watch me, to fuck me, to dominate, humiliate her femme.

Then she was on her knees next to me, the boss kneeling behind her, grabbing her tits roughly, pinching her nipples, scratching her tits. My girl cried out, and the boss's right hand, closest to me, slid down and brushed lightly between my girl's thighs. "Put your ass in the air," she ordered. I moaned louder.

"You make my dick so hard," said the boss, as though she'd said this to a million girls, each time a little differently. "You make it strain through my skirt, you make it so fucking erect. I want you to take it however I want, and first I want you to beg." It hurt to hear my girl beg, like in the hetero pornos she always made fun of, "Please, please, give me your cock. I need dick. I need it. Oh!—" The boss slid into her. "I just can't, oh god, be satisfied without you filling my, oh god, my tiny hole with your, please, big, big, cock. I'm such a little— oh, ow! Yeah—whore, I want it so—ah!—bad!" They'd done this before, maybe many times, and she knew exactly what this woman wanted her to say. She'd made me say stuff like that, slapping me and telling me what a slut I was for wanting cock, but when I'd even mentioned turning the tables she'd always just laughed. With her right hand, the boss gripped my girl's tit, letting her nails sink in. She thrust in and out of her, moaning. My girl leaned forward, her face in the mattress, her ass even higher in the air. "Tell me how you want me to use you, slut," said the boss, and my girl replied quickly, "I want you to, nnnnn, penetrate my tight pussy with your hard—hard—cock, please! I wanna be your—fuck!—little toy, I want you to use me, ah! Hurt me, yeah! Please give me your hard, thick, cock!" She was well trained, I thought bitterly. I was wet, jealous, hurt, angry, turned on—"Do you like this?" asked the boss, finally getting into the game. "Do you like hearing me fuck your girl just like she fucks you? My hard cock is sliding in—and out—and in—and out—of her tight, slippery pussy." She reached down and smacked the side of my girl's face, and my love started screaming words that weren't even words, just sounds, in tune with the hard slap of the boss's hips against her ass.

I moaned, straining at my bonds, crazed, aroused, humiliated beyond pride.

"Oh, God," cried my girl. "Oh, please, please, please, please, FUCK!" Shaking, screaming, sobbing, she pushed back against the boss in a last spasm. My cunt throbbed as she cried out and collapsed on her haunches. The boss slapped her ass. "Please," I begged, humbled, confused. "I'm sorry, I'm so sorry I tried to control you."

"I forgive you, honey," gasped my girl, unhooked her bra, and wiggled out of my lingerie. "I love you," I was about to say, but the words were stopped by the cock, sticky with my darling's come, that the boss pushed insistently, brutally, into my mouth. As I gagged on it and pulled on my restraints, three fingers slid quickly into my cunt. I gasped and braced myself.

The assault wasn't as rough as I feared. They pushed me, but not to the limit of pain. I knew not to come, but as my girl fucked me lubelessly and the boss hit me, hard, across the face with each thrust, so that my lips and cheeks felt swollen as my cunt, it was hard not to. She'd pulled the dick out of my mouth and spit on my face, and now I was moaning abjectly, too turned on for jealousy or anger.

"Now we're going to fuck you, really fuck you," said my girl. Her voice sounded a million miles away through the red haze of fucking. "We're going to gag you, you little whore," she advised me, stuffing something in my hand with the hand she pulled out of me. My underwear, pulled off her pussy. "You won't be able to speak. This is your safe word—you can drop it if you need to." I whimpered my fear, confusion, and consent. We had never taken it this far. The boss shoved a smooth, soft ball in my mouth, then wrapped cloth around it, lifting my head to tie it. She wrapped something else around my eyes. "Ready?" she whispered. I didn't know who she meant. Maybe both of us. My jaw began to ache again.

Then the pain began again. Clips tight on my nipples. Whipping stinging my inner thighs, as I tried to moan and spread them apart. A closed-fisted blow to the face. All the while, a hand brushing over my pussy, too slow to let me come. "She forgives you, but you deserve this," said the boss, hitting my face again. "You bitch, running around on her and calling it something nice. Nonmonogamy, huh? And now when she's finally getting her own, you make her feel like shit. You whore. You hypocrite. I have to do this, you understand?" The whip stung my breasts, bad enough to bleed. It wasn't ours. "Otherwise, it's over." She slammed her fist into my face one last time, and I tasted blood. My fist stayed clenched around the panties.

Then fingers thrust into me, so many fingers, stretching me, using me. Both of them? My nipples ached, face throbbed, thighs stung. I breathed through my nose. So many fingers slamming into me, rubbing me, bringing me so close. Lube on them this time, and my girl saying, "Let's do it," and *pop*. Everything was a blur of pain, fucking, arousal, my cunt filled up with my girl's small fist, and my aching, bruised cunt being used, being pleased, and then *pop*, and I saw fireworks behind my eyes. Two fists? And as the pain mounted, I came, my cries muffled by the gag, reduced to a blind, dumb fuckdoll, and I saw God, felt forgiveness, just like on Yom Kippur, and I came and came and came.

16

The Game

Alison Tyler

And her bosom lick
And upon her neck
From his eyes of flame
Ruby tears there came
While the lioness
Loos'd her slender dress
And naked they convey'd
To caves the sleeping maid

William Blake

Angela called that first party, almost two years ago, a trial by fire. Having to meet the entire band at one time. But, honestly, I preferred it that way, plunged into the group without a chance to step back, to move away from the flames.

Still, I was scared. I tried to control my nerves as I slid off her Harley, then waited while she set her gloves and helmet on the rack. We'd parked her bike in the circular driveway, already filled with other, more decadent bikes, and we walked past them to the front of the house.

"Guess we're the last ones here," Angel said, leading me up the stairs and into Deleen DeMarco's Hollywood Hills estate. "That's good. You'll get to know everyone in about five seconds flat—then

Published by The Haworth Press, Inc., 2006. All rights reserved.
doi:10.1300/5328_17

you can stop trembling and enjoy yourself." I nodded and gripped her hand. As a model, you'd think I'd be used to meeting celebrities—especially since I'm considered one myself. But I was fairly new on the scene. And meeting the members of Objects—the band with the most number one hits in the country—was disconcerting, regardless of how many fashion shoots I'd done.

Angel pulled me along behind her, whispering assurances to me: "You'll do fine. They'll love you." We brushed past the multicolored balloons that filled the entryway, lolling against the molded doorways and fluttering softly up to the ceiling.

A poster of the new album cover, *Objects of Desire,* was taped to one wall. It showed Angel, Deleen, Beauty, and Arianna totally nude with Keith Haring–style arrows pointing to their breasts and cunts. Lola, the cherub of the group with her blonde ringlets and innocent smile, sat naked in her wheelchair, staring up at the rest of the group.

As I looked at the picture, I realized how each band member derived power through individuality. Angel's tattoos were starkly severe in the black and white photo, as if they'd been carved into her body. Arianna had painted stars and stripes on her breasts to make them more patriotic. Deleen was like a mad sorceress. She winked at the camera with an almost evil smirk, and rubbed her hands together with glee. Beauty, who's half German and half Native American, had braided her thick, black hair into a solid rope—it made her look dangerous and mean. She stood sideways between Deleen and Arianna, and her braid hung down her back, past her shoulder blades, almost to her waist.

"That's the uncensored version," Angel told me. "The public receives a model with black X's covering the indecent parts."

I stared, fascinated by the curves and dips of the women's bodies, their unique shapes, but Angel pulled on my hand, leading me into the sprawling living room. The lights were dimmed, and I almost stumbled over a white cat walking up to greet us.

"Hey, Shazzam," Angel picked up the kitty. "I'd like you to meet Katrina."

I shook a fuzzy paw, and Beauty, staked out on a matching sofa, said, "Where are your manners, Angel? You introduce your lady to a pussy before us?"

Angela shrugged, set Shazzam gently on the ground, and said, "Everyone, I'd like you to meet Katrina. Katrina, this is everyone." She looked around the room, "Well, almost everyone. Where are the hosts?"

Arianna, reclining on a matching red leather chaise lounge with her girlfriend, said, "Somewhere in the kitchen." She was covered by a petite Asian beauty named Sara, draped casually over her like a shawl.

"You should check out the spread," Beauty told us. "Tessa got the Sleeping Buddha to cater."

Angel and I turned as Tessa appeared in the doorway, caught beneath the iridescent light filtering through a gathering of balloons. Tess is a true Irish redhead, her ivory skin sprinkled with millions of freckles like golden confetti. They seemed to sparkle across her nose and shoulders and over her cleavage, and I wondered if they covered her entire body, then blushed at the thought.

Deleen came up behind her carrying a glass of champagne in each hand.

"Hey, Angel. Who's the babe?"

"Deleen, really," Tessa admonished. "You're frightening her."

"This is Katrina," Angela said, her arm behind me, pushing me toward them. I shook hands with Tessa. Deleen, passing the champagne on to Arianna and Sara, took one of my hands in both of hers and kissed my fingertips.

"Charmed," she smiled.

"Help yourself to food," Tessa said, ignoring her flirtatious lover. "We've got a feast spread out in the dining room, buffet style."

Angel and I piled up plates, then walked back into the main room and settled onto the floor against a flood of satin pillows. Tessa came to sit by my side. She had on a strapless dress with a black bodice and a short skirt of fluffy lace. Her slender waist was accentuated with a wide velvet ribbon. I complimented her on the look and she said, "Thanks. Easy on, easy off," and then leaned across me to ask Angel a question, rubbing her breasts slightly against my knees.

I wondered if she'd done it on purpose, and then looked at her startled as she asked me a question.

"I'm sorry, what?"

"Do you know Lola?"

"No. I know *of* her, but we haven't met."

"She should be here later," Tessa said, looking at Angel to include her in the conversation. "Lo was meeting with a publisher in New York about doing a book of photos. They say she's the next Herb Ritz." She paused, as an idea came to her, "You know, she ought to take some of you." Tessa said.

"The two of you together," Deleen interrupted. "Now, *that* would be a picture."

I saw Angel nodding in agreement, but turned when Arianna leaned up on the sofa, Sara moving with her lover's body as if she were another limb.

"Add Sara, too," Arianna insisted.

"And, um," Beauty fumbled as a gorgeous strawberry blonde strolled in from the kitchen holding a bottle of mineral water. She walked up to Beauty and snuggled against her.

"Liz," she purred.

"Yeah, and Liz," Beauty finished, lamely, and the rest of us laughed, transforming an awkward moment into a rather silly one. Liz didn't seem to mind. She curled her long limbs around Beauty's, protectively, like an owner.

"I wouldn't get too comfortable if I were her," Tessa whispered to me. "Beauty left her last girlfriend on the plane when she met this one," Tessa nodded to Liz who was now kissing Beauty's earlobe. "Beauty's always had a problem with the word *commitment*."

Angel excused herself, then, to get more food, and Tessa took this opportunity to lean even closer to me. Her body pressed against my side so that I could feel her fragile ribs, the warm, bare skin of her upper chest on my arm.

"How long have you two been hiding out?" she asked me when Angel was out of the room. "We haven't seem much of Angel since the recording ended."

"A month," I told her, thinking in my head that it was thirty days exactly since she'd come with Melanie to the fashion shoot at *Zebra*.

"And you met . . ."

"Through Melanie Samuel." I waited for the recognition to appear in Tessa's eyes.

"The journalist?"

I nodded.

"You're on the cover of *Zebra* this month, aren't you?" she said, getting it.

I nodded again, giving her a quick version of the smoldering look they'd had me do for the shoot—the one currently appearing on every newsstand. Lashes lowered, head tilted, lips pouting.

"You seem different in person," Tessa said, smiling at me. "So much younger."

"That's the makeup," I explained. "But it's what Angel said, too. It's what she liked about me, I think, the person beneath the image." Everyone in the business knows about it, but only a few people allow others into their shell.

Angel had said, "Can I talk with you?" And I told her, knees trembling at the thought of talking with Angela McMorrow, lead singer in the hottest band in the country, "Hang out until I get this makeup off." She'd waited, outside the dressing room, chatting with Melanie who kept yelling for me to hurry up. I came out in a T-shirt and ripped jeans, my normal attire, and Angela looked me over and shook her head.

"You're younger than all that, aren't you?" she asked, glancing toward the lights and the fancy dresses hanging from a metal pole in wardrobe. "I'm the same age underneath," I grinned. "You just have to look beneath the surface."

Angel had nodded, moving in close to me as Melanie withdrew to answer her cell phone in private. "Yeah, I would like to do just that, Katrina. I would like to see what's lurking beneath your surface, peel you open, spread you out, learn each of your secrets for myself."

Then Melanie had returned and things continued as normal—at least until the next time Angel and I were alone. Still, I didn't say any of these things to Tessa. She would know all about duplicity, two-faced worlds, being the partner of Deleen DeMarco—someone whose little black book contained the number of every "in" person in Hollywood.

Angel came back then, now sitting on Tessa's side, and she gave me a look over Tessa's head that I took to mean, "How are you holding out?"

I shrugged back at her and then said, "Please," as Deleen stopped in front of me with a fresh bottle of champagne. It surprised me at first that there wasn't any "help" at the party, but I was glad for it, glad for the low-key atmosphere. I could tell that these people were for real—not needing the constant stroking of fans or media.

The house—mansion, really—was as kickback as they were—set up for comfort, not appearances, although all was stylishly done. There were pillows everywhere, velvet and satin striped, with butter-soft leather sofas. I hoped to decorate my own place in a similar fashion someday, wanting to be able to walk into a room, eyes closed (or blindfolded), and enjoy the surroundings by touch only.

By my third bubble-filled glass, I was leaning against the cushions, listening to Montage croon on the stereo, drifting in a warm fulfillment. I paid scant attention to Angel and Tessa who were discussing the promotion for *Objects of Desire*. I watched as Arianna and Beauty gossiped across the space between their sofas, Sara describing her latest nude centerfold in *Planet X* magazine, and Liz, a first-class cabin attendant, explaining how Beauty had stolen her heart at 32,000 feet.

I wondered what had happened to the girl Beauty had been with, and I thought about asking Tessa, but she left to fetch a joint. When she returned to the living room, she was tottering on her spangled high heels.

"Want some, Angel?" she asked, collapsing on the pillows on Angel's left side, turning my lover into a "person sandwich" with Tess and me the bread.

"Naw, I'm saving my voice."

"Katrina?" she asked.

"Sure."

Marijuana goes to my head quickly, especially when I'm drinking, so I only took one hit. But Tessa apparently had been smoking in the bedroom before coming out. She was flying, and while I lit up, she leaned seductively against Angela and said, "You have the most beautiful eyes, Angel. You know it?"

Angel tried to brush her off, nicely, by saying, "Deleen's the one with the killer eyes." Angel turned to me, "Did you know that Del's eyes have no color?"

I was more stoned than I'd thought, because this statement tripped a string of bizarre images in my mind. "What do you mean?" I finally managed to ask.

"They're almost perfectly clear. She usually wears shades or colored lenses to hide them. Del!"

Deleen looked over from her lazy-lioness position in the hammock chair.

"What's up?" She was gone, too.

"Come show Kat your eyes."

"Send the kitty over here."

I got up, also a bit unbalanced, and wove my way to Deleen's corner. She turned a floor lamp around so that the light shone directly in her eyes, and I drew in my breath. They were like glass, perfectly clear irises with liquid black pupils in the center.

Deleen smiled at me and said, "I always wear contacts for public appearances. I wouldn't want to scare anyone."

She put her hand out to steady me. I'd been rocking in place, and her fingers were like flames licking at my skin. Startled, I stumbled back to the pillow corner. Tessa was now in Angel's lap, her dress hiked up to her thighs exposing the purple ribbons of her garters as she straddled my lover. Angel didn't seem uncomfortable, but I could tell she was humoring Tess.

"You don't mind, do you Katrina?" Tessa grinned at me. "Angel has the most inviting body. I wanted to be closer to it."

"Go ahead," I said magnanimously as I leaned against the wall, letting it support me as I slid to a sitting position. "Do what you have to." I wanted to see how far Angel would take it, wanted to know what I'd be in store for in the future. At the moment, she seemed to be letting Tessa call the shots.

Deleen got up to open another bottle of champagne, and I saw a frown on her painted lips.

"What are you up to, Tess?" she asked, her buzz obviously worn off. Deleen's demeanor surprised me, considering how she'd flirted with me when we'd met.

"Just goin' for a ride," Tessa slurred, leaving no doubts that Angel was to be her horse.

Deleen clicked her tongue against the roof of her mouth, and then sat down on the nearest sofa, forcing Arianna and Sara to move aside. They protested for a second before resuming their positions: Sara had undone Arianna's leather jeans and was very quietly sucking on the strap-on dildo that Arianna wore in a harness. The darkness of the room had concealed their activity, but they didn't seem to mind being revealed. Arianna's moans and Sara's kittenlike suckling noises testified to that.

"What is it with you, Tessa?" Deleen's voice was very softly menacing. "It's been three hours since you last came, is that too long for you?"

Tessa looked at Deleen through clouded eyes. "I'm just entertaining our guests, Del," she said.

"Uh-uh, baby, I'm not going to play that game." Deleen slid her hand through her silvery hair, apparently trying to calm herself down. Deleen's hair is completely gray and has been since her teens. She wears it combed off her forehead, and it falls like an old lion's mane straight down her back. "Get your little ass over here."

Tessa stood up quickly, a worried look replacing the lecherous one she'd worn only a second earlier.

"Now," Deleen ordered, when she saw Tessa hesitate.

Angel watched the whole scene with her features set. She appeared emotionless, a statue, but I could tell she was getting turned on. I was already able to read her expressions, the slight wrinkle in her brow or tightening of her jaw. I settled against her and she put an arm around me, gently turning my face to kiss my lips.

Tessa cautiously walked the rest of the way over to Deleen, as if condemned. As soon as Tess was in reaching distance, Deleen grabbed hold of her waist and threw Tessa over her lap. Tess struggled, realizing suddenly what her Mistress meant to do, but Deleen held her firmly, scissoring one leg over Tessa's two squirming ones to keep her in place. Deleen lifted Tessa's dress by the hem, pulling it up to reveal a lavender lace G-string and matching garter belt.

"Katrina, would you mind bringing me my Harley gloves?" Deleen asked me, her voice unreadable except for the power in it, the command. "They're on the table in the entryway."

I looked at Angel to see if I should, but all she said was, "Go ahead, Kit-Kat, it's Del's party."

When I stood up, Deleen added, "Oh, and get me some K-Y, too, won't you? It's in the bathroom cabinet—the one in the hall." My heart racing, I left the room, gathered the tube of gel and the leather gloves, and walked back to Deleen who still held the upended Tessa over her knees.

"Thanks, sweetheart," Deleen said as I handed her the items. I turned to sit down next to my Mistress again, feeling weak and confused. Angel pulled me to her, positioning me between her legs so that I could feel the wetness that pulsed through her jeans.

Deleen slipped Tessa's G-string down her thighs, but left the garter and hose in place.

"Better calm down, Tess," her voice was hypnotic, and I realized suddenly that everyone in the room had turned to see what was going on. Sara and Arianna, after struggling into semi-upright positions, were watching intently. Liz and Beauty, who'd been up to something on their own plush sofa, were now mellowly regarding Tessa, Beauty softly explaining to Liz how Tess and Del's relationship worked. I heard Beauty say, "Don't worry, Lizzie, it's just how it is."

Deleen had her worn leather gloves on, and she squeezed a generous supply of the jelly onto one finger and then spread Tessa's ass cheeks with the other hand. Tessa continued to fight, but her slight frame was no match for Deleen's more powerful build.

"I said, calm down, Tessa."

Although Deleen hadn't raised her voice, there was a note of danger in it, one that made me sure that if I were in Tessa's position, I would be still. Tess must have sensed it, too, for she was suddenly quiet, yet I could tell her muscles were tensed to escape if Deleen would give her the chance.

"Tessa wants to come," Deleen said, addressing the rest of us as a group for the first time. "She has an insatiable appetite." As she spoke, she worked the K-Y around and into Tessa's asshole. When she slipped a gloved finger inside her naughty lover, Tessa started to protest again. Deleen put her lips close to Tessa's ear, but we all heard her hiss, "Once more, baby, and I'll get the studded gloves."

Now Deleen had two fingers inside her, and moved them in and out with increasing speed. She used her thumb on Tessa's clitoris, and Tess moaned, an obvious sound of pleasure that set off titters from Liz and Sara.

"Like that, don't you?" my Mistress whispered to me, and I nodded, leaning against her, feeling the hard synthetic cock that she was packing beneath the soft denim. Angel put both arms around me, protectively, as we continued to watch Deleen's progress with Tessa. Del was making her come slowly—bringing Tessa close to climax, then teasing her down. When she'd forced three fingers into Tessa's asshole, Tess started to move against her Mistress, fucking Deleen's gloved hand, working her body on it, but Del would have none of that.

"Tessa, don't," she said, a warning in her voice. It was obvious that Deleen did not want her lover to take any form of control, and I could tell that it took every ounce of Tessa's strength for her to follow this command.

"I'll make you come in my own sweet time," Deleen promised, before turning her attention to me. "Katrina? Tess was . . ." she cleared his throat before saying, "*riding* your property. Would you like to be the one to punish her?" She paused to look at me before continuing. "Because as soon as she comes, she's going to need to be disciplined."

The blood drained from my cheeks, and I turned immediately to Angel for help, but my Mistress shook her head, leaving the decision up to me, *testing* me, I thought. Flashes of conversations with Melanie replayed themselves in my head. "Leather," she'd said, "Bondage and dominance. Sex games. Wild, wild parties."

"I couldn't," I whispered.

"Another time," Deleen said, letting me off with a reassuring smile. Then, in a completely different voice, a darker voice, "Did you hear me, Tess? You'd better try to slow it down, because I'm going to spank your little bottom as soon as you come."

Tessa started crying, and I knew it was because she was close to orgasm. And that, humiliating though it might be to come in front of everyone, being spanked would be worse. Deleen continued finger-fucking her asshole and stroking her clit. I noticed how gently she stroked Tessa there, and understood that Beauty was right, that despite what Deleen had said, this was a game, with Tessa a willing player.

And then, with everyone's attention focused on her, Tessa flushed, closed her eyes tightly, and let her body finally respond to Deleen's attention. She arched her back, tense with concentration, and came in a series of powerful shivers, electricity running through her body.

The roomed seemed lit by her energy, a shower of metallic sparks, alien green and copper, vibrating in the air. She was truly stripped, as if Deleen had peeled her layer by layer, leaving a nude and shimmering soul for us to see.

How awesome it must feel to be that free.

17

Lap Dance Lust

Rachel Kramer Bussel

We pull into the shadowy parking lot in some corner of Los Angeles. I look around the deserted area, wondering where exactly we are, only half caring. Most strip clubs in L.A. are located in tucked-away corners like this one.

I'm a little apprehensive as we walk around to the entrance and part the strings of beads to enter Cheetah's—a strip club, a real live strip club! I've been dreaming of just such a place for years but have never worked up the courage to actually go, until now. I'd heard that Cheetah's was "women friendly," and from the crowd I can immediately tell it's true. There are plenty of guys but also a decent number of female customers who look like they're having a good time.

My three friends and I take ringside seats along the surprisingly empty stage and animatedly set about checking out each new dancer. Many of them are what I expected—peroxide blonde, fake boobs, very L.A., and very boring. Some have a spark of creativity and feign a glimmer of interest to tease out one of the dollars we hold in our hands, but many pass right by us or stare back with vacant eyes.

We watch as one girl after another maneuvers around the stage, shimmying up and then down the shiny silver pole, twisting and writhing in ways I can't imagine my body doing. It feels surreal, this world of glamour and money and lights and ultrafemininity. I look and stare and whisper to my friends. Though I'm having fun, the

Published by The Haworth Press, Inc., 2006. All rights reserved.
doi:10.1300/5328_18

place starts to lose its charm when I have to get more change and still no girl has really grabbed my eye. I settle in with a new drink and a fresh stack of bills and hope that I won't be disappointed by the next round of dancers.

When the next girl walks out, I'm transfixed. She's the hottest girl I've ever seen. She's wearing cave girl attire, a leopard-print bandeau top and hot pants—all tan skin, natural curves, and gleaming black hair. She looks shiny, like she's just put on suntan lotion. She slithers along, making eye contact when she passes us, crawling back across the stage, putting her whole body into the performance. She toys with her shorts, thumbs hooked into the waist, before sliding them down her long legs to reveal black panties. I know that she's the one for me, that I really like her and am not just an indiscriminate ogler, when I realize that I preferred her with her shorts on.

After her performance, I offer her a wad of dollars. "Thanks," she says. "I'm Gabrielle."

"Hi," I say shyly. "I really like your outfit."

"Me too," she giggles, then smiles before waving her fingers and gliding off the stage.

"Oooooh, you like her. You should get a lap dance."

"Yeah, get a lap dance! Get a lap dance!"

My friends are practically jumping up and down in their excitement, making me blush.

"Maybe."

"No, no, you should get one. She's totally hot."

"I know, I know, but let me think about it, okay?" They're so eager for me to lose my lap dance virginity, I'm afraid they may drag me over to her.

I need to get away for a minute, so I go to the bathroom. To my shock, I find her sitting inside, casually chatting with a friend. "Oh, hi," I stammer. "Is this your dressing room?"

She laughs. "No, but it's almost the same quality." I smile at her and then go into the stall, nervous at having spoken to her. When I emerge and begin to wash my hands, she admires my purse. I tell her about it and then take out my sparkly lip gloss. She asks to try some, and I hold it out to her, watching as her finger dips into the red goo.

We talk a bit more about makeup and then she says, casually, "Did you want to get a lap dance?"

Did I? Of course! "Yes, I'd like that," I say.

"Great, just give me a few more minutes and I'll come get you."

I practically float out the door and back to my friends. *I'm going to get a lap dance, and I arranged it all by myself! Ha!* I feel like gloating. I wait patiently, trying not to let my excitement show in a big stupid grin.

After a few minutes, she emerges and summons me, leading me to the other side of the stage, against a wall where I've seen other girls pressed up mostly against old men. She seats me on a plastic-covered couch, then takes a chair and places it a few feet in front of me. "So people can't look up your skirt," she tells me. I smile to thank her for her kindness; it never would've occurred to me. I give her some larger bills, and we talk for a minute or two before a song she likes comes on.

And then, quite suddenly, it starts. She pushes me so my head is tilted back against the wall, the rest of me pressed against the sticky plastic, my legs slightly spread. She stands between my legs, then leans forward, pressing her entire body along the length of mine. She smells like sweat and lotion and some undefinable sweetness, and I breathe deeply. Even her sweat smells good, like baby powder. Her soft hair brushes against my face and shoulders; her breasts are pressed up against mine. Then I feel her thigh against my hand; she's climbed up on the couch with me. This is definitely not what I expected. I've never been to a strip club before, but I thought I knew the deal—I'd seen *Go*, right? You can't touch the dancers or you'll get kicked out. But what if they're touching you? What about her hand gliding along mine, the outside of her smooth thigh touching my arm, her slightly damp skin setting mine on fire? The look she gives me is priceless: as her body moves downward and she's crouched near my stomach, I look down and her hooded eyes are on me, her face a vision of pure lust, her mouth slightly open. I'm sure it's a practiced look, but it feels as real as any look I've ever received, and it enters and warms me.

I think I know what I'm getting into; I've read all the feminist arguments, the sex worker manifestos. This is just a job and I'm a paying customer: one song, one lap, one transaction. But all of that background disappears, likewise my friends, my family, L.A., everyone else in the club. It's just me and her, never mind the music; it's that look as she slides between my open legs. I swallow heavily. I can't move, and I don't want to, ever again. I just want to sit here and let her brush herself against me again and again as I keep getting wetter. And then her hand reaches up, delicately turning around my necklace, a Jewish star. It's the sweetest gesture, and something only another femme would notice or care about. She gives me a little smile as she does it, and I give her one back.

The song is almost over, and she gives it her all. Her body pushes hard against mine, pressing my chest, stomach, thighs. She's working me so good this huge bouncer walks over and glances at us suspiciously, but she turns around and gives him a look that tells him to move along. I like knowing that whatever she's doing with me is enough out of the norm to warrant the bouncer's attention. I feel ravished in a way I've never felt before; it's pure sexual desire, concentrated into whatever messages her skin and her eyes can send me in the course of a five-minute song.

When the song ends, I give her a generous tip, and she sits with me for a little while. She takes my hand in hers, which is delicate and soft, and I revel in her touch. It's tender and sensitive, and I need this, need to hear her sweet voice tell me about her career as a singer, her friendship with a famous musician, her upcoming trip to New York. I need to hear whatever it is she wants to tell me, true or not. My head knows certain things: this is a strip club, that was a lap dance, this is her job. But inside, inside, I know something else. I know that we just exchanged something special. It wasn't sex or passion or lust per se; it was more than, and less than, each of those things. It was contact, attention, and adoration. Call me crazy, but I think it went both ways.

After we talk, I go back to my friends, but I feel a bit odd. I know they were watching, but did they see what really happened?

"That was some lap dance."

"Yeah, that was really amazing for your first time."

"She gave you her real name? That's a big stripper no-no."

"I think she liked you."

I nod and respond minimally, still in my own world. For the rest of the trip, whatever I'm doing, wherever I am, part of me is still sitting on that plastic-covered couch, looking down at her, breathing her scent, reveling in her look.

I haven't gone to any more strip clubs since, or gotten any more dances. How could they ever live up to her? I don't know if I want to find out.

– 18 –

The Manicure

Nell Carberry

Last week, when I had some time to kill, I noticed that my nails were in sad, sad shape. I felt gray and washed-out, invisible in the big, loud city. But as I wandered through Greenwich Village at sunset, the air was bright, like someone had opened a bottle of champagne and let it spray. So I found a little nail parlor on one of those streets that goes at cross angles to everything else. The manicure shop was painted pink and red, like the inside of a womb.

Within the pulsing room, there was only a single manicurist, a small Asian woman with gorgeous brown eyes.

"I was going to close up," she said. She glanced at my hands. "But I can help you."

She wore a long pink cotton smock, and her ID badge read KAREN. I asked her what her real name was, and she looked annoyed.

"That is my real name."

I was embarrassed. What I'd meant was someone so beautiful should have a beautiful name. But the damage was done. I told her my name was Nell.

Karen locked the door and turned out all of the lights except the one over her manicurist's table. She practically pushed me into a chair and began to file at my ragged hands.

"Shouldn't I pay you first?" I said.

Published by The Haworth Press, Inc., 2006. All rights reserved.
doi:10.1300/5328_19

"It depends on what we're going to do," she said. She smiled, I think. "You don't take very good care of your hands," Karen said, "and they're beautiful hands. You should be punished for what you've done to your hands." At least, I thought that's what she'd said. The fumes from the polish and the soaking fluid were making me woozy.

She'd filed and soaked my nails, then went to work on my hands with pink lotion. Outside, it was getting dark, the wind was rattling, and I looked toward the door.

"Look only at me," Karen said.

My hands felt boneless. My groin felt warm, weightless.

"I really should pay you," I said, and my voice came out all soft and dark, too.

The door rattled, but it wasn't the wind. It was a woman trying to get in. She was dressed in black jeans and a shiny red silk shirt, and even in the dark, I could see she was desperate. She yanked at the door.

"No more customers," Karen shouted.

"Customer!" the woman shrieked. "I'm not a customer, you bitch!"

Karen shook her head. "Crazy people in New York," she said, looking at me sympathetically. "You would never do such a thing, would you?"

"No," I said, more fervently than I expected. "I'd never do that to you."

Karen wore some kind of perfume, roses and spice, something off, like jazz, but right, like jazz, too. The woman outside howled some more.

"Hey you, you in there with Karen. Get out now!"

Karen held my gaze with hers.

"If you ignore her, she'll go away," said Karen. "And you want her to go away, don't you?"

I looked only at Karen's eyes. I heard the woman walking away. I wanted to turn around then, but Karen tightened her hands around mine. How could such a tiny woman have such powerful hands?

"You wouldn't be rude like that, would you, Nell?" she whispered. "Not after I've done so much for your hands . . ."

That's when I saw the man step out of the darkness from the back of the shop.

I must have passed out.

The next thing I felt was a mouth on my mouth—smoky, male, wet.

It was now completely dark outside, and inside the shop was lit only with a couple of high-intensity lamps.

My legs were cold.

My legs were naked. My cunt exposed.

Karen worked on my cuticles as if this were the way she did all her nail jobs.

The mouth continued to explore my face, a tongue on my lip, a nip on my ear. I was dizzy, and my eyes wouldn't focus. I had been tied to the chair and stripped from the waist down. Sensations came and went. The male mouth traveled over my ears, licking, and down my neck, biting. My clit began to swell, and sweat, and trickle. The moisture hit the plastic of the seat, making it sticky. Karen gave me a glance, and stood.

"Don't you ruin my chair, you sloppy girl," she barked. Suddenly, she tilted the light down to the floor. My stubby square toenails had been painted bright red. They looked like the feet of a slut. My clit grew some more. I didn't recognize those feet as my own.

Karen noticed me looking at the color. "You like it? I call it 'Wench.'"

I turned back to the shop window. Karen hadn't yanked the metal grate down or pulled a curtain. If anyone had looked in, they could have seen us plainly: a half-naked woman being gently mauled by a silent man in tight black jeans, a white cotton shirt, and a ponytail, while being watched over by a stern, tiny mistress. I couldn't really see the man's face, but I could smell him. I hated men who smoked, but not this one.

"Show me her breasts," Karen snapped, and without warning, the Mouthman grabbed the front of my white Oxford cloth shirt and yanked it open. The buttons fell on the floor with a clatter. Somehow that made me hot, too.

"What an ugly bra," Karen spat. "We'll have to do something about that."

Mouth pulled a switchblade out of his tight jeans and flipped it open, like a biker boy. Carefully, he placed it on the material between my breasts and slit the fabric. He was gentle, but still he drew blood. Karen sighed and picked up a cotton ball. She dabbed it with rubbing alcohol: I could smell it rising in the air. She swabbed my wound down hard, and the sting made me gasp.

But my nipples got hard, and my cunt was slick with juice. My shirt dangled from my arms, and my bra was ruined.

"I would never have taken you, if your hands hadn't been such a mess," Karen whispered. "Now, I'll have to do all of you."

Mouth flung my shirt into a corner, along with my bra. Occasionally, I could sense people stopping outside, staring into the window, wondering if they really saw what they thought they saw in the shadows.

My wrists were bound to the arms of the chair, just a little too tight. Then they gagged me with a ball gag. There was a click of metal: clips made of silver filigree grasped my nipples fiercely—again, a little too tight.

"No sound," Karen ordered as she finished. "No talk, no moan, no pant." The Mouth said nothing, only opened and closed his knife once more.

Then Karen yanked on the chain between the nipple clips, and something between a pant and a grunt escaped from my mouth, despite the gag. I waited for a whip, a slap, a blow.

Instead, Karen sat down deliberately and pulled the manicure table to the side. She grabbed a bottle of bright red polish, leaned into me, and painted the pinkie finger of my left hand. She smelled like heaven. Her jazzy perfume was breaking down, mixing with her sweat. I wanted to lick it off, even though I'd never touched another woman. She rose from her chair and perched on my left leg to finish the job, careful not to touch me anywhere else. This was my punishment—that she would sit right next to me, right on me, but draw no nearer. I tried to look on the bright side: I thought, this might not be so bad. Stripped naked by a dangerous man. Painted like a whore by a beautiful woman. I could be a silent, good little girl through that.

Then Karen nodded to Mouth, who had donned a pair of black rubber gloves when I wasn't looking. His smell had changed. He, too, was sweating, and his erection was obvious. I tried not to think ahead, tried not to wonder whether I'd get to see any more of his body. Then, he walked directly behind me and tied a blindfold around my eyes. The sour-sweet smell of the polish rose in the air.

Blind and mute, I felt as if I could smell everything in the room, as if my skin had doubled in size. Karen was on the "fuck you" finger, stroking my palm with one hand while decorating it with the other.

I would be her good girl. I could be quiet. Then, I felt a rubbery hand stroke my mound as Karen was stroking my palm Mouth went to work below while Karen worked on my hands. What a bitch she was, I thought. That woman had been right.

I writhed in the chair, but I kept quiet. I ground my ass into the sticky, cheap plastic of the chair, trying not to come, trying to avoid his hand, ever advancing. . . . I yanked at my wrist restraints. I was only trying to do what Karen demanded: to absorb the pleasure without a sound. Then, someone slapped me hard on the face. It was Karen, I guess: the slap was scented with perfume and lotion.

Karen hissed, "Ruin this nail job, bitch, and you'll never leave this place."

"Let's teach her something," said Mouth. His voice was smoky and dark, too. My outer lips ballooned at the sound. Everything was making me hot. How could I possibly do what Karen wished? But I wanted to. I knew I wanted to.

Mouth's hand withdrew from my crotch, and Karen stopped her nail job. I felt ashamed. I had failed her. I couldn't even get my fucking nails done without failing.

I felt Mouth grab the back of my chair, dragging me across the shop, dragging me toward . . . the storefront window. I could tell, even with the blindfold, that there was a streetlight shining outside, and that we were close enough to the glass to give anyone a very good view of my nail job.

"Will you be a good girl, Nell?" Karen whispered in my ear. I wanted to feel her tongue there, too, but it wasn't going to happen.

Karen yanked at my nipple clip chain. "Will you be a good, quiet girl?" I nodded, biting my cheek to keep the sounds inside my mouth.

I was a liar. I wanted to come. I wanted to scream. I wanted Mouth to plunge his hand deep into my cunt, and Karen to suck on my tortured tits. But I wanted to please her. The truth was, from the moment I'd sat down in that chair and put my hand in her hand, I was hers.

Karen kept up the pace of my nail job, while Mouth worked me below, kneading my mound until he flowed onto my clit, teasing it between two fingers. Sweat poured off my neck, my breasts, down my legs. I could hear Mouth begin to pant himself, and outside, I sensed, people were gathering.

Karen switched to my other hand, and Mouth's fingers drew patterns around my labia. How big was the crowd watching me?

I didn't know. I could hear a couple of people talking outside, another tapping on the glass, tapping. The blood rose in my chest, and I could feel my pale skin turn red from desire. I wanted to move my hips against Mouth's persistent motion, press hard against his long fingers, but I knew, I just knew, this was wrong.

"It's a bigger crowd than usual," Mouth said, and I could feel him smirking. The ball gag was making my mouth dry, my jaws tired. Bigger crowd than usual? I thought. What the hell did that mean?

And then, as Karen began painting my right hand, Mouth slid two fingers into me. I bit the inside of my cheek as his fingers found my G-spot and stroked it slowly. At the same time, Karen brought her mouth close to my breasts and just . . . breathed.

Outside, the crowd was quiet, but I could feel them watching. "They usually give up by now," I thought I heard a woman say, but maybe I imagined it. With his other hand, Mouth began exploring the crack of my ass. Karen withdrew her breath.

"Only four more fingers to go," Karen said brightly. As if in response, Mouth slid a third finger into my cunt. My knees shook, and my shoulders quivered. The ropes cut into my legs, and my circulation slowed.

"You clean up good, Nell," Mouth said mockingly. I felt him kneel in front of me, to one side of Karen, both hands wedged deep in my crotch. My asshole was still tender, untouched. I could feel his eyes on my clit and my cunt.

"Three more," said Karen, and for the first time, I heard some heat behind the ice. More heat against my crotch: it was Mouth, doing what Mouth did best. I twisted, as if I imagined that I could still avoid him. Karen slapped my breasts.

"You almost ruined that one," she shrilled.

"Either she's melting, or her juices are dripping off the chair," said Mouth.

"And she looked like such a dull little thing when she came in. But I knew you for what you were, Nell," said Karen.

Mouth now lapped me in earnest, from cunt lips to the tip of my clit. I heard a thump, thump, thump.

"They're pressing themselves against the glass, Nell, because they want a piece of you," Karen said, as she finished with my index finger, the one I liked to use to touch my breasts. Below, Mouth shoved his tongue into my cunt and licked the deep red walls inside me.

I was desperate not to come until Karen was done, but I didn't know how I was going to hold off. I thought about taxes, Republicans, white vinyl belts. I thought about bad TV movies, and Barry Manilow. But Karen was on the last digit now, my right thumb, and she was massaging my palm again. Nothing was working. I imagined a world where everyone, even John Denver, got tied down, worked over, and painted up like a slut. And we all loved it.

More thumps against the window. I thought of Hitchcock's *The Birds*, the thud of the predators.

"They all want you, Nell," said Karen. "But you're mine, aren't you?" Suddenly, my eyes filled with tears, and I nodded.

"All done," said Karen. And everything stopped. The Mouth withdrew, with a final tug at my clit. Karen dropped my hand. Outside, silence. I was on the verge of coming, and I suddenly felt completely alone. Were they going to leave me here? Was this my reward for obedience?

Karen whipped off my blindfold, untied the gag, and Mouth undid my bonds. He put his hands under my arms and forced me to stand. I shook, but I didn't fall.

And then I saw them: a crowd of twenty outside the glass, men, women, mouths little O's of lust, their sweaty hands applauding. I was naked, my hands and feet sparkled red, the color of the whore I was, the whore I wanted to be. I was swollen, I was ashamed, and I was Karen's. I wanted to be Karen's more than I wanted to moan, more than I wanted to come.

I turned, and there she stood, in a pink smock and nothing else. Nothing else, that is, except a black leather harness and a white marble dildo. And a mean gleam in her eye. I wanted to ask her permission, but I had lost my voice.

"Bend over the chair," she said. I eagerly complied.

But then she shook her head and gave me a mean little smile.

"No. Let's wax your legs first."

Gumshoe in a Cocktail Dress

Shelly Rafferty

Because it's become nearly standard operating procedure for my local bookshop to offer me a reading when my latest book is published, I have spent most of my career regarding these events as necessary and relatively benign flashes of self-promotion. But when my most recent, *Gumshoe in a Cocktail Dress,* broke the best-seller list a month ago, I knew my celebrity would be ratcheted up a notch.

At the podium, I surveyed the roomful of—dare I say it?—*fans,* as I breezily shared a few anecdotes from the writing life. From their tiny tables littered with spoon wrappers and espresso cups, my readers adored me with rapt attention, laughed in all the appropriate places, and reverently stroked their copies of my book.

I recognized a few faces. My friends Jen and Connie had alerted the local lesbian reading group, and consequently, many of the leather-jacketed, close-cropped, and Earth Mother varieties were sprinkled throughout the crowd. I caught an eye here and there and nodded appreciatively. I was delighted and charmed they were all there.

Until Tricia Corbin walked in.

The competition was in town.

❧

"Not your usual attire," Corbin whispered in my ear. Her perfume was faint, intoxicating. She was leaning over my left shoulder as I

Published by The Haworth Press, Inc., 2006. All rights reserved.
doi:10.1300/5328_20

wearily signed the last few copies and shook some hands. Her finger-tips grazed my skin so lightly I shuddered. "And the dress is quite brave," she continued. "I never thought you'd be playing this in character."

Neither did I. The cocktail dress—red, sequined, and very, very short—was a far cry from how most of my readers saw me. My ordinary dust jacket photos characterized me as an unthreatening academic: I wore the requisite blazer and turtleneck. But on campus and in my political work, the up-close version generally offered me in jeans, double-pocketed shirt with the sleeves cut off, and beret.

The cocktail dress had been a lark, my publicist Margaret's idea.

"You're not trying to suggest that I'm predictable?" I asked Corbin.

"Well, you're bound to cause a stir in the community. . . ."

"Frankly," I said, "the community could use a stir."

Tricia Corbin's infectious laugh surprised me. She leaned in close again, even as I pushed another signed copy across the table. "Let me take you for a drink?"

I leaned back a bit, intrigued. "All right."

As she stepped away, she let the back of her hand graze the nape of my neck. Her nails were longer than I expected.

She waited until I finished my chat with the last of the autograph hounds. She found a chair near the self-help titles and made small talk with one of the bookshop's owners while I put my briefcase and pages together. I noted that she'd crossed one leg over the other, a silky ankle exposed under the tapered hem of her wool trouser leg. The pump was smart, subtle, and a rich, black leather. As she talked, she turned a delicate key ring through her slender fingers, and the two gold rings on her left hand were not to be missed. For an instant, I wondered if she was wearing panties.

Tricia Corbin's own work was better known than mine. Her sprightly mystery series, featuring lesbian immigration cop Edith "Edie" Cutler, had attracted a healthy and eclectic readership over the past ten years, and she'd made enough to give up teaching and write full-time.

Corbin and I were not well acquainted. We'd met before, of course, but only in passing, at some gathering of local writers for one of the book clubs. We weren't friends, not by a long shot. We'd rubbed shoulders on a few feminist panels, and had chatted casually one evening at a reception for a mutual friend. A stretch of the imagination might characterize us as colleagues. And certainly we knew each other as competitors.

I found my Burberry raincoat and tossed it over my arm. I caught Corbin's eye, and she made her excuses. "Here, please," she insisted, reaching for my briefcase, "let me carry that."

"Aren't you going to be embarrassed to be seen with me in this?" I slipped a thumb under my spaghetti strap and tugged it slightly.

She smiled. "On the contrary. I *like* to be seen with ladies. . . ."

"I'm no lady, and you know it," I said.

"That's what I'm counting on," she answered. She slipped her hand under my elbow. "I'll buy," she said. "Shall we go?"

To my great surprise, we ended up on the fortieth floor of the swankest hotel in the city. The bar was full of straight people and patronizing waiters, and a decent jazz quintet patterned the air with a sulky piano. We got a table near the windows, and for a moment we looked down on the traffic and lights flickering in the streets below.

In the car on the way over, we'd made small talk. Although I felt extraordinarily self-conscious in the cocktail dress, I knew I had crossed my legs and turned toward her in an imitation of some ingenue I'd read about in a bad romance. It was strange, powerful, wearing that little and feeling so strong. In the garage, I had even let her open my car door.

I ordered a club soda from our red-jacketed waiter; Corbin asked for whiskey.

"You wouldn't like something a little stronger?" she challenged. "Somebody told me you're a beer connoisseur."

Again I slipped a finger under the strap of my skimpy, satin frock. "I'm protecting my image. Don't you think a can of Budweiser would disrupt this little illusion?"

"It looks good on you," she said quickly. "Not at all what I expected."

"I left my power tools at home. Is that what you mean?" I didn't wait for her to answer. I knew I was right. "What brought you out tonight?"

"Truth? I liked your novel. I mentioned it to my editor. He said you were giving a reading, an experience which, parenthetically, I abhor. You seem very at ease with the crowd. You laugh easily, field questions amiably. You're generous and patient. I could use some of that."

"I'm still teaching," I admitted, somewhat sheepishly. "I suppose that keeps me loose."

"In any event, I admire you. We get compared a lot, you and I. Not so much by reviewers, although McDonough did call you my 'heir apparent'—but you know what I mean. We're at the top of the lezzie literary hit parade."

"Well, you are," I said, genuinely trying to be gracious.

"*We* are. You're right beside me. . . . Does fame make you uncomfortable? No doubt you've had a cadre of groupies . . ."

I had to smile. I'd had my share of fan letters, a few obsessive-compulsive cases of puppy love, and one persistent graduate student who found me good fodder for her thesis. "Well, it's hard to resist their attention, at least at a superficial level. But I know their affection's not rooted in any 'real' place. They don't know who I am."

Corbin turned her gaze to the night sky. "They haven't got a clue. They see something in our hard-boiled heroines, in the serial monogamy, in the 'I'll be a lesbian no matter what it takes.' Don't get me wrong. I appreciate my readers. But they think I'm living the charmed life of a movie star. It's like being typecast by your own main character."

"So I shouldn't make any assumptions that you have anything in common with Edie Cutler."

"I'm queer and I like pretty girls. That's where the similarities end, I guess. I'd hate to think I'd given away all of my secrets in my books."

"So, you're not making any assumptions about me, right?"

"Well, that's just wishful thinking. I came with pretty much the same expectations everyone else has. I thought for sure you'd be in your usual uniform, talking about kickboxing, politics, crime fighting."

"You must have been disappointed."

"Quite the contrary. To be honest, I don't think we'd be here right now if you weren't wearing that dress."

"It's not an invitation. It's just a dress."

"If you say so. Don't get so defensive. You're very beautiful."

The way she was staring at me unnerved me. I don't think anyone had ever told me I was beautiful. I considered myself rugged, maybe even a little handsome, but beautiful?

Tricia Corbin was certainly beautiful. Her silk blouse was open at the throat, and I could tell by the way she moved that her shoulders were delicate, the planes of her shoulders smooth, the back of her neck an elegant arc of the softest skin. Her hair had been shaved down close to the skull, but the buzz had hung on to the deep auburn color that complemented her dark brown eyes.

She had beautiful hands, too. Proportional and strong.

"I feel at a disadvantage," I confessed suddenly. "If I was 'in uniform' as you call it, we wouldn't . . ." I hesitated. "You wouldn't—"

"You miss your boots."

I finished my club soda. "Right."

"'Cause you want to kick my ass or something."

I thought about that for a minute. The banter was fun, seductive, challenging. Under other circumstances, I'd be punching her in the arm by now, or robbing her blind at the pool table. But in my little cocktail dress, with my breasts straining at the fabric, my hands positioned politely on the tablecloth, I had given myself some secret permission: To not be rough. To not be aggressive. To allow myself to be seduced. All I could think about was fucking her.

I studied her lips, her mouth. "Or something."

Corbin, for her part, seemed to know how these things went. She'd walked into my speaking engagement and seen the flag of my dress as a signal to play the game. I suspected that who I was had little to do with the way she played. But she liked the dress, that was for sure. I began to wonder if she would be the one who got to ask for the drink, the check, the kiss good night.

Had I given all that away, putting on the stupid dress?

"Do you think I could? Kick your ass?"

Corbin smiled. "Not in that outfit."

"And if I wasn't wearing it?"

"Are you seeing someone?"

I wasn't. "Is this a date?" I asked nervously, suddenly warm.

She eyed me carefully, weighing her words before she spoke. Under the table, her hand found my knee and I immediately felt the rush of dampness in my crotch. As she spoke, she stroked the inside of my thigh, slowly. Her eyes didn't leave mine. "I've never dated a butch before," she began. "All of my women have been high-heeled, dangly earringed, and immensely sexual. You appear to be something of a paradox."

"You think I'm a wolf in sheep's clothing?" I asked. "The dress is throwing you off." I felt her index finger at the hem of my dress, tracing the line where it crossed my leg.

"The dress," Corbin said slowly, "is leading me on."

"That's not the dress," I answered quickly. Again, her fingers, caressed the weave of my stockings, gently, and slipped under the hem of the dress. I signaled our waiter. He scurried tableside.

"Yes, ladies?"

"Check, please," I said suddenly, leaning forward. Corbin's hand fell away. "We should go."

Tricia Corbin began to object, fumbling in her black leather clutch as I daintily dropped a credit card on the waiter's tray. "I said I'd pay," she said.

"You will," I smiled. I nodded toward the door. "I need to get out of this dress."

"Right," said Corbin, getting to her feet. "You definitely do."

To make a long story short, in the elevator on the way down, I convinced Tricia that we should get a room. Maybe it was the way she had pressed me to the back of the car and kissed me, her mouth open, her tongue mingling the taste of whiskey across mine.

The suite was large, with enormous windows. I drew back the curtains to let in the night, and Tricia quickly mixed us both a drink from the minibar. "I can't get over you in that dress," she began, as she handed me a scotch.

I returned her toast. "To dressing well," I smiled. I sipped the strong stuff and set my glass on the desk. I let my hand rest on the placket of her blouse; I stared into her depthless eyes and felt the circle of her pearl buttons under my thumb. I tilted my head toward the bed. "Do you want to . . ."

I didn't need to finish my sentence. "I'm going to undress you," Tricia said. "Turn around."

Hesitantly, I turned and her hands fell to my hips, and slid down to the hem of my dress as she moved in to kiss the back of my neck. She tugged gently at the zipper in the back of my dress and effortlessly the dress came up, over my head, and was dropped into a silky pool at my feet. "Leave the slip on," she whispered, as her thumbs pulled at the waist of my hose. Her hands were so assured as they traveled down my legs. My panties disappeared with the stockings.

I turned around and reached for her. She unbuttoned her blouse as I relieved her of her trousers and stockings and whatever else was underneath; then her mouth was on mine again and she kissed me hard. Her fingertips found my nipples, teasing them into arousal. She maneuvered me toward the bed and ripped the comforter off, even as she eased me down and back. She'd left her blouse on, but her breasts pressed forward through the open silk, and she covered me, stretching her lengthy frame over mine. I could feel the brush of her soft pubic curls, slightly damp, against my own.

"I'm usually on top," I breathed into her ear.

"Not tonight," she answered, as she slid to my side and reached into my cunt, stroking my clit and measuring the depth of my wetness, first with one finger, oh, so slowly, then with two. "Just let me take you."

I inhaled sharply as she entered me again, deep, slow, and I tensed, willing my cunt to swallow her hand. I didn't want her to stop. I found her wrist and squeezed it, rocking my shoulders toward her mouth. She nibbled at my neck, and moved her mouth down across my chest; she bit at the edge of my slip, taking the lacy edge between her teeth, and tugged at it. I wanted my breasts in her mouth and I pushed her away, suddenly. She fell to her back and I climbed atop her and tore my slip off over my head. "I don't know if this is standard femme behavior," I started, pinning her hands over her head. I leaned over her and rested my left nipple at the edge of her lips. "But I don't care."

Her mouth was a hungry animal, drawing the sallow tautness of my breast in, and I released her wrists so she could touch me; straddling her, I knew I was marking her abdomen with a trail of my juice. Her mouth chewed at one nipple, then the other, until my breath started to rasp. Her hands grasped my ass and I knew I couldn't wait much longer. The flush in my face was hot. Sweat began to bleed from my temples, and my heart raced like a timpani. "I want to taste you," I murmured into her hair.

"No, it doesn't work like that," Tricia whispered. Her voice was confident.

I'm not sure how it happened, but she dragged me forward until my cunt was poised over her mouth, and her tongue was inside me, slathering my vulva and reaching for my cervix, until we found a rhythm, and I stayed there, meeting her thrusts with a steady tempo. At the edge of my orgasm, she suddenly held still. Blood pounded in my ears, and my short, deep breaths were accompanied by a delicious tremor that sent all of my muscles into tiny convulsions. "Finish me," I said.

And in a flurry of movements with her mouth and lips and tongue she went after me, eating like there was no tomorrow, until in a rush of hot fluid, I let her fill me and I came hard, and fell away in a tangle of silk and sweat and stuporous contentment.

For a few minutes I didn't move, and Tricia wrapped her strong arms around me and held me, as I waited for my heart rate to return to normal. Her breath behind my ear was warm, and I could feel the pounding of her heart against my back. Slowly, her hand found its way over my shoulder, and she reached under my chin and turned me toward her.

"You okay?" she asked, smiling.

I nodded. "That was so fucking—"

Her fingers on my lips stopped me. "The little red dress," she said.

"If you say so," I answered.

– 20 –

Trash Talkin'

R. Gay

I met Mia in high school. We were just friends then, and I gravitated to her because she had a Southern drawl that sounded like she was pouring honey over every word. She was a daddy's girl in the worst way. Her daddy, Old Man Spencer, called Mia his princess and his little lady and her bedroom looked like one giant confection, all pink and sugary. The best part was a bench for two in front of a huge dressing table with a wide mirror gilded in gold. The top was always covered in hairbrushes and ribbons, bottles of perfume and lotions, and of course, there was her makeup—powders and mascara and eye shadows in every hue a girl (or stylish boy) could imagine. We spent countless hours painting ourselves like Brooke Shields and Christie Brinkley, our narrow shoulders pressed together, legs crossed, right over left. We were determined to be as stunning as our imaginations would allow, though looking back, I can admit that we were somewhat deterred by the limitations of late-1980s couture. I fell in love with Mia because she could shape my eyebrows without making me cry and knew the difference between plum and grape.

I was not a daddy's girl—never even knew mine. What I did know was that I was going to get out of Valdosta, Georgia, and hanging on to the tail end of Mia Spencer's star was the fastest way to do that. She took pity on me, I think—a little Puerto Rican girl who came from the proverbial wrong side of the tracks and spoke without thinking,

Published by The Haworth Press, Inc., 2006. All rights reserved.
doi:10.1300/5328_21

more often than not. My mouth has always gotten me into trouble and it's my mouth that changed things between Mia and I. I was sitting on the edge of my bed, on a Tuesday morning, looking up at Mia who was staring down at me, her eyebrows furrowed, lower lip tucked between her teeth as she held my chin in her hand. I fidgeted and she squeezed my chin harder.

"Sit still, Mami, or I won't get this right," she said.

I batted my eyelashes and stilled. She had taken to calling me Mami since we moved to New York where we heard Spanglish more than anything else. It made her feel more *urban* or so she said. Mia started tracing the outline of my lips with a MAC lip pencil, for we only used MAC products—Spice, for contrast. And I don't know. She was smelling good, and she was wearing a threadbare tank top that I could see right down, and a pair of my boxers. Her dirty blonde curls were piled atop her head save for a few stubborn strands that kept falling into her eyes which, like I said, were staring at me with this intensity. The next thing I know, my hand is wrapped around her wrist and I'm falling back, pulling her with me, and I'm kissing her even though my lips are only half done. I heard the pencil fall to the floor and her breath catch in her throat. I felt my thighs slide apart and press against her sides. And then her left hand was planted against my chest, pushing me away, wiping her lips with her right.

"Jesus, Lettie, why do you always have to go too far?" Mia said. She rolled off the bed and stalked out of the room. I could hear water running in the bathroom and cabinet doors loudly opening and closing.

I stared at the ceiling, rubbing my stomach, and I couldn't help but smile. I was going to turn that girl out. Because I hated girls like Mia and all their friends who befriend girls like me to reassure themselves that they are part of their very own rainbow coalition. I do my part of course, adding a little extra *boricua* to my walk and talk—rolling my r's and popping my neck, giving a little extra shimmy to my shake when I'm strolling the block. I paint the picture that they want to see and keep everything else to myself.

Mia and I met in her daddy's peach orchards, where my mama worked, when we were both fourteen. For whatever reason, mama had to bring me to work with her one afternoon. She told me to stay out of the way so I started wandering through the orchard, eating bruised peaches that had fallen onto the ground.

I was about to take a bite of a fresh peach when I heard a sharp little voice say, "What do you think you're doing?"

I looked up, and there was Mia, hands on her hips, chin jutting forward looking every inch the little princess I would soon learn that she was. "What does it look like I'm doing?" I asked, taking a bigger bite than usual, never looking away. White girls like her did not impress me.

She shrugged, picked up a peach for herself, and we've been friends ever since, going on eleven years now. We came to New York seven years ago to attend Columbia. I majored in business; she majored in art history. Then, because we had nowhere else to go, we stayed, for the shopping, if nothing else. We've done everything together over the years—we even came out together sophomore year, when we grew weary of trying to pretend that the girls we had spending the night in our dorm room were just friends that we shared the same bed with. A lot.

When I think she's calmed down, I go look for Mia, who is lying on the futon mattress in our living room, watching something on television. I sit atop her legs and drag a finger along her bare upper arm. "You mad at me, *querida?*" She loves when I call her *querida* because I told her it was my nickname for her and her alone.

Mia buries her head into the mattress and I know I'm forgiven because I also know that I'm doing exactly what she wants. I've been watching her, the way she leaves the bathroom door open just so while she's stepping in the shower, how she walks around the apartment in next to nothing, how she dresses in the outfits she knows I love, how we're more affectionate than any given circumstance warrants—it's all out of a bad high school romance novel. Neither of us have had a girlfriend in over a year even though the opportunities have been plentiful. I continue to assume we're waiting for each other. I know all about this little dance and so does she. I kiss her cheek, letting my lips linger, then retire to my room to finish getting ready for work.

When Mia calls me in the afternoon, I shake my head when my assistant asks if I'm in. She arches an eyebrow but takes a message anyway. Instead of focusing on a merger of two small bookstore chains I hike my skirt up over my thighs, twirl my chair around, and brace my feet against the glass window. I spread my legs and stroke my clit hard and fast. I think of Mia and the weight of her body falling against mine. When I come, I'm tired. It's hard work loving and hating someone at the same time.

Mia is meeting me after work for shopping and drinks, so I don't bother washing my hands. When I lean in to kiss her cheek, I want to leave the scent of me on her arm. At 5:30 sharp, she's in the lobby of my building, wearing a dark brown suede sleeveless dress and matching shoes. Her makeup, as usual, is flawless—Film Noir lipstick and Bamboom eye paint, just a touch of Blunt blush. I would never have thought those shades might work together, but on her they do and I tell her this as we quickly embrace and strategize about the evening's targets. This morning has been forgotten, or so she makes it seem, holding my hand as we head uptown in the back of a cab, her perfectly manicured fingernails lightly grazing over my knuckles in a steady circle. I so appreciate the attention to detail. Meanwhile, the cab reeks of unwashed people, the seat is torn, and the cabbie is taking the wrong route but I'm ignoring all of it, slowly but surely inching closer to Mia until our heads are practically touching. She turns and again our lips brush together.

Before she can turn away, I trace her lips with my thumb, sliding just the tip between her lips. Mia closes her eyes, and I can feel her teeth gently biting my thumb. "Let's stop driving each other crazy," I whisper.

"Were you in the office when I called earlier?"

I nod and slide my thumb from between her teeth, replacing it with the tip of my tongue. I let my hand slide down her dress, over her breasts, to her knees. They're clamped shut, so I tap my fingernails (Naked Tip nail lacquer) against her knees before snaking my fingers between them. The higher my hand reaches, the more her grip loosens. Mia is kissing me back now, breathing in short little bursts. She tastes like wine and cigarettes. I now know that she lied when she said she quit. There is a smudge of my lipstick (Viva Glam III) on her cheek in not quite a lip print. From the corner of my eye I can see the cabbie staring at us, so I cock my head downward for a moment, watching as his eyes cast toward Mia's now open thighs and her panties pulled aside, my fingers dancing along her pussy lips. By the time we get to where we're going, I only smell her.

The next hour is a flurry of groping between clothing racks and trying on dresses and skirts we won't buy and me putting that extra *boricua* into my strut. I know Mia likes that. Our last stop is at the Boutique Missoni, where the salespeople look positively famished. I am bored by stores like these with their slick floors and slick walls and three outfits for sale but Mia loves them—again with feeling urban, and her trust fund makes it possible. I sit on a plush bench and watch her surveying the inventory. My shoe dangles from my toe and each time I catch her looking at me, I slide my fingers under my nose and her cheeks redden. She must have discovered modesty while I was at work. Eventually, she waves a gauzy striped blouse and matching skirt and motions toward the dressing room. I follow, and once we're inside I shut the door, loudly, and turn Mia around so that she's facing the wall. She drops her selections to the floor. I pull her skirt up, her panties down, and I kick her legs apart with my left foot.

I nibble the back of her ear and slide two fingers along the crack of her ass, then along the dark underside toward her cunt which is hot and wet and quivery as my fingers tease. "Am I going too far?" I ask Mia.

She nods, but pushes her ass toward me. Opening my hand, I slap her ass twice. Mia exhales, and she says, "Mami, I like that."

I'm not surprised. Girls like Mia like it a certain way. Then again, so do girls like me. I slap her ass a third and fourth time, slide my hand over her cheek and back toward her cunt. While she's trying to catch her breath, I slide my fingers inside her where it's tighter than I thought possible. The walls are pulsing, gripping my fingers, and I realize that this is an intimate thing I'm doing. Resting my chin against her shoulder, I slide my other hand around front, beneath her dress and up toward her breasts. With a little effort, I work the bra cup out of my way and begin twisting her right nipple between my thumb and my forefinger to the same beat of two fingers sliding in and out of her pussy. She presses herself closer to me still and I can smell the MV2 perfume she's wearing and her shampoo and the scent of tobacco still clinging to her hair. I sink my teeth into the soft tissue of her neck just left of her chin, flicking my tongue as I bite hard and then harder.

There's a moan rumbling at the base of her throat. Mia's lips are pursed shut. She's afraid to let the sound out, afraid to admit that she wants this. "It's okay to let that out, *querida,*" I say. "You know you like this shit."

I've thought about a moment like this for a long time. It feels as good as I imagined.

The breath she's been holding hisses from between her lips. She reaches back for me with her right arm, her fingernails digging into my side. Her legs are trembling. So is my arm. She slides the fingers of her left hand through my hair, curling her fingers into a tight fist of pale skin and dark tufts of my hair. Her lips, now slightly swollen, their color smeared, crush against mine in a sloppy kiss that is all tongue and teeth. When she does moan, the sound travels down my throat and into the pit of my chest where it stays. It's fitting.

We stay like that, awkwardly entwined. We're both sweating and sticking to each other. My suit, a skirt and jacket number from Donna Karan's collection last year, feels impossibly heavy. My feet are slipping in my heels. I start to fuck her hard, thrusting my fingers into Mia's cunt until her body allows me no further, holding myself there until she starts to whimper, then retreating, until she whimpers. I call her nasty names in a voice a few notches above a whisper—tell her that she's a slut, a whore, *mi puta* who will do any dirty little thing I tell her to. The only word she keeps saying is "Yes." It's the only word I want to hear.

She's close to coming because her pussy is thick wet slick and four of my fingers have made their way into her and she keeps rolling her head from side to side. I stop talking, fucking her now with silent deliberate thrusts that I hope hurt as good as they feel. I slide my right hand back down her stomach to her clit—small, but hard and swollen and sensitive because I've barely touched it before she is moaning, loud enough for me to know that I can do anything I want. I press against her clit until I can feel the sharp bone beneath, stroking slowly—slow enough that I'm driving myself crazy as well.

"Is it my pussy?" I ask her. She says nothing, so I stroke her clit faster, bringing her crazy close to coming, then stop. "Is it my pussy?" I ask again.

"Yes," she says, choking.

"Are you going to give it up again?"

This time she answers much faster. "Yes."

"Good," I say, leaving my fingers inside her as I stroke her clit again in tight fast circles. "Because I'm going to take it when, where, how I want it from now on."

I drag my tongue from her chin up her cheek. I imagine marking her. When Mia comes, I cover her mouth and nose with the hand that was on her clit, feeling her body shudder, feeling her chest constrict, feeling more wetness on my fingers wedged inside her. Slowly, I slide out of her pussy, my fingers instantly cold. She turns around to face me and I slide my fingers deep into her mouth. She swallows them obediently, suckling them clean. I slide my fingers beneath my skirt and into my own wetness then return those fingers to her mouth. She moans loudly, pulls the taste of me into her, and reaches for me with her lips. Her arms are wrapped around me so tightly I can hardly breathe, and there is a desperation, a hunger in the way we kiss. I imagine what Old Man Spencer would think if he saw his little princess now. When I've had my fill of her, I tell Mia it's time to go home. She tries to get herself together but I shake my head. I want her to walk out of here with her dress wrinkled, her shoes in her hand, her hair tousled, makeup a shitty mess. It's a better look than one might think.

We leave the dressing room with the outfit she was going to try on in a crumpled heap on the floor. We walk past the automatons and into the cool Manhattan night air. Mia hails a cab for us, and as we get into the backseat, I can see that she's crying. Mia reaches for my left hand and brings it to her lips for a moment, before holding it in her lap clasped between both of hers. I turn to her and smile, before returning my gaze to the street. I'm still in love with her, but the memory of Mia with the stain of mascara along the arc of her cheekbone will satisfy me for quite some time.

– 21 –

Alicia

Dahlia Schweitzer

"I want to learn how to make you come," she whispered in my ear.

I could feel her breath hot on the back of my neck, her hand snaking its way around my waist, her hips pressed behind me, but the only thing that registered were those words, those words and the space between us. Her breath continued, slow and steady, while I stood there, making my palms and my neck sweat, while she waited for my response. I didn't know what to say. I knew who this girl was, even though I hadn't seen her face all night. I closed my eyes and let my mind refresh my memory. I closed my eyes, held onto the bar with my hands, and let Alicia fill the space behind my eyelids. I couldn't resist smiling while I pictured her, knowing that, when I turned around, it would be her mouth inches from mine.

Her breath continued on my neck as she waited for me, knowing that she had me and, with that fact solidly assured, she had all the time in the world to wait. I gave it another fifteen seconds, indulging myself in the mental picture I'd drawn, and then I turned around to see the real thing.

God, Alicia was the hottest thing I'd ever seen. She stood at least six feet, her black hair cropped short and boyish, her hips hung low, and her arms lean and well-defined. She'd been a track star in college and never lost her runner's figure. Her eyes, which stared straight into mine so unflinchingly that I had to look down, were the kind of blue

Published by The Haworth Press, Inc., 2006. All rights reserved.
doi:10.1300/5328_22

that makes you realize how often you are disappointed in the sky. It was impossible to look at her lips without thinking of eating them.

The thing that got me most of all about Alicia, the thing that made me get wet and quivery even when I saw her from a block away, was her wallet chain. A million punk rockers wear them and look ridiculous, but on her the silver strand that ran from hip to ass was hypnotic and sexy and made me want to fuck her like nothing else. There was something about the way it hung, gently cresting off her waist, swinging ever so slightly as she moved, the little loops glittering in the stray light, that made me want to grab it, to yank it, to pull it out of her pocket, wrenching her to me.

Until tonight, I'd only stared at the chain, fantasizing about it. One lucky night a week or two earlier, she had stood in front of me at the bar, and I delicately ran my finger over it while she ordered her drink. She didn't notice, of course, and I didn't say a word. How could I? It was Alicia, after all.

I figured that would be the closest I'd come to her and her chain and those perfect hips, but then tonight—tonight her breath had been on my neck, her words still lingering in the air between us. I just looked at her while she looked steadily back at me. We held it like that for what felt like an hour—an hour when the bar grew silent and everyone else vanished. My world existed merely to hold her across from me, until she smiled—the grin racing to split her face, lips revealing small white teeth—and then life hit Play again. The music surged back into my ears, and I almost flinched from the shock.

"Hey," she said, tilting her head like John Wayne, "did I scare you?"

"Oh god no," I rushed to respond, my mind frantic to get the words out quickly enough to allay her fears but still slowly enough to make my reassurance appear convincing. "Not at all. I mean—"

"Prove it."

I looked at her, too stunned for an instant to say anything, before figuring what the fuck. I dove right in. I grabbed the chain with my right hand, her waist with my left, and pulled her to me. I don't remember which hit first—her lips or her hips—but before I knew it, both of them were pressed up against me, my tongue tasting hers for the first time.

She tasted like whiskey and cigarettes, like motorcycles with a hint of lip gloss. I held her to me, afraid that the second she pulled back for air she'd realize she was kissing the wrong girl. I kept our lips locked, running my tongue against her teeth, hoping I'd keep her distracted until—until what? I don't know, I guess until I'd either had enough (which would never happen) or until she'd been kissed long enough to fall under my spell.

Not quite believing my luck, I savored her taste while my hands ran over her hips, the hips that I'd stared at from across streets and across rooms—so slim and yet so low. She had the Western stance with the boyish figure that killed me every time, and I couldn't get enough of her. I felt the ridges of her pants, the seams on her pockets, the chill of her chain, the rough fabric of her jeans, and the smooth hint of her underwear along her waist. I felt it all—quickly, rapidly— eager to consume her before she could disappear.

I had no idea why Alicia had decided to kiss me that night, but I wasn't going to ask any questions. I wasn't going to say anything, in fact, because I wouldn't give her the opportunity to reconsider. I wouldn't stop kissing her until she made me. I kept my tongue in her mouth, my hands on her waist, my fingers wrapped around her chain, desperate to absorb it all.

I felt myself falling into a daze, the voices around me disappearing, the world becoming full of only her and the rhythmic bass beats from the DJ's records. My eyes closed, all I saw was black, and all I felt was her. I couldn't think of anything more perfect, until she pulled her head back to look me in the eyes, and then the ground opened up beneath me. I could barely look back.

"Hey."

I smiled at her nervously. "Hey."

"I meant it," she said.

"What's that?"

She stared at me for an instant before leaning over to place her lips against my ear. "I want to make you come." There was a pause while I felt her hot breath on my face, and I wondered if I'd be able to keep standing. "Will you teach me?"

I leaned forward just enough to bring my lips to her ear. "Where should we go?" Alicia pulled her head back and gave me a steady look. "I figured we could get started here," she said, as her hand slid up my skirt, pushing aside my underwear.

I had to grab the stool beside me for support. I couldn't breathe. All I felt were her cool fingers pressing against my wet thighs as she kept staring straight into my eyes. "Do you, I mean, I don't kn—"

"Shh," she said, leaning over, her lips mere inches from my face. "Don't worry—no one's watching."

I looked around, barely able to move my head while every part of my body was focused directly between my legs. In the slow motion of my gaze, it appeared to be true—no one *was* watching. We were in the corner of the room, and my back was to the wall. Alicia was facing me, so whatever she was doing to me was blocked from view by her body. The room was dark, and most of the other girls seemed more concerned with finishing their drinks and finding dates than what we were doing, but still—my brain couldn't quite process what was happening to me.

Just as I started to come to terms with the fact that this gorgeously sexy girl had slipped her fingers up my skirt and into my underwear, my lungs froze, my heart stopped beating, and the world came to a sudden halt when she suddenly shoved her fingers inside my pussy, up through the warm, wet space and against the front wall, sending waves of electric pleasure into my entire body.

I felt the very unglamorous feeling of my eyes rolling back in my head as I slumped against the back of my stool, my hands hanging weakly at my sides, control of my body having been handed over to the six-foot figure who was still staring intently at me. No one had ever made me feel like this before, and I didn't think it was simply because no one's fingers had ever been this long.

I couldn't move; I couldn't do anything but sit there and let her press inside me again and again and again, each time my body reeling with pleasure and pure sensation, each time my pussy filling up with wetness, my clitoris swelling. With every touch, the feeling heightened and I became less able to respond like a functioning adult. I was convinced that everyone in the bar must be staring at me in this ridiculous position. I tried to get Alicia to stop just long enough so that I could collect my senses, so that I could look around and make sure people weren't pointing, so that I could figure out what, exactly, she was trying to get from me. I tried to push her hand away, but she just leaned over, closer, and whispered in my ear:

"I'm not going to stop. I'm not going to stop until you tell me something else to do." I couldn't get the words out. I knew I should have something to say, but I couldn't say it. At first I couldn't because my brain couldn't form the words, and then I couldn't because Alicia had started licking my lips. I didn't know which sensation was more acute—her tongue, gently flicking at the outer edges of my mouth, or her fingers, which were still pressed far inside me. I felt like I had become a vessel for pure sensation, and there was no room left for anything else.

My entire body tried to curve around her fingers. I didn't care anymore that people were talking and smoking and drinking all around us. I couldn't quite forget that they were there, but I couldn't see straight enough to see them. I sort of heard them, but they were drowned out by the buzzing in my ears, my hearing apparently sacrificed as my other senses took over. I smelled Alicia, her scent wafting toward me with every move she made, filling my nostrils and lungs as her fingers filled the cavity between my legs. She smelled like hair products and perfume, beer and cigarettes, leather and sweat. Just like she seemed larger than life, her scent seemed to consume anything else that might have been in the air. I took in huge gulps of it— that is, when I was remembering to breathe.

When I wasn't remembering to breathe, my body was bent around her fingers, pushing her in, deeper and harder, making her fingers slide into the space they were made to fit. Just when I thought I couldn't feel anything more, when the pleasure couldn't possibly get any more intense, Alicia did an extraordinary thing that I can only attribute, again, to the length of her fingers, or perhaps her remarkable dexterity. While keeping two of her fingers pressed solidly against my G-spot, still maintaining pressure and movement, she placed her thumb on my clitoris and began to rub in small, methodical circles. If it hadn't felt so incredible, I might have passed out.

I slumped further back in the stool, my face set in an expression of complete rhapsody. By this point, I was sure I was making a spectacle of myself, but what could I do? There was no way in hell I'd let Alicia stop; all I wanted was more, more, more. I didn't think I'd be able to breathe again until she'd finished coaxing me slowly and skillfully to orgasm. So I lay back, just barely aware of the people and the noise surrounding us, wondering how she managed to fit her fingers so far inside without letting up pressure on my clitoris.

I could feel the pleasure coming in waves, rolling up from between my legs, making my stomach tense up and my lungs contract. Her fingers would press against my G-spot and then slide out, tantalizing me as they grazed the opening, then slipping their way back in to repeat the pressure. In and out, slowly building up speed and momentum, all the while never letting up her methodical rhythmic pressure on my clitoris.

"Do you like it?" she asked, breathing into my ear. I envied her that ability to breathe, that ability to inhale and exhale. I felt like steel girders had replaced my lungs as I clenched the sides of the stool in an effort to utter some kind of response.

"Well?" she asked again, that grin back on her face as her fingers slid back out of my pussy and ran down my thigh, leaving wet trails behind them.

"Oh god, don't stop," I said, before I could think of anything else to say, before I had a second to realize how weak desperation always sounds.

"What's that?" She smiled at me, her fingers now making wet circles on my knee.

"I asked you not to stop." I tried to make my reply sound cool and easy, not as if I was actually making a fool of myself in the middle of a crowded bar, my voice a pathetic plea, my entire self bent backward on the chair to facilitate whatever angle she selected.

"So you liked it then?"

"Yes. Yes, yes, yes."

She leaned over close, putting her lips directly outside my ear. "Anything else you want me to do?"

I didn't answer. Alicia stood back and gave me a long stare before leaning back over to continue, "I really want to see you come." The world swirled around me. I tried to breathe. "Will you tell me how I can do that?"

How she could do that? My entire insides were aching. My entire body was a tightly wound knot of sexual frustration. I was convinced that there must be a puddle between my legs. My underwear was drenched, my clitoris screaming for attention. I felt hyperawake, so desperate for release that she could have touched me and I would have melted on the floor in a mess of sighs and moans.

She stood in front of me, and I felt like looking at her might be pleasure enough—it would have been pleasure enough if I had forgotten how amazing her fingers had felt and how intensely I wanted them back. Just looking at her right hand, as it rested on my knee, made it impossible for me to think of anything but those five fingers and what they could do to me.

"I want you back inside me," I told her. "You're killing me. I want more. I want your fingers back where they were, and I want to feel my fingers inside you." She gave me a huge grin.

"That sounds perfect. Come." She grabbed my hand in hers and pulled me behind her. I grabbed my coat and hurried after her. We went to the back of the bar and turned to go down the stairs.

"What's down there?"

"Don't worry," she replied, over her shoulder, as we made our way into the darkness, "it's the storage room. I've got a key."

I followed her into the dimly lit room, past some empty liquor boxes, behind a couple of shelves of beer bottles, to a red vinyl couch littered with some paper and stray cups. She brushed the debris off and pushed me down on the couch. Standing over me, she reached under my skirt and pulled off my underwear, never letting her eyes leave mine. She glanced briefly at my underwear before tossing them to the side. I saw her smile to herself when she noticed how wet they were. Then, pushing my legs apart, she turned her attention back to me. She ran her hands down my thighs, right hand on left leg, left hand on right leg, running them over the curve of my thigh, circling my knee, going down to the edge of my boots. She lingered there for a second before bringing her fingers slowly back up my leg, stopping on my knees for what felt like an eternity, while I spread my legs as far apart as I possibly could. Oh god, I wanted her fingers inside me— just seeing them on my legs, noticing their delicate length and perfect shape, made my insides ache.

Her ripe red fingernails stood out in the dark room, looking almost black against my white skin. Still looking straight at me, Alicia squeezed my knees and, with a small sigh, kneeled down between my legs. I couldn't believe it. Her body was now officially between my legs, her hands making their slow way up my thighs. I could feel her hot breath on my skin while her face came closer to me.

Her fingers pressed into my thighs, inches away from my clitoris, which was aching to be touched, and my pussy, which was aching to be filled. As if she was completely unaware of how desperately I wanted her to cross those few inches, she grabbed my thighs and stared at me. Her nails dug into my skin, the little red orbs making perfect circles on top of my flesh. I moaned, a combination of frustration and complete desire. Her fingers deep against my thighs, she pulled them back, pulling my pussy lips apart in the process. I inhaled sharply, feeling the cold air rushing inside me, in marked contrast to the hot wetness between my legs.

Grinning at me, she leaned over and flicked my clit with the tip of her tongue. Feeling as though I might drown in red naugahyde, she skirted over the outside of my pussy with her tongue, using just enough pressure to make my skin feel like it was on fire. I arched my hips at her, craving a slip of her tongue, her fingers, *something* inside me, but she just shook her head and pulled back.

With perfect precision, with impeccable slowness and care, Alicia took her first two fingers and slipped them into her mouth. The sight of those fingers disappearing between those red lips nearly killed me. I watched the red nails slide in and out the matching lips—red on red against white. The part of my brain that could still think appreciated the aesthetic perfection of the moment—but most of my brain had rushed between my legs and was an aching mess. I'd stopped wondering why Alicia was doing this and just wanted her to take it all the way.

She pulled two very wet fingers out of her mouth and pressed them flatly against my spread pussy lips, her wet fingers making flat circles around my lips. She started to push in as though she wanted to put her fingers in me the long way, her fingers parallel to my lips, the tips at my clit, the palm cupping my ass while I slipped even further forward on the couch.

"How does it feel?"

I was so dazed and dizzy, I didn't even realize that she was speaking. Her fingers slid out, bringing me to attention by the loss of her inside me. I looked down for a second, but, before I could see anything, she replaced her fingers. Assuming that my silence meant I needed more, this time it was three. She let some spit leak down from her mouth and onto her hand. It was starting to get sloppy—my juices mixing with hers—and I knew I was leaking everywhere. I could hear wet sounds coming from between my legs.

The tightness I felt when she introduced her third finger had changed to a satisfying fullness, and I arched against her, trying to push her deeper inside. I could feel myself relaxing inside to accommodate her, while her pinky finger tapped against the lower part of my pussy, occasionally brushing against my ass. She must have been able to tell what she was doing to me, since each time she licked at my clit, more of my fluid leaked down my crotch. I could feel a small pool of moisture building up under me and I wondered, briefly, if it was possible to stain naugahyde.

Her fingers came out again, and I was freshly distracted by the thrill of feeling her slipping them back in. They felt amazing. I'd never felt anything this far inside me, never felt so full and alive and electric, as though every skin cell on my inner walls had just been awakened. The combination of fingers inside and fingers outside sent a dizzying overload of sensation to my brain. It was almost too much to have it both ways, but, at the same time, all I wanted was more pressure, more rhythm.

As if sensing my overload, and loving the power it gave her over me, she took her left hand and, while keeping her right hand inside me, pushed my tank top up to my shoulders, pulling my bra down, underneath my breasts. Leaning over, she ran her tongue up my stomach, to the center of my chest, and then in looping circles around my nipples. Totally teasing me, she flicked her tongue over their surface momentarily before pulling back to run her mouth back over my neck, chest, and waist.

Gradually, she brought her tongue closer to my nipples, running back and forth over them, her spit sending liquid streaks down my chest. While her tongue licked, her perfect white teeth closed over the tips of my nipples, not biting so much as just pressing down around them. The combination of the pain and the pleasure made me dizzy. I tried to put my arms around her, to pull her close, but between her movements between my legs and her movements across my breasts, my arms were useless.

Just as the sensation became too acute, she slipped her hand out and spread her two fingers into a Y shape before leaning over to lick the exposed part of my pussy. It felt like she had just spread the most exquisite trail of fire, leaving me quivering in her wake. Pleased with my response, she continued to run her tongue from bottom to top over and over again, each time leaving me more of a wreck than the time before, as every part of my body appeared to rush between my legs.

Gradually increasing her pressure, she never let up her perfect rhythm. Each time, she would start at the bottom, just at the base of my opening, and then she would slowly run her tongue over the opening, letting it linger just enough to gently caress the surface inside, before making her way up to my clit, where she would press just a bit harder, make two or three of the tiniest of circles, and then slip her way down to start over. I was just barely aware that my nails were digging into the naugahyde on either side of my legs.

As she coaxed me to totally inexperienced heights of agony and frustration, a victim of her slow and methodical technique, she sent me reeling by slipping her fingers back inside me—never once letting up on the rhythm of her tongue. With that combination, it was over in less than a minute. Between the internal pressure and the external pressure and the smooth softness of her tongue and the persistent pushing of her fingers, the stimulation on the clitoris and inside my pussy, on my G-spot and everywhere, I crumbled.

With a huge moan, the tingle started at my toes and rapidly consumed my body. Something unintelligible came out of my lips as my body fell limply against the couch and Alicia, with one parting lick, slowly drew her fingers out from inside me. I just looked at her in awe. I had no idea who this beautiful creature was, or why she had chosen me, but I wasn't going to ask any questions. I couldn't even talk, for starters, and, in my daze, I was even more transfixed by her beauty than before. She looked at me for a moment and then stood up. Leaning over, she gave me a delicious, lingering kiss, full of my taste and hers and the intensity of what had just happened. I tried to mutter something about how it was her turn, but she shook her head and gave me one more kiss. "I'm more than satisfied," she said. "I've been wanting to do that to you for a long time." With that, she gave me one more kiss and helped me stand up.

"Leave your underwear down here. It'll make it easier for me to touch you later tonight." I just stared at her as I followed her back up the stairs. Watching her hips move in front of me, as the silver chain swung just so, I couldn't believe what had just happened, I couldn't believe that I remembered how that chain had felt in my hand, or that we were going back upstairs to do it all again.

Two Girls in a Basement

Cheryl B.

I think we are all in agreement that two of the greatest things in life are Led Zeppelin and Breasts.

Tim Wells

We were what you would have called mall chicks, typical Jersey girls with painted-on stonewashed jeans, tiny fringed T-shirts stretched tight across our tits, and long hair that invited petting. Our nails were perfectly painted rectangles that extended way past the tips of our fingers, shining like new linoleum.

The summer of 1989, I graduated from high school, and although I didn't plan on it, I was about to figure out I was a lesbian. That summer I moved out of my tiny childhood bedroom and into my parents' basement. I didn't know what I wanted to do with my life, and I couldn't afford to live on my own. But I couldn't stand to hear their fighting anymore. So I bought a soundproof door at the Home Center where I worked as a head cashier and had my ex-boyfriend Guido (yes that was really his name) install it for me. That way I could think, figure things out.

As he worked, I stood below him on the stairs and inspected my acrylic nails, which in my memory of that day were done in a bright purple with alternating white and gold stripes. Occasionally I handed Guido a tool from a big orange box he'd brought with him or gave

Published by The Haworth Press, Inc., 2006. All rights reserved.
doi:10.1300/5328_23

him a rag to wipe up the sweat that had gathered on the hairs that poked out from underneath his tank top mingling in with his gold chains.

When he was finished with the door Guido pulled it closed and we were alone on the stairs leading down to my new "apartment." He did a good job and I told him so with a hug and a peck on the cheek.

Guido pulled me toward him and put his hand on my ass. "How's about a little candy, Lina?" he asked as he squeezed my left butt cheek. Guido was five years older than me and we'd been dating since I was sixteen. My parents wanted me to marry him because he was a plumber and "you always need a plumber."

I looked down and saw the bulge in Guido's pants growing. I could feel his eyes burning hopefully on the top of my head. He wanted a blow job. I can't say I wasn't slightly tempted. Guido, for all his Guido-ness, was a good-looking guy and during our relationship he got a blow job every day, sometimes more. Normally, I would happily get on my knees for him, mouth hungry, eyes wide. Not so much out of lust for Guido—I don't think I was ever even in love with him, but I just liked doing things with my mouth.

But that night was different. That night was Girls Night In, something I'd read about in a magazine, probably *Cosmo,* where as a show of your female independence you're supposed to hang out with your girlfriends, leaving the guys to themselves or something like that. Besides, Guido and I had been broken up for over a month and rumor had it that he was seeing Christie who was a total bitch not to mention a complete slut. He could get her to blow him.

"I don't think Christie would appreciate that too much," I teased him, playfully pushing him away from me. But really I wanted him to leave. I had to get ready for my guests. Actually it was only one guest, Tammy. Most of the girls I invited already had plans with their boyfriends; one actually said her boyfriend wouldn't let her come. So much for female independence.

"Where'd you hear about Christie?"

"Oh, you know, around," I said, looking at my watch.

"You got something better to do tonight?"

"Yeah, you know I told you I was going to have the girls over."

"Oh, yeah, the women's lib thing."

"No. It's just like a sleepover."

"That's kind of hot, all you girls snuggled in together," Guido said dreamily.

"You sicko," I said. Why wouldn't he just leave? "Oh you, get out of here," I said, playfully punching him. I opened the door which led into the kitchen. My parents were fighting. Dad sat at the table in a dirty T-shirt, his tiny boom box in his hands, trying to find his favorite country music station. Mom was over by the sink, angrily scrubbing a pot. "Are you staying for dinner, Guido?" This could pose a problem. Guido really liked my mother's cooking. Maybe they should get together.

Tammy would be over in less than an hour and I needed to get ready. Before Guido could answer I said, "Oh no, he's on his way out. He's a very busy guy," and led him to the front door.

I turned my cheek as he leaned in to kiss me on his way out.

He looked at me, pointing his finger, "Don't be turning into some dyke on me." And then he added in all seriousness, "Don't drop the soap."

"Have a good night, Guido," my mother called from the kitchen as I closed the door on him.

Tammy was a new friend I met a few months ago in aerobics class. Turns out we both pretended to have cramps one day and wound up together in the locker room of Living Well Lady sneaking cigarettes by the window.

I noticed a gold bracelet she wore around her slender wrist: a cut-out heart covered in tiny diamonds on a thin rope chain. It sparkled in the light coming in from the window and reflected off the tiles in the bathroom.

"I like your bracelet," I said.

"Thanks," she answered, taking another drag off her cigarette.

"Can I see?" I held out my hand and she lifted her wrist. I fingered the diamonds, touching the soft skin on either side of the bracelet. "Nice," I said and for some reason I didn't let go of her hand right away. Suddenly I was confused; I wasn't sure if I was appraising the bracelet or the skin on the underside of her arm.

"Got it from the boyfriend," she said taking her wrist back and in-specting the bracelet herself, "for Valentine's day."

"Cool," I said, taking a final drag off my cigarette before stubbing it out on the windowsill. As I did this, I snuck a look at her and noticed for the first time that her silver leotard had a cut-out midsection. Her stomach was a combination of firm and curvy. I wanted to touch the skin in the center; it had a beautiful, bronze sheen, the perfect tan. I was filled with a strange combination of jealousy and attraction and I totally lost myself in the gaze. I continued to watch her. Her lips when closed were a glossy, pink bow. When she opened her mouth to take another drag off her cigarettes her teeth were like perfect white chicklets, her tongue wet and red . . .

"So you got a boyfriend?" she asked. I quickly stopped checking out her tongue and shook my head.

"No. I mean yes, his name is Guido," I said, embarrassed although I didn't know why.

She smiled. "Yeah, I know what you mean. Sometimes I think it would be good to be single again too."

I smiled shyly at her and we became friends. Over the next few weeks we shopped together, modeling clothes for each other in the dressing room of Macy's. Tried on high heels together at the mall and helped each other into lingerie at Victoria's Secret. At one point while I was buttoning her into a black lace bustier, her blonde hair brushed against my hands and I had the urge to slip my hands around her waist, push her against the wall, and rub myself all over her. Instead, I dropped my hands to my sides. But I swear there was this bizarre sex-ual energy flowing between us. I think she felt it too, because we could hardly look at each other the rest of the day.

Now she was due to come over in like twenty minutes! And my basement room was a mess! And I barely had my makeup done! And I hated all my clothes! Tammy usually wore short skirts. So I decided to wear tight jeans as a contrast. I put on my push-up bra and pulled a cut-off Bon Jovi T-shirt out of my drawer. I splashed a little perfume on my wrist, smudged some blue eyeliner on my lids, and gave my long, dark hair a once over with a generous spray of Aqua Net. I turned off the overhead lights and turned on a few old table lamps. I took my

favorite tape out and placed it by the stereo. I poured some Doritos
into a bowl. Put out a few Diet Cokes and took a long sip from a bottle
of Jack Daniels, then threw it under one of the cushions on the couch.
I wasn't much of a drinker, but I thought I could use a little booster. I
slipped my feet into a pair of heels I'd bought with Tammy one day.
They were her favorites, pointy toed with a four-inch spiked heel in a
midnight blue that matched the blue in my T-shirt. Tammy said they
made me look like a porn star. And sitting there waiting for her on my
parent's old couch, I felt like the sexiest woman on earth.

At this point, I have to make a confession; the Girls Night In thing
was just a front. I put the invitations out there knowing the other girls
would decline. I just wanted Tammy to myself.

I heard the doorbell ring upstairs. She was right on time. I'd already
instructed my mother to let her in. And I could hear Tammy's heels
on the floor above following my mother down the hall to my basement door. I was so nervous, I was shaking. I stood at the bottom of
the steps and could see the doorknob turning, my mother's voice bur-
rowing its way through insulated steel repeating the "Berlin Wall"
line. As the door opened the light from the kitchen shone in, and I
could hear the Judds droning from my father's radio in the background.

Tammy stood at the top of the stairs in a pink skirt so short I could
see her baby blue panties. Her hair was big and blonde and wild. She
made her way down the stairs in her fuschia spiked heels. My mother
stayed on in the doorway as I regarded Tammy coming toward me.

"I've never heard of this, two beautiful girls hanging out in a smelly
basement when you could be out on dates," my mother said. "I don't
know where you kids came from."

Tammy reached the bottom of the stairs.

"You look great," I said.

"So do you, Lina," she said and I could tell by the way she looked at
me that we were there for the same reason.

"I swear if I had your figures I'd be out playing the field. I wouldn't
be sitting in some basement full of my parents' old furniture," my
mother continued from the top of the steps.

"Thanks, Ma," I said as I made my way up the stairs to lock the door.

"Remember, you're only young once . . ." she continued as I closed the door and locked it.

By the time I got down the stairs, Tammy was already sitting on the couch, one long leg tucked under her while the other stretched out across the couch. She was taking a sip from the Diet Coke and fingering the dingy material on the couch.

"Sorry about the furniture; it's kind of crappy," I apologized.

"I think it's so cool you did this. It's like you have your own little place. I'm still sleeping in my little room in my parents' house. There are still unicorns stenciled on the walls!"

I crossed the room and stood in front of her sprawled leg on the couch. I expected her to move the leg for me to sit down, but when she didn't I sort of slid in underneath it, placing her fuschia heel on my lap. Suddenly I felt like a guy or like I was the guy or was playing the guy's role or something. I needed a drink. I reached under the couch cushion where I'd stashed the Jack Daniels and pulled out the bottle, taking a long sip. I offered the bottle to Tammy even though she doesn't really drink much either. She took a bigger sip than me.

I tried to make small talk. "So have you seen the new clothes at The Limited?"

I realized I'd begun running my hand up her leg. Her skin was unbelievably smooth and I wondered what she used, whether she shaved or waxed or . . .

Tammy reached forward, pushing me back on the couch. She straddled me, grinding her hips into me, and kissed me in a way that I could only describe as "with abandon," as if she wanted to swallow me whole. It really knocked my socks off. But I was not to be outdone. I pushed her off me and got her flat on the couch, I reached my hand up her shirt, felt the lace of her bra, and I swear I soaked my panties right there on the spot. I could feel the wetness in the confines of my tight jeans.

"Ohhhh," I moaned. I reached down and kissed Tammy, mashing my mouth into hers. I worked my hands around her back to unsnap her bra and to my amazement did it on my first try! Tammy quickly pulled off her tiny shirt which I noticed was airbrushed JERSEY GIRLS BEST IN THE WORLD! We both looked at the shirt and began giggling.

"I guess I picked the right shirt," Tammy laughed.

She picked the right shirt and the right skirt and the right panties, which to my surprise I quickly pulled off and felt between her legs. Tammy pulled her skirt up further, at this point it was practically a belt, and spread her legs for me. I don't know if there is such a thing as a moment in which you "turn gay," but if there is it was that moment looking down at Tammy. It sounds cheesy, like something from a bad porn film, but the thought of my hands, with their long, purple nails, grazing her neatly shaved pussy is something that to this day still turns me on. I can still feel her heat and the wetness and the uncontrollable excitement let loose in my body. I was a baby femme-top and I didn't even know it.

We kissed and rubbed some more, got my pants off, sucked each other's nipples; she fingered me, her hot pink nails making a circle around my clit. Somehow I wound up kneeling in front of her on the floor. And I buried my face in her, at first poking around with my tongue trying to figure out what to do. She ran her hands through my hair and she moaned, spreading her legs farther apart, moving her pussy closer and closer to me. And I just went for it, licking her in tiny circles, then long laps, then little flickerings on her clit until I felt her stiffen, then shake and moan. And I swear as she came I felt the earth move, the room spin. She pushed my head away from her.

"Please stop. I'm gonna fall apart." She laughed, falling back on the couch and closing her legs.

I sat down next to her and we both began giggling.

"It's a good thing I got the soundproof door," I said.

"I'm sorry, was I loud? My boyfriend says I'm loud."

I could feel myself frowning. "Let's not talk about him now."

We sat there, my head on her shoulder and amazingly, I began to drift off.

"Hold on there," Tammy said, touching my face. "It's your turn."

"Oh really," I said.

"Oh, yeah," she said getting down on her knees.

"Wait," I said, "I forgot the music."

I got up and crossed the room to the stereo, and in true Jersey Girl form picked up my Led Zeppelin 4 tape, popped it in the player, and pressed repeat.

– 23 –

Cup Cake

Tanya Turner

Ever since I was little, I've always wanted to be a baker. I remember getting ready for my fifth birthday party, helping my mother make the cake. I stirred and mixed and spilled flour all over the floor, and got to lick the sugary batter off the spoon. She let me help her frost my pretty birthday cake, holding the soft, mushy tube filled with the sweetest of pastes, keeping my wobbly letters that I was so proud of, and by the time we were done, it looked like a child's painting, though perhaps a gifted child's (I hope), with pretty roses made of pink, white, and red icing. And it tasted divine, though I can't take much credit for that. So it's no surprise that the minute I graduated high school, I moved to New York City, home of everything cool and delicious, and instead of going to college right away, got an assistant job at a bakery. And not just any bakery, but Rainbow Bakery, so named because it lies smack in the heart of Chelsea, the gayest of the gay neighborhoods. And it also features cupcakes in a rainbow of pretty pastel colors. We like to display them in rainbow motifs, or other holiday-themed decorations. Our special food coloring can match our frosting to your bridesmaid's dress, and we're known for our creative and outlandish designs.

I also love my job because they let me close up, and turn a blind eye when I stay late and use the kitchen as my own experimental funhouse—concocting new treats, testing out recipes, generally mak-

Published by The Haworth Press, Inc., 2006. All rights reserved.
doi:10.1300/5328_24

ing a sweet, sticky mess of the place—as long as I clean it up and don't
do any damage to the ovens. I bring in my own ingredients and feel
right at home, a mad scientist crafting the perfect concoction, making
the most delicious morsels ever to touch the tongue. I was looking for
something, something that would let me know that this was my true
path, something that the moment it touched my tongue I'd be in
heaven. I wanted to taste something unlike anything I had tasted before, quite a task considering that I've spent most of my life consum-
ing desserts as meals, sampling every cake, cookie, and pastry I could
get my hands on, but I enjoyed it. It never felt like work to me, but
simply a step on the road to sweet discovery. Occasionally, I'd get a
little lonely, would long to be part of one of those couples delicately
feeding each other beautifully decorated cupcakes, licking the pink
and purple frosting off each other's fingers, dessert as foreplay, but I'd
let those feelings go as soon as they welled up, wanting to stay focused
and determined. There'd be plenty of time for love once I created the
perfect cupcake, so I set to work, happy to be in the warm, sweet haven of my kitchen.

I was working late on my own special recipe, trying to create the
perfect cupcake for my upcoming birthday party. Instead of gallons of
alcohol, for my twenty-first I wanted sugary delights, baked goods
galore, all made by me. I wanted to prove to my friends and myself
that I'd done what I'd set out to do when I moved to New York—be
the best baker I could be. My family thought I was a fuck up, the ultimate failure for passing up a college education to do what I could have
done from the safety (and frugality) of my mom's kitchen. But they
didn't understand. New York was a cupcake buyer's dream, where
the best ones fetched as much as four dollars, where they were treated
as a delicacy, not simply a child's treat. I wanted to make my mark on
the world, at least my little world, and needed time and patience and
inspiration to concoct the perfect cupcake. I was wearing a summery
yellow dress, matching today's pastel shades of frosting, looking for
all the world like some kind of homemaker, save for the turquoise and
magenta streaks in my otherwise bleached-blonde hair. And the nose
ring. And maybe the chipped fingernails and ratty fishnets. Well, my
version of a housewife, the kind I might be someday to my rock-n-roll

playing punk-rock dessert-loving wife, whipping her up a batch of cookies before band practice, prancing around in an apron, feeding her every chance I got. The kitchen was my home, my domain, and this kitchen, so grand and glorious, made me feel like a queen.

I was just getting all my ingredients ready and swirling colors, trying to find the perfect shade that said *me,* when there was a knock at the door. I looked up, expecting a co-worker who'd forgotten something, but instead found a slightly older woman, looking like a modern-day Donna Reed in a pink raincoat and a bright yellow sundress. I recognized her from a few recent visits, during which she'd sampled nearly every concoction we offered and left bearing huge bags weighted down with cakes, puddings, and other tasty treats. I had wondered at the time how she stayed so slim, for even though she had to have twenty years on me, she radiated youth and vitality. I was curious about her visit, since the closed sign on the door tended to ward off any curious passersby, and I cautiously walked toward the door, opening it a crack.

"Hello? We're actually closed right now. Can I help you?"

"Hi. I've had a little baking emergency and was wondering if I could use your kitchen for an hour or two; I'm in the middle of a recipe and simply must test this out. I'm a frequent customer here; you can ask Sharon, the owner, and she'll tell you that I'm here at least once a week buying treats for my kid's soccer team. I was just hoping that I might prevail upon you, and I'll even share my creation with you, but it's really quite vital that I use your kitchen." Even though her words sounded like she was asking for a favor, her body language said that she wasn't going to take no for an answer. And with her pink raincoat and steely gaze, I somehow wanted to let her in, this tough-as-nails mom with a sweet tooth. Maybe I'd learn a thing or two from her, and besides, I had all night.

It turned out the Mystery Woman knew her way around a kitchen, which I found out quite quickly as I watched her deftly start sorting and counting and planning, her fingers moving nimbly around, as if she'd baked in this very room all her life. She didn't so much take over as take charge, pushing forward like I wasn't even in the picture, except that every few minutes she paused to give me a small smile or a saucy wink, and I was so amazed at her chutzpah that I just shut up and let her dominate my workspace, sure that she would concoct something sweet and delicious. As I watched her work, I realized that what I truly wanted a bite out of was her ripe, fleshy ass; the way she moved about in her sundress, so sure of herself, efficient without being brisk, made me want to suckle at her tits and rub myself against her. It didn't matter that I didn't know her, that she was almost old enough to be my own mother, that she'd just invaded my "office" and could get me in major trouble with the management, that I was sublimating my own baking dreams to let her work her magic with the ovens. No, none of that mattered as the sweet smell of her cupcakes filled the air, the already-sugar-perfumed room filling with the scent of arousal, of desire, of secrets and magic.

When she offered an outstretched finger to me, painted in a gorgeous lilac frosting, I opened my mouth, savoring the sweetness that seemed to explode right on my tongue, pure sugar. My whole body, not just my taste buds, was alive, supercharged with the goodness of glucose and arousal, and I sucked her finger further into my mouth while keeping my eyes locked on hers. She didn't look away, but instead teased me with her fingertip, sliding it along my tongue, pressing it into my bottom front teeth, urging me to clamp down on it, a hint of things to come. I took a step closer to her, her finger still between my teeth, the tension in the air now inescapable. I let her pull her finger out and she reached behind her, eyes still on me, and came up with another fingerful of frosting, but this time she took her left hand, the clean one, and ripped my blouse right open, buttons falling, and smeared the sweet confection all over my chest, covering part of one tattoo, getting my best lace bra dirty, but I didn't care. She looked different now, not quite the simple, motherly type, but something more, something raw and animalistic, younger.

I didn't know anything about her beyond that moment, and probably never would, but I knew it took a lot more than Donna Reed to barge into someone's workplace, take over, and then seduce them with sugar. She had my full attention, my body on high alert, as she slipped a finger inside my bra, massaging my beaded nipple with the cool frosting, then peeling down the cup and sucking up every last drop of it. She lavished my nipples with so much attention I thought I would pass out. Instead of going directly to biting them, she lavished them with her mouth, making them so wet they were almost soft. Her tongue darted back and forth, flicking, teasing, long after the last drop of frosting had been licked clean.

"And now, my dear, it's time to show you how to bake." Before I could sputter out a protest about the arrogance of such a statement, the wrongness of it, she pressed her sticky fingers into my mouth, effectively shutting me up. "Just watch and learn," she said, and before I knew it, she was molding the batter I'd been creating when she arrived into the cupcake dishes, quick as a flash but very careful, fastidious as she whipped them into shape. Not the smooth, flat surfaces I was used to, perfect placeholders for the frosting that was our pièce de résistance, but instead rounded on top, with a little point. Oh my goodness! That was a nipple, and her cupcakes were breasts. It was amazing, and I burst out laughing, but she kept right on working them into shape, then slid them into the oven, without a care in the world.

"Now try the real thing," she cooed at me, and swirled some of the sweet, pretty icing around both of her nipples, but I didn't even need that enticement. This maternal enchantress had already worked her way into my brain, arousing all of my senses, and I sucked her nipples greedily, unsure whether this would be my only chance. I toyed with them, licking along each one, and almost unthinkingly brought my hand up between her legs. She didn't object as I toyed with her panties, scrambling to get inside them as I kept sucking her nipples long after the last traces of sugar had vanished. Her nipples had gotten warm, matching the soft, wet pussy I found waiting for me. I opened my eyes, looking up at her for a moment, and the change was startling. She'd lost ten years, at least, maybe more, her face free and relaxed, no longer supermom but super, sensual woman, letting me in deeper and deeper as I pushed against her slick passage. The air was getting hotter as the cakes baked and I shoved my fingers into her, desperate to please her. In what seemed like only a few moments of the most frantic, urgent fucking I could imagine, she came, collapsing onto the floor as I held her close to me, both of us worn out from the effort.

But she was the first to recover, sitting up, smoothing her hair, then standing and daintily taking the tray out of the oven, frosting them with the air of a true professional. They looked marvelous—round, soft tits, painted a rainbow of colors, truly good enough to eat, edible erotic artwork worthy of the kinkiest frosted display cases.

"Those aren't for your son, are they?"

"No," she smirked at me, not looking ashamed in the least. "They're for my girlfriend. Thanks for the kitchen. You should see mine sometime." She sashayed out of there, with her breasts and her breast cakes, leaving the air filled with the scent of sugar and sex. I leaned against the wall, panting, amazed. If this is what being a baker is all about, I'm in it for the long haul.

– 24 –

Sugar

Diana Cage

Well past midnight a faint clanging registers above the din of the vacuum cleaner. After the third ring I recognize the faraway bell sound as *phone*. In a rush to beat the voice mail I bloody my shin on an errant CD rack.

Sugar's shaky voice comes through the receiver. She is crying and I can't make out most of her words through an unmanageable slur. She's had too much wine and one of the mild tranquilizers that her doctor gives her. She suffers from anxiety. She can't sleep. She worries too much about things like aging and rape and racial tension. She cries about turning thirty. I suspect she really loves me.

When her outburst subsides I hobble to the kitchen and staunch the flow of blood from my shin with a dish towel. Sugar whispers to the receiver, "I need to see you, Gwen. I'm lonely." I reassure her, tell her how much I love her, that I want to see her, too. She falls asleep while I am softly whispering to her about what a good girl she is and how much I want to fuck her, push my fingers into her cunt, and make her cry.

Sugar loves to lie in bed all day watching old movies. She could stare at the young Ava Gardner for hours. "Look at her eyes; look at the way she wears her eyeliner," she always says. It took me forever to stop trying to imitate the film actresses she adored. During the first year of our relationship I was a platinum Dorothy Malone, a wounded

Published by The Haworth Press, Inc., 2006. All rights reserved.
doi:10.1300/5328_25

Barbara Bel Geddes, a cool, detached Catherine Deneuve. After we watched *Faster, Pussycat! Kill! Kill!*, I dressed like Tura Satana. I ground the gears of the Toyota and sped through the streets of San Francisco, looking for necks to break.

I met her on a weekend trip to Los Angeles. I spotted her shoe shopping on Melrose. We shared a mirror at Retail Slut, each of us posing seductively for the other. The straps of my 1980s Prince-inspired lingerie slip kept slipping down and exposing my nipples. We agreed that her blonde hair and blue eyes contrasted romantically with my jet black hair and ruby lipstick. I showed her the barbed-wire tattoo across my sacrum; she showed me the ankh on her breast.

We reached a pinnacle of vanity and lust when the salesgirl told us we looked like the vampires from *Daughters of Darkness*. Sugar pulled me into the dressing room and pinned me to the wall. Her height gave her an advantage, but I grabbed a handful of her bleached hair and pulled her head back till she whimpered aloud. The sound made my cunt throb. She pushed up my dress and pulled my G-string to the side. "Please," I said as she slipped three fingers into my soaked pussy. She kissed me softly on the neck and I urged her on with little hip thrusts. She whispered, "Can you come like this?" I answered her by tightening up and digging my short, painted nails into her shoulder. Then I came hard, letting out a high-pitched wail and slumping forward against her chest. The salesgirl knocked on the dressing room door and said, "I'm going to have to ask you two to leave." Sugar smiled wickedly and took my hand. "My turn," she said as she pulled me out of the store.

Her apartment is just off Sunset, behind the Whisky. She has no furniture, just a closet full of clothes, a huge bed, and a full-length mirror propped against the wall. Her bathroom counter overflows with tubes of liquid eyeliner, body glitter, and sparkly nail polish. There are bottles of expensive booze lined up like bowling pins in the kitchen. In the empty living room there's an oil painting: A blonde woman with heavy sixties-style pastel makeup, like a young Elke Sommer, reclining naked on a fur rug, her body a collection of exaggerated curves. One breast juts toward the ceiling, a prominent pink nipple perched atop it.

"I want to fuck you with a dick," I said to her as we collapsed on her bed.

"There's a cock and a strap-on in that box." She pointed to a black leather harness and a bright red dick. I pulled it on as gracefully as I could and coolly pressed the head of the cock against her upturned ass.

"Lube," I asked.

"Under the bed," she whispered.

I felt around and found a small bottle. I drowned the bright rubber cock in it before slowly pushing it against her perfect asshole. When I grabbed her hips she said, "Oh god, fuck me. Oh my god." We fucked languidly, content to gaze at ourselves in the mirror across from her bed. She ejaculated when she came, gushing all over the sheets and soaking both of us. We fell asleep among the wet sheets and woke up hours later, disoriented and still turned-on.

We were crazy for each other from that moment. We saw each other every weekend despite the 400 miles between our respective cities. Sugar hates to fly, so I'd fly down to Los Angeles and she'd drive back up with me. She once drove all the way from Los Angeles to San Francisco with one hand on the steering wheel and one hand in my crotch. In the visor mirror I could see her fingers sliding through the vertical folds, disappearing and reappearing, making a slick *tic tic* sound. With one leg out the window of a rented Lexus I came to an extravagant climax. Semis drove by and honked in congratulations.

I hang up the phone and give up rearranging the furniture. The pieces are still in disarray—as if they were interrupted while dancing. In bed I lie awake, fingers on my throbbing clit, imagining the sound of her voice and picturing her beautiful face when she comes.

A few days later in a fit of desperation, she flies up to see me. When I answer the door there is a tall, slender woman in ridiculous shoes posed next to three huge suitcases. "I'm sorry, I'm groggy. I took too many Dramamine." She begins dragging in the first bag. "I was crying on the flight. I couldn't stop. When the stewardess came around I said, I'll have four bottles of vodka. She didn't protest at all. Just set them down on the tray in front of me." Sugar cries all the time. I guess it's part of her charm.

Sometimes she cries after she comes. In the beginning she would beg for me to fuck her hard, harder. And I'd do it. Each time I came when she did, without her so much as touching me. She liked a hand across her throat as she got closer. Not choking her, just resting on her fragile neck like a threat. I never squeezed, but I often wanted to. Once she gets her suitcases inside, she pulls her movie star sunglasses to the end of her nose, a nose shaped entirely different from the one nature intended. Her big L.A. swimming pool eyes are puffy and red.

She leans forward and throws her arms around me theatrically. I know she'll stay for too long. She does it every time. She tells me she'll be here a week, and a month later I'll be begging her to book a flight home. For the next six weeks, I'll be late to work every day. I'll eat out every night. My bank account will be depleted. I'll buy bikinis at Versace that I will never wear. And I will have tons of raucous, emotional, and thrilling sex.

After a few moments she does a perfunctory check of my appearance. I'm in a T-shirt and jeans.

"My gawd, what's happened to you? You look so *normal.*" When she says normal it sounds like someone else saying *slug* or *sewage.* She stoops to wrestle a pair of high-heeled sandals from her feet. "New?" I ask.

Sugar doesn't work. She shops, spends weekends in spas, goes to yoga religiously. She doesn't understand that I have responsibilities. "I think the reason that you and I get along is we both understand the necessity of multiple pairs of black shoes." She's always dropping bits of wisdom like this.

She sighs and says, "I really have to rest, Gwen. The flight left me exhausted."

Though the flight from Los Angeles to San Francisco takes only fifty minutes, I grab her suitcases and say, "Take a shower; you'll feel better."

Half an hour later she is naked, leaning over the sink shaving her pussy. One leg is propped on the basin. Her razor is a heavy silver men's model. Her strokes are light and she runs a hand over the unshaved area to guide the blade. When she turns around to show off a job well done, I kneel down to closely inspect her handiwork. I trace my tongue along the lips of her cunt, teasing her until she's wet. Her clit is large, larger than any others I've seen. I lick it lightly and force her to ask me for more. She grinds against my face in response and wants me to make her come immediately, but instead I tease her, knowing she'll beg for it. Instead, she pushes me backward with her foot and pins me to the tile. I feel her teeth against my shoulder, and a moment later she bites me so hard it breaks the skin.

"Love me, Gwen. I want you to love me," she says. I feel two of her long fingers slip into my cunt, wet already. It's been wet since she walked through my door in her stilettos. She presses hard against a spot at the top of my pussy that almost hurts, but I don't want her to stop. She fucks me roughly, the same way she likes me to fuck her. The tile is cold but I'm getting so close and if I can only get a little bit more I would come. She feels me open up and slides in two more fingers, pushing in and out, but still, I can sense the rest of her hand and I want it inside me. "More, God damn it," I tell her and she tucks her thumb into her palm and pushes into me. I scream at the top of my lungs as the widest part of her hand enters the tight ring of muscle at the opening of my cunt. Once inside, she remains perfectly still, simply filling me. I realize that my mouth is open and I'm reaching for something, but I don't know what it is, because all I can see and feel is the woman above me, staring at the place where her hand disappears into my body.

Sugar talks me down, cooing warm words into my tingling ears. "You are so pretty, Gwen. Your voice, your hair. I love you, baby. You are everything." When she says these words to me, I melt inside. "We have what it takes, Gwen. We can make each other happy." And I believe her at that moment. Because she is earnest. She means it. I don't reply. I can't. I'm breathless and spacy, I've fallen into the hole that Sugar often sends me. She overwhelms me. Instead of speaking, we curl up on the cold tile floor and she holds me with an urgency that makes my clit jump.

Later we will eat, shop, sleep. I will roll my eyes at her extravagance and bicker with her over small things. I will want her to leave, to give me back my space and my normal life. But not now. Now I just revel in her naked body and her need.

– 25 –

Power Sharing

Tania Britton

I was so bored. This had to be the lamest play party ever: a bondage/fetish party after *Dyke March?* What were the organizers thinking? The owners of the dungeon did not look happy either, as they checked in the stream of giggling, middle-of-the-road, baseball-capped, bridge-and-tunnel lesbians. These were definitely not future clients. My floor-length latex dress was clammy against my skin: The windows had been left open to keep us cool during all of the hot action. Heh. I didn't predict much of that tonight. We were all gonna freeze.

I made my way to the snack table and absentmindedly popped a few cherry tomatoes while deciding if I should leave. Tessa and Jasper were on their way to get a rope bondage lesson, but I could always call and have them come to my house instead. And some girl from a magazine was supposed to come take pictures. . . . But of what?

"Whoo-hoo!"

I looked over to see a chubby pint-sized baby butch playing rodeo king on the same vaulting horse where I had received my first caning. She was bucking and jolting, waving her cowboy hat high, and sending her look-alike audience into a relative explosion of snickers and eye rolls. Ha ha. Isn't S/M funny.

"What the hell do you do with that thing?" one of them asked.

"I dunno . . . Ride it!" the cowboy replied with a cheeky grin.

Published by The Haworth Press, Inc., 2006. All rights reserved.
doi:10.1300/5328_26

I was suddenly titillated by the idea of giving these cute little bois a lesson in the proper use of dungeon furniture. I felt the blush creep into my cheeks and a tingle spread across my labia. I imagined myself grabbing the cowboy's hair and pushing her facedown into the horse's leather, as I calmly lectured her friends on the importance of the element of surprise in domming. I would pull a flog from my garter belt and give her the proper punishment for disrupting the dungeon's somber tone.

"Naw, man. People whip each other and stuff in these places. I can't believe we paid ten bucks for this shit. I don't wanna get whipped; I wanna get *laid*."

This little butch looked and sounded just like a frat boy. I suddenly felt like I was back in my scary rural high school. What the hell were these kids doing here?

I was jolted out of my judgmental musings by the feeling of someone's eyes locked on me. My eyes followed my sixth sense over to the door, where a pair of buff straight-looking jock dykes shot me evil stares as they whispered in each other's ears. I watched the taller of the two "inconspicuously" point at my $280 thigh-high black vinyl stiletto boots and laugh into her hand. When she caught me looking, she flipped her goddamn ponytail and coolly stared at the wall. Her friend was a bit slower, though. I locked eyes with her mid-guffaw. Sorry little ex-cheerleader bitch. I'd show her a thing or two about S/M. I was ready to grind my boot heel into her cheek.

My rage must have shot through my stare, because she immediately dropped the smile, her skin went pallid, and she pushed her friend back out the door, into the waiting elevator.

Good, I thought, *I got rid of two of them. Now if only the rest of these fakers would leave, so we could have some fun.*

But then I felt more eyes on me. I heard more snickers. I came to.

I realized that there was no "we," only *I* didn't belong. I looked down at my petroleum-based fetish ensemble and realized how freakish I must have looked to all of these girls, who were furloughed from New Jersey or Long Island or Connecticut but once a year. I was part of a museum exhibit to them, a glimpse into an alien world. I felt drained, powerless.

I slumped away to the back cell to retrieve my bag of supplies, said my necessary good-byes, and got on the elevator. Someone else would have to serve as tonight's freak show.

On the elevator trip down I questioned whether I should have stayed, as research for my thesis. I thought of the conversation we'd had yesterday in my Gender and Power seminar. My professor had argued that the male gaze had been so incorporated into the female psyche that we are actually the objects of our own gaze. I was suddenly questioning whether the cute little Southern girl in the class, Amelia (my one straight-girl crush), had been right when she rebutted, "Men just crashed our party. The female gaze has *always* been centered on other females." She had argued, with much documentation behind her, that the male gaze was rendered benign and largely irrelevant when compared to the jealous, judgmental, controlling female gaze, which she hypothesized caused anorexia, among other things. "The gaze that destroys is that of envy, which robs you of your right to even enjoy a sexualized gaze, male or otherwise," she had asserted in her sharp, sexy twang. Male or otherwise. I'd forgotten about that. Hmm.

I wondered what Amelia would think about this kind of jealous cattiness in a lesbian setting, where the male gaze really was irrelevant. And what of the masculine butch gaze, which "othered" the femme, thrusting us into the heterosexual paradigm against our will? I imagined us entangled in lustful make-out sessions behind closed doors, where no gaze could objectify or belittle us. Our orgasmic bliss would even shut up the judgmental voices of our foremothers in our heads. You know, I really hadn't read enough Foucault to handle this topic alone. I would have to ask Amelia out to coffee.

The gods have a wicked sense of humor. When I opened the elevator door, Amelia was standing right in front of me.

I immediately objectified her. How could I resist? She was wearing a Catholic schoolgirl outfit. A tight white blouse perfectly enveloped her pert, alabaster breasts; the navy, green, and red plaid skirt was tailored well above her knee, exposing milky white thighs and hinting at the lushness hidden beneath; white kneesocks and Mary Janes added a professional finish to the jailbait look. Though the ringed leather choker was a bit out of character, it hinted at her inner kink and defined her long, elegant neck. Her strawberry blonde hair was restrained in a tight, low ponytail; incorrigible waves fell across her back and shoulders. Her full, smooth bangs rode her arched eyebrows that shot up in surprise. Her naturally rosy lips were accentuated by an innocent sheer gloss; they widened into a mischievous, pleased smile, exposing quirky, benevolently wide teeth. Her green eyes sparkled as they locked with mine.

We stood there, silent, an electric charge building to a potentially deadly intensity in the three or four feet between us. I quivered when her eyes moved down to take in my transformed state. At school I was . . . a nerd. No other way to put it. But right now, when I imagined myself as she saw me, I relished her gaze. It warmed me as it traveled centimeter by centimeter down my five-foot-eleven-inch body (thanks, dad). First it soaked in the way my black eyeliner rimmed my haunting, almond-shaped, chocolate brown eyes (thanks, mom); how my blood-red lips offset my supple, golden skin. It admired the blinding shine of my raven-black hair escaping from its bun in wild spikes. I imagined it swooning over the perfection of femininity exhibited in my curves, wrapped in a floor-length black latex dress with red piping and a Nehru collar, a torturously seductive slit exposing my entire right leg and hip. I felt it stop and fantasize about the delicious promise held in the space between the top of my boots and my red thong, which peeked out ever so slightly when I moved.

My own gaze was directed into her eyes, which held so much laughter and joy. She was here, she was queer, get used to it! But I couldn't adapt to the fact that she stood before me, let alone open my mouth to say hello. I was horrified by my own idiocy. I had written her off as straight because she was *femme,* as countless people had done to me before. While I was busy deriding myself, the elevator doors closed, and I was sent back up to the thirteenth floor, sputtering and kicking the wall for the entire trip.

I immediately raced back to the cell, flung down my bags of gear, and bolted into the bathroom (the only room in the damn place with any *light*) to check my hair and makeup. A little shiny, but easily remedied by a quick blot of the forehead and nose with a paper towel. I was happy to see my hair was still perfect, and my breasts resisted gravity, held taut by my dress. I ran-walked back down the hall to see Amelia and her equally kinky-looking friends (where had they come from?) checking in and signing the release form.

I paused and watched her for a moment, gathering my courage. What would I say to her? How serious was she about BDSM? She was clearly in another league from the rest of these kids, but how hard could I play without freaking her out? Our seminar had only seven people. My life would become a living hell every Tuesday if I fucked this up. I decided to play it safe.

I sauntered up behind her, flashing my most playfully flirtatious smile. "Hey, Amelia."

At first, she didn't respond. She looked at me, wide-eyed, and cocked her head to one side, twirling her ponytail between her fingers. She batted her eyelashes a few times, and then opened her mouth to reply in a perfect British accent. "I'm sorry, who?"

"*Amelia* . . ." I repeated quizzically, shaking my head in confusion. I looked to her friends for backup, but they just shrugged and walked off smirking, with a "See ya later. Have fun."

"I don't know Amelia, but I'm Emily. Is that close enough?"

I stammered and sweated. She had begun the game without me. "Uh, yeah. I mean, definitely." I decided to experiment with upping the ante. "You've sure grown up since I last saw you, Emily. I didn't realize it was you."

She curtsied deeply. On the way up, she thrust back her head, arched her back, and placed one hand on her hip, with a mischievous smile. "Are you pleased with how I've grown, Mistress?"

Now my throat parched. This was one of my favorite games, but I'd never played it with someone so . . . so . . . so *pubescent*. She was aping the thirteen-year-old cocky hypersexuality perfectly, sending my frustrated inner schoolmistress into a frenzy. My clitoris pulsed angrily as my juices soaked my underwear. I wanted to grab her and ram my fist into her, fucking her wildly into the registration desk while screaming "Yes, you perfect, cruel little slut," biting her smooth flesh, tearing into her button nipples, and clenching her ponytail, thus arching her head back and sending her gasps up into the air to be heard by the entire stupid city.

But instead I had to take a deep breath.

It was my dom duty to stay cool, to figure out her weaknesses and needs and slowly draw her to her edge. I could always jack off later. I now eyed her inquisitively, looking for holes in her armor. Ha. I found it. She thought she knew how I was going to answer. She was wrong.

I sighed.

"No, I'm not pleased, you petulant little bitch."

As I walked closer to her, my eyes bored into hers, awaiting any movement that would let me know I'd gone too far. None came. Instead, her pupils dilated, letting me know her pussy had just been flooded. I was on the right track.

She tried to look frightened as her chest heaved lustfully. "What do you mean? How dare you call me that!"

I shook my head. This was too much fun. Like a whip, my arm reached out, grabbed her by the hair, and snapped back, pulling her head to my chest, her ass into the air, and her spindly legs flailing to retain her balance.

"Do you know why you've been sent here, Miss Emily?"

She stuck out her bottom lip defiantly and remained silent. She was begging for it. I gave her a light, sharp slap on the ass to reward her acting skills. "Emily" yelped adorably in return. I looked over to see the Dungeon Mistress smiling with approval and nodding. *Fuck it,* I thought, *if we have to hold a two-person play party, so be it.*

I leaned in close to Amelia's ear and raced through the rules of play in a whisper, though I was pretty confident she already knew them: "Okay, the safe word is *abort*. The word for when you need a break is *pause*. When you're ready to return to the scene, you say *begin, start, ready,* whatever you want and we'll come back. Just remember *abort*. *Stop* doesn't work because most people like to say *stop* when they don't mean it. If you understand and you want to play, say 'I've been a naughty girl.' If you don't understand or aren't sure if you want to play, say 'I've been a good girl,' and we'll stop right here. Once play starts, we can stop anytime. No matter what you decide, I'll take care of you afterward and make sure you leave the scene centered. Do you understand?"

She stayed silent, panting, against my chest, for what seemed like minutes. She gazed up lecherously into my eyes. I felt like she was fucking me with them, like somehow her gaze was sending imaginary fingers to haunt my G-spot. I was weakening. That manipulative little . . . She was doing this on purpose. She was fucking with me.

I ground my fist further into her scalp and twisted it around. "I said, Do. You. Understand."

She laughed and licked her lips, relishing the pain. A trickle of saliva dribbled down the right side of her mouth, tempting me to lick it up, and her huge vicious eyes taunted me. She giggled her way through a response. "No, I don't understand, mistress. I don't understand why you're being so *mean*. I can be such a good girl for you. I'll do whatever you want. I'll start, I'll pause, I'll abort, whatever you like. Just please *stop* hurting me." With that she broke into explosive laughter again.

Wow.

This was a fucked-up way to play.

She was destroying my rules. Tearing them to shreds. I knew she wanted me to play, and play hard. She wanted me to play harder than I ever had, in that she wanted me to play without a safe word. What the fuck was I supposed to do? I understood her intellectual reasoning, in that life really has no safe words, and I trusted that I understood her body language, but I could get into some deep shit if any of my fellow doms found out I had gone off the edge. Still, this was the hottest girl I'd ever played with. The hottest girl I ever would play with. The. Hottest. Girl. I knew I had no choice. There was no going back from here. She was smarter than me. I would have to overpower her with something other than reason. But first I'd have to make sure she knew who was in charge.

As my look hardened, Amelia pouted. "You're no fun, *Miss* Britton. You're the meanest schoolmistress I've ever had."

I gasped and widened my eyes as though offended, though I was really marveling at the fact that she remembered my last name.

"Meanest?" I let go of her hair. "Oh, no, not that." I pushed her away. "I'm sorry, I don't intend to be mean. I don't know what's gotten into me."

With that, I smoothed her skirt, adjusted her collar, and patted her hair.

"There. All better. You're right. You are a good girl, and good girls don't deserve such awful treatment. It was good seeing you again, Emily, and I wish you all the best in your studies."

I walked away, off to the cell where my equipment was crumpled in a corner. I yanked my bags out from under an entangled butch couple making out on top of them and set to work removing the necessary accessories. Twenty feet each of the white nylon 3/8" rope for the kotori-shinju, which bound her breasts and arms, and the sakuranbo, which bound her "cherry," and fifty feet of the extra-strong, extra-expensive yellow 1/2" for the kotori, the suspension harness, which suspended her from a hook in the ceiling. That would hold her and serve as an awesome lesson for my students. I poked the making-out couple out of their stupor. "Do you know what time it is?" The top thrust out her watch for me to scan while still stabbing her victim with her tongue. It looked like bad boy porn. I was glad to concentrate on making out the numbers. I muttered to myself. "Almost seven. They'll be here soon. Good. Thanks."

My own victim shuffled remorsefully into the room moments later, as expected. She had sobered up from her power-drunk elation and remembered that it wasn't much fun to top a top. She squatted down next to me and eyed my movements as I removed a leather blindfold, some six-foot cinch rope (I'd almost forgotten), and a bottle of lube. I stopped and turned to her, asking her with my eyes what she could possibly want.

"What'chuh doin'?" she asked shyly, in more of a cockney accent than the proper BBC announcer British she had employed before.

"Getting ready to teach a lesson." I returned my gaze to the tool bag, mysteriously shuffling items around inside of it to get her attention.

"A lesson?" Her eyes brightened and her shoulders perked up. "What kind of lesson? I need to be taught a lesson. Can I come?" She grabbed one of the ropes and began fiddling with the ends.

I grabbed the rope back out of her hands in a huff and placed it back down on the floor. I savored the power implicit in my silence as I sized her up. "I'm not sure if you've passed the prerequisites necessary for this lesson."

"Oh." She looked down, defeated, and began fiddling with a loose thread on her skirt instead.

"But I do need an assistant in order to perform a demonstration." I raised my eyebrows and stared at her appraisingly. "Would you be willing to volunteer for such a task?"

She demurely lifted her softened doe eyes to meet mine and responded slowly and sweetly. "I would be honored, Mistress Britton. I've been a very, very naughty girl. I'd like to make it up to you."

With that, she fell down to her hands and knees and crawled low on the floor to me. Her skirt fell aside to expose a round ass covered by white, ruffled panties. I stared at that ass with full concentration as I felt her hands wrap around my foot. I looked down to see her watermelon-pink tongue swirling around and around, wetting my left boot, her lips puckering and sucking on the bridge of my foot, her cheek catching against the vinyl covering my shin. When she was done, she sat back on her bottom, took my right boot in her hands, lifted it up, and stuck it between her breasts. She shoved them up and together, pushing into me, forcing my foot to fuck her tits harder and harder while gasping as if I was shoving it deep into her body. Finally, she brought the boot up to her face. She slowly, seductively opened her mouth wide and stared me deep in the eye as she pulled my heel closer and closer, finally wrapping her lips around it and taking it all the way down her throat. I shuddered and melted, my eyes rolling back into my head. When I opened them, I looked down at her body, only to notice a dirty smudge from my boot across her chest. That was it. This was too much. I wanted her now.

Luckily for me, I had Tessa and Jasper to stand in for my willpower. When they walked up, my eyes were glazed over with desire, my posture slack. I was moaning in rhythm with Amelia's thrusts. I'd given in.

"Whoah, sister-friend, what's goin' on here?" Jasper walked up behind me, took my face in her hands, and began gently slapping my cheeks. "Hey, Tessa, I think she's on something."

I just smiled up at her blissfully and giggled. "Hi! What are you guys doing here?"

"Uh, removing the spell this girl's put on you." Tessa leaned down and pulled my boot out of Amelia's mouth. She looked Amelia right in the eye. "Hi. I'm Tessa. Who are you and what have you done to our friend?"

Tessa had a vested interest in this topic. She'd tried to top me a number of times, and I had argued that I was untopable, that the only way I could get off was domming. I hadn't been fucked since I was fifteen, and I planned to keep it that way. Tessa wasn't hearing it. She was as big a femme top as myself, as stubborn as me, and fifty times more jealous. The fury seared through her eyes seeing Amelia's confident smirk and my slack jaw. If she wasn't topping me, no one was. However, Amelia had just given me psychic head, and for the first time in my life I was damn well ready for her to go ahead and do whatever else she saw fit. If they had shown up an hour later I would have probably been strapped to the St. Andrews Cross with a dildo up my ass. And with this girl in charge, I would have liked it.

Amelia stuck out her hand and shook Tessa's. "Amelia Ross, how are you. Tania and I are in school together." She leaned back on her arms and awaited my response. I lurched forward in shock. What the hell was she doing? Tessa and Jasper didn't know my real name. They surely didn't know I was in school. And who told her she could step out of character like that? I quickly stepped in to do damage control.

"That's right. I'm her *teacher*. Right, *Emily?*" I rose to my feet, yanked her up, and slapped her on the cheek. "Permission to speak was not granted, pupil."

Before she could respond, I stuffed a ball gag in her mouth and was talking again. Even with the ball gag in her mouth, she was a vision of consternation. I tried to ignore it and hoped Tessa and Jasper would do the same. Hell, she wanted to play hard, right?

"Emily here has generously offered to be our model today."

Tessa and Jasper nodded. Thankfully, they hadn't noticed the security breach. Behind them, I noticed a few onlookers who had poked their noses in and noticed there might be something brewing. They stood waiting in the doorway, hesitant and unsure. I looked over at Amelia, who was standing patiently. She didn't seem that annoyed with me anymore. She actually seemed to calm down with the gag in her mouth, as though she finally felt comfortable with how I was treating her. This one wanted to be forced into submission.

I took a deep breath, handed Tessa and Jasper one roll of white rope each, and began my lesson. As I spoke and began demonstrating suspension methods and knots to them, I remembered my first kinbaku, rope-tying, lesson in Tokyo, where I was in Amelia's shoes. I had been terrified. I checked on Amelia, looking into her eyes with a smile. Her eyes smiled back. She was doing fine. I winked at her and continued my lesson while privately reminiscing. I had been nowhere near as confident and brash as Amelia was. I was a demure little nineteen-year-old wanna-be who saw subbing as a way to make money without penetration. Luckily for me I ended up in one of the better houses in Japan, where nawa-kesho, the art of rope, was performed only by a true nawashi, or rope artist, who had already been in my shoes. She had trained me to become a jo-osama, a powerful mistress, to make thousands both practicing my craft and being practiced upon. She had been kind and gentle to me. Now, ten years later, I would honor her memory by being the same way with Amelia.

"Okay, any questions?" Jasper and Tessa shook their heads. "You remember your bowline, Portuguese bowline, and square knot?" They nodded. "All right. I'm going to stop talking now. Follow my lead and be ready when I ask for your help. Tessa, hand me the blindfold."

Amelia and I were entering into a whole different realm now. I wondered if she realized, wondered if she would like it here or would want to go back to our crude S/M role-play. I bowed deeply to her and expressed my gratitude that she was letting me show her my love of the art, shibaritai. When I came back up, her eyes were closed and her neck loose, showing that she had entered into absolute submission. I walked behind her and wrapped the blindfold around her head. I felt her let out a deep breath as I wrapped my arms around her and began gently caressing and massaging her from head to toe. I removed her shirt and kissed my way across her chest. I reached behind her to unsnap her bra and, leaning in close to her ear, startled her with a whisper. "Just shake your head if you feel any numbness or need to stop and I'll take the gag out of your mouth, okay?"

Amelia nodded. I slowly disrobed her, finally unbuckling and shaking off her Mary Janes, leaving her in kneesocks so she wouldn't get too cold.

I asked Jasper to obtain the ropes to bind her sakura, her little cherry, her delicious ripe fruit. I bent down to begin and my nose filled with her smell. Jasper passed me the rope, which I sent around Amelia's waist once before tying the first knot. I then reveled in tying the "joy knot" over her clitoris and watching her squirm into it, forcing it into place for maximum sensitivity. I leaned down and rummaged around my bag, procuring a remote-control silver bullet, which I popped into place between the ropes and her mons. Once I had secured the final over-the-hand knot between her buttocks, I flicked the switch on the remote control and let myself get lost in her moans and squeals as she bucked and swayed, getting closer and closer to orgasm. I began playing with the intensity of the vibrator, pushing the rpm's higher or lower in response to her breath, keeping her ever on the verge of a higher and higher wave of bliss. I stopped before she could come, and left the vibrator on its lowest setting for the duration of the scene.

Now it was time to tie her shinju, or "pearls." Her breasts really were pearls, round and smooth and precious. I took special care not to snag her skin at any point as I wrapped and tied the rope, separating and lifting her breasts, clamping her arms to her sides, sending the nipples up and outward to be sucked, kissed, bitten, clamped . . . I shuddered for a moment at my proximity, at all the options for pleasure. I then leaned in and took advantage, breathing ever so lightly on her nipples, flicking them with my tongue and giddily watching them harden before pulling away to teach my pupils about the most basic, and most potentially dangerous, form of suspension bondage, the kotori. I was going to make her fly, to forget she was human, to forget she even had a body. The first time I had experienced this, and, actually, every time after, I had entered into the deepest meditation of my life, a state of completely blissful nothing, yet a connection to everything. I had experienced something deeper and more spiritual than orgasm. I hoped she would feel the same.

Tessa and Jasper wrapped her ribcage once more, right beneath the shinju. As we tied the back and connected cinch ropes under her arms, Amelia started to sway. I got nervous she wasn't breathing and went to remove her ball gag and blindfold. She began shaking her head frantically, then switched to nodding just as violently. I took the gag out of her mouth and she immediately seethed at me. "No! I'm fine! I was shaking my head, but then I realized that meant to remove the gag, so I started nodding to tell you I was fine. Please don't stop!"

Her eyes were glowing vibrant emerald green; her cheeks were red and her skin radiant. She was more than fine. Seeing her happiness sent a smile shooting across my face and energy shooting up my spine. Impulsively, I kissed her. She kissed back, deep and soft, sending more of her vital feminine energy through me. When we pulled away, we shared a loving look, and then I replaced her ball gag and blindfold before my students and I finished the final ties and prepared to send her up to the skies.

Jasper used a ladder to climb up and send the suspension rope through the ceiling clamp. It pulled her upright, rendering her body even more statuesque and her breasts even more prominent. Once the rope was secured, I gently pushed Amelia forward, letting her feel the rope's ability to carry her weight for a while before lifting up one of her legs. This was Tessa's specialty, so I let her shine. She wrapped Amelia's knee as high as her thigh, then tied that to the ceiling rope. With one leg up and one sweet, socked foot on the floor, Amelia looked too vulnerable and precious for words. I stepped in here for a moment and placed myself between her legs. I checked and adjusted all of her ties, and then reached down between her thighs to check and adjust her vagina. I slid a finger between the rope and her right lip, probing and finally plunging my finger into her wetness. She grunted like a wild animal, fucking my hand until her knee finally buckled, leaving her with her full weight on the rope. "She's ready," I shared, and Tessa and Jasper pulled up her free leg, tying it expertly. As they did, I shoved my finger deep inside of her, pushing out a low, satisfied groan. Now Amelia really was flying, anchored to the earth by only my one finger inside her.

"What is this called?" Jasper asked, pointing to the suspension ropes. "Tsuri," I replied, as I caressed Amelia's skin with my free hand. "That's nice," Jasper replied. I smiled. It was nice. I felt Amelia relax into the bonds. I wasn't sure which action relaxed her, so I brushed her face softly as I recited its different names quietly in her ear. "Tsuri. Nawa-tsuri. Tsurusu." I pressed into the knots below her shoulders, tapping into the acupressure points underneath and sending healing energy to her center. "Shiatsu tsurusu." Amelia cooed gently, finally afloat in the ecstatic state I had hoped for her.

Suddenly, she began quaking like a leaf and screaming. Tessa and Jasper looked absolutely freaked at first, but I reassured them and told them to focus on her. It was a natural part of the process. Her endorphins had risen, her energy was flowing perfectly through her body: she was having an orgasm. Tears streamed from the blindfold and her body's spasms shook the building. I moved away to leave her to her bliss, free of any distraction from her soul's resonant voice. The orgasm never really stopped, but it subdued, and I released her from her binds after only ten minutes. The first time was too intense for more than that. I let her fall slowly into my arms as Tessa and Jasper undid the ropes one by one, and then curled her up in my lap and held her tightly, massaging her energizing face points, rocking her, and humming to her gently as we breathed together.

When I finally opened my eyes and pulled my focus outside of the three-foot-wide circle that bound Amelia and I, I saw that the room was packed to overflowing with women, a silent, reverent audience whose gaze cast its singular focus on us. There were all kinds of dykes; every subculture, every race, every gender orientation was represented. And they were all saturated with love: hands were held; heads were on shoulders; noses were nuzzled. We had created a circuit of loving energy that filled the room; the electricity shooting through us flowed through everyone and everything. It was a different party altogether, yet these were the same people who had been there in the beginning: I recognized the rodeo king, the frat boy, the make-out butches . . . Even the bitchy ex-cheerleaders were back, now beaming as they gently massaged each other's breasts and whispered sweet nothings into each other's ears.

Jasper and Tessa quietly rewrapped the ropes, smiling at us. When she was done with the last rope, Tessa walked over and covered us in blankets, kissing Amelia on the head as she finished. She walked back over to Jasper and shot her a mischievous, sexy look before putting her arms around her. No one moved for a few minutes, and then people began to channel the energy we had sent through them. Their hand-holding turned into caressing; heads moved from shoulders to breasts and stomachs; nuzzles turned into kisses and bites. The silence was broken by gasps and moans, the "crack!" of hands on asses, thrusting and sucking noises emanating from moist crevices. Now it was Amelia's and my turn to watch and be inspired; we fumbled passionately under the blankets, hands finding nipples and thighs and the folds of labia. Before I knew it, our fists were inside each other, rocking each other gently on the waves of our own private song. Amelia had asked to keep the blindfold on, so I had left it; now my eyes were rolled far back into my head. No one was watching anymore. No one was judging, no one was dissecting, no one was comparing, and no one was ashamed. There were no spectators and no objects; we were all part of the same big universal show.

Mercy's Pocket

Tulsa Brown

The young woman traipsed into the nightclub behind Mercy as if she was a dark, long-legged giraffe who'd fixed on a mare as her mother. Mercy Lawton was five-foot-nine-inches from her spats to her gleaming, bear-greased hair, and the woman's sullen gaze glowered over it. Six feet if she was an inch. At the piano, Alphonse whistled quietly through his teeth.

"The Lord sure knows how to stretch it," he said.

I was beside him on the stage, with a broom. I'd been sweeping and singing. Alphonse and I called that a rehearsal, even though we'd been working together four months and I could slide into a song as smoothly as a red silk glove.

Now I felt my throat close tight. Where had Mercy found this one?

The door eased shut, squeezing out the bright afternoon glare that had powdered the tables and chairs with dust. Mercy swung toward the stage, a jaunty stride that made her pocket watch sway on its chain. She was wearing a houndstooth zoot suit.

"Afternoon, Alphonse. How are y'all?" Mercy said.

My stomach twisted. Mercy hadn't been in her hometown of Mobil, Alabama, for twenty years, but she pulled down her drawl like a bedroom blind. It was her wooing voice. I knew it well.

She looked up at me. "Anna-Marie, this here's Cecilia, who's my headliner starting Friday. I want you to fix her up and make her at home. Find her a crib and a dress."

Published by The Haworth Press, Inc., 2006. All rights reserved.
doi:10.1300/5328_27

I was clenching the broom handle as if to choke it, but the words were cool and powdery. Snow. "We don't have anything that would fit."

"Then you take her to Patson's and buy her one. On my account."

"But Miz said—"

"And you tell her what *I* said." Her dark eyes flashed a warning. "She can come around Saturday night and get it all. Mercy Lawton pays her bitches' bills."

Cecilia was gazing at Alphonse's battered upright.

"Is that the only piano you have?"

Mercy whirled on her. "Christ Almighty, girl! Where do you think you are? The Cotton Club?" She stalked away, shoes clicking hard on the cement floor. Cecilia's sleepy eyes opened with surprise, and I let go my first easy breath. I would outlast this diva, too.

"Headliner" was a term of flattery in Mercy's joint, the Pan Handle. There was no marquee outside the tall tinderbox, no orchestra to lift a torch song to the rafters. We had Alphonse on the piano and an occasional trumpet or sax man who was drifting his way through Harlem, looking for a night's crib. Still, by selling hooch in the back room Mercy managed to pay the rent, and she held one high card that lifted her above the other speakeasies: Thomas "Fats" Waller was a personal friend.

Fresh from his success on Broadway with the score for "Hot Chocolates," Fats didn't light up the little club very often, but Mercy made sure his name hung in the air like cologne. I'd seen him just a few times in my four months at the Pan Handle: a sleek, laughing, well-fed seal of a man with a smudge of a moustache. He never stayed long enough to hear me sing.

"He's a good man to know," Mercy said once, her voice a rasp of pleasure. "Something to have in my pocket."

She thrust her naked hips higher, forced my tongue deeper into the pink, fruity folds of her sex.

We were all in Mercy's pocket.

Was there a woman in Harlem in 1931 who didn't believe she could be Bessie Smith? Who didn't sing while she washed dishes or waited tables for dimes in Cook Alley? I did, and that's where Mercy had found me. She hadn't let me finish my shift but swept me down beside her for lunch, a dashing, gleaming beau from the first glance. I liked her brashness, felt it kindle in my belly and lower. And she owned a nightclub.

"You're so pretty. Dolled up, you'll be Christmas," Mercy said.

"But I can sing, too," I said. "You heard me."

"Of course you'll sing at the Pan Handle. You'll open for me." Her smile was crumpled, naughty. "You'll open."

It wasn't exactly the compliment I'd been fishing for but I took it. I soon found out what Alphonse and everyone else already knew: Mercy had a sharp eye and a tin ear.

"Oh, you're good enough, Anna-Marie," Alphonse assured me. "You're better than most everything she's had through here in a year." But his kind eyes told me a wailing tomcat might have fit that bill, too.

"Again, Al," I said, my hands clasped at my waist. "Let's just take it from the top again. Please?"

I practiced until my throat was sore and the notes were smooth, if not luminous; I hunched around my hope as if it was a match in the wind. But I discovered one silky truth: I could be Christmas when I wanted.

I'd always thought I'd dressed well enough. In a frilly blouse and four-gored skirt I'd turned heads and earned handfuls of dimes. But behind the curtain at Miz Patson's Evening Boutique I held a length of fabric I'd never seen the like of. It was as if someone had laid a sunset in my hands, thin and weighty, scratchy with sequins.

When I zipped up the short back, the slinky fabric embraced me. I straightened my shoulders to keep my tits in the cups, and my curvy body felt taller than it ever had. I padded out to the mirror barefoot, surprised by the sensation of my bare thighs caressing each other, and the way the slit made the fabric lick my left leg, again and again.

The store hushed. In a chair, one elbow on each armrest, Mercy pressed her fingertips together. Even from a distance her eyes seemed smoky. I turned to face the full-length mirror and was astonished by the stranger. She was an orange-gold sunset *and* the dark night, breasts sitting high and round, tugging the beaded straps to taut lines. I gazed, mesmerized by how the slightest sway made the colors cascade from amber to vermilion. I wasn't on fire, I *was* fire. A torch.

"Someone get this lady a pair of spikes," Mercy growled, her voice deep with fresh hunger.

Friday night I had the shoes, the dress, and paste diamonds, too, sitting in a ring of stars around my neck. I'd spent hours creating a new face, eyelids dreamy with false lashes, lipstick that looked like a glossy red butterfly poised on my lips. I felt beautiful, powerful. I didn't walk onto the stage of the Pan Handle, I claimed it, heart pattering.

The stage lights blinded me. The audience was a crowd of shadowy mannequins, but I could see Alphonse perfectly at the piano. He looked back at me and lifted an eyebrow of approval, just before he struck the first chords of "Frankie and Johnnie."

I opened my mouth, and the brilliant sunset flowed up from my body and out of my throat, swept over the house in a wash of sound I'd never known I could make.

❧

I walked fast when I was angry, even in heels. They were shorter, more square than my singing shoes, basic black with a strap. I was all business now, suffering in an itchy fitted tweed suit in July, but the sacrifice was worth it. Not only did I have to sweet-talk Miz Patson, but I would have boiled in oil before Cecilia Dumas outflashed me.

She sauntered a defiant half-step behind, bare legged and in flats, her simple cotton dress the color of cotton candy. It struck me as a church dress, or a girl's frock made too long, and that suited her mood: a bored, sulky child. How old was she? I didn't know. I'd hardly gotten a handful of words from her. I wouldn't have cared except I was looking for the string to trip her with.

"Did you bring sheets with you?" I tossed the question over my shoulder. "Alphonse is going to want them."

"I don't need sheets. I can do whatever you want."

Ah, she understood the lingo but it was a stock answer, the well-worn response of someone who didn't read music.

"Well, you need 'em anyway," I insisted. "Alphonse will want your version and key."

"My sheets are Tchaikovsky."

I stopped on the sidewalk and swiveled around to look up at her. For the first time I noticed her high cheekbones, and eyes as large and liquid as a calf's.

"What the hell are you saying, girl?"

"I'm a classical pianist," Cecilia said. "Honky-tonk and blues are *not* difficult, if you've heard them at least once."

"Has Mercy ever heard you sing?" I blurted.

"She never asked. She saw me standing with the gang inside Hubbert's Review Hall."

I nodded. I knew that place, a rotating carousel of talent, headliners sliding down and hungry nobodies scratching up.

"She walked over and said, 'Aren't you a long, cool drink. What's your name?' I told her it was on the signboard outside. She didn't even go look, but offered me twenty-two dollars a week. I was only making twelve."

"So you're not a torch? Nobody pays you to sing?"

A smile broke over Cecilia's face like a misty dawn. "No. But sometimes they pay me to stop."

I started to laugh. I couldn't help it. My fears had blown out in a single puff and it was so funny, so fitting. Mercy deserved this, the tin-eared wolf.

Cecilia's grin widened along with me, broke to show white, straight teeth, a tiny gap between the front two. Damn, she was pretty. And so young. I saw her more clearly now that the mask had lowered. Bored? The girl had just been terrified.

"What's going to happen now?" Cecilia asked. Then, softly, "I need the twenty-two dollars."

I looked up at her. "Well, first we're going to get you a dress."

Miz Patson wasn't happy to see us, since I wasn't there to pay the bill. But she perked up when I gave her Mercy's news; Saturday was good enough. The showy old bird clucked around Cecilia.

"If you've got half as much talent as you've got legs, you'll be a sensation," Miz said. "Come to the back. I haven't got but three dresses long enough."

One blue, one black, one red. For a moment Cecilia seemed dazzled by the gowns, three different holidays on hangers, but then she slipped behind the curtain without a word. I took a step after her and stopped. My desire surprised me, not just to see the result, but to create it. I wanted to pull the Sunday-school pinafore down and slide the shimmer up, dress her like my own lady doll.

The thought was a sweet nip between my legs and I squirmed, tingling with a new itch. I'd never dressed another woman.

Cecilia's head poked out from behind the curtain. "Anna-Marie, would you give me a hand?"

She'd chosen to try the blue first, a form-fitting pastel satin that had two swaying rows of ruffles at the hem. It was sleeveless and plunged in the back to a deep heart's point. I stared at the impossibly long trail of her spine and the tantalizing shadow at the base of it, where her ass pulled the fabric into an alluring gap.

"It should fit on top but it doesn't, and I don't know why," Cecilia said.

"You need to 'fall into' the brassiere. Here, bend over."

She did and I reached into the front, cupped the hot, soft handful of her little breast, and lifted it forward. Then the other. The spike of desire made my knees weak. My clit felt suddenly thick, seemed to push against my panties like the tip of a tongue.

When she straightened, Cecilia's breasts filled the bust perfectly, pressed out small, glossy curves in the blue fabric. I tried to pull my gaze away, but to my amazement new highlights were forming and I stared, mesmerized by the delectable call of it. Hard nipples under satin.

When she touched my hair, I woke.

"It's so silky," she said. "How do you do that?"

"Iron it. I'll do yours, if you want."

"Yes, please. I don't even own a lipstick." But her smile said, *I'm not as young as you think.*

"I'll do your makeup, too," I said, and the rush of want made my voice smokey. If I'd been singing then, I would have melted all of Harlem.

We walked back to the Pan Handle silently, each of us lost in a private dream. I could sense her secret glances from above and the flattery stoked me. I felt bold as well as hungry, and my desire cast a protective net around her. How could I save her from the disaster I knew Friday night would be? How beautiful did she have to be before they no longer heard her sing? Then there was the other obstacle, the one I never seemed to know my way around.

Mercy was waiting in the foyer, dapper in evening gear, although the Pan Handle didn't open on Thursdays until 8 p.m. She was wearing a pin-striped suit and red bow tie, a bright splash against her white shirt, crisp with double starch. I knew because I was the one who'd washed it.

Mercy's dark eyes gleamed as she looked over Cecilia and her shopping bag. "Well? You gonna show me what I bought?"

The tall girl had fallen back behind me in the narrow hall. I felt her hand below my left shoulder, a hidden touch. A plea.

But my chest had seized and any brave words I'd planned fused together in a cold, frightened ball.

"Not yet. I'm not finished with her. You'll get it all tomorrow night," I blurted. Cecilia's hand fell away from my back.

"Well, I thought the lady would have dinner with me," Mercy said.

Cecilia stepped past me and swung around Mercy, her face a hard, sienna slate. "I'm not hungry."

"You've got to eat sometime, Cotton Club girl," Mercy called after her. She turned to glare at me. "You could have softened the bitch up."

I caught Cecilia on the stairs, tried to clasp her elbow. She shrugged me off like a cheap coat. "I guess you need the twenty-two dollars, same as me."

I let her go.

My bedroom was on the second floor, a broom closet that also served as my dressing room. But the door had a lock. I don't know what time it was when Mercy began to pound on it.

"What the hell are you doing, girl? The house is full, Alphonse is waiting. Get your ass down there and *sing!*"

"I'm sick," I said to the ceiling.

"God damn, you'll be worse than sick when I'm done. You hear me, Anna-Marie? They'll find you floating in that pretty dress . . ."

Eventually she gave up and slipped over to the other door, a *real* broom closet where I'd set up a cot for Cecilia. Mercy Lawton turned to Southern syrup.

"Oh, come on, sweet thing. You don't have to sing tonight, just let the people see you. Give 'em a sip of that long, cool drink. I'll put a little something in your cup, too."

Nothing. Mercy suddenly hammered the wood, a wham that went through me like a spike, even across the hallway. "You'd better damn well be ready tomorrow!" At last I heard her mutter down the stairs. "Fuck, I hate show business."

I lay on my bed, watching the gray, unchanging ceiling, feeling leaden. How heavy could four months be? And why did every ounce of it lay on me today? I knew I was done; I realized I had been for a long time. The problem was the *going*. I had a few dollars squirreled away, but Mercy didn't like to let go of anything she thought belonged to her, whether she used it or not. Especially in tonight's mood. There was a back door to the Pan Handle, but I'd have to walk the length of the club to get to it. And me sneaking away didn't help the woman across the hall.

I thought of Cecilia behind me in the hallway, her hand on my back. What pockets we put ourselves in, I thought, and how fast they got deep.

I pushed myself up. She had to know that.

She didn't answer my knock.

"Cissy," I said quietly to the wood, "I'm sorry. I'm not brave. And maybe I'm a slow learner, too. But there's something you should know, girl. In a real job, they pay *you*, not the other way around." I paused. "I'm walking out of here tonight. You can come if you want. Or you can wait and see if she's any different with you."

Long, terrible seconds. I felt my pulse on both sides of my neck. At last the door opened a hand's breadth and her face hung above me like a dark, beautiful moon.

"My name's Cecilia," she said.

We were going to do this Mercy's way, or make it look like it. Doll up, flutter around the floor once, then slip out the front door.

"I've got some suds, not much but enough for a few days. If we have our dresses, it'll be easier to land work. Or we could pawn them."

Cecilia's brows gathered. "But I haven't paid for mine. She might call the cops."

I thought of the busy back room with two little slats in the door, one to take in money, the other to hand out slim bottles. "Sure. The same day she phones Herbert Hoover," I said. Then, "Close your eyes."

She obeyed and I began to smooth blue shadow over her lid with a little sable brush. I held her chin with my other hand, entranced by the sensation of her warm skin and delicate jaw, the nearness of her long, elegant body.

It seemed so intimate to touch her this way. I became fascinated by Cecilia's contours, the shape of her cheekbones, the curves in her voluptuous lips. Did I still have the plum color rouge in my drawer? What shade of lipstick would be right? I felt a quiver of nameless excitement. Mercy's brashness had drawn me to her—it was so different from me. But decorating Cecilia was like stroking myself in a secret place.

And she'd given herself over to me. Cecilia sat, hands folded calmly in her lap, as trusting as a child. Sometimes her eyes quivered beneath the lids, or her mouth widened in a smile—I was tickling. Yet like me, she was all patience.

It was July. The air in my bedroom was close and ripe with the scent of us, powder and the deep places of a woman's body. I could smell myself, the almost-ocean fragrance between my legs, the sharp, damp suggestion rising from my bra straps and skirt waistband. I stole glimpses down Cecilia's neckline, remembered the plump swell of her breast in my hand, and squeezed my thighs together.

"I know that song," Cecilia said.

"What song?"

"The one you're humming. It's 'Ain't Misbehavin'.' I could play it for you sometime."

She opened her eyes and I caught my breath. Oh, I'd done the liner perfectly! There was a feline quality to her face now, both sly and luminous, a brown-eyed tigress.

I was still bent toward her, balancing myself with one hand on the chair's arm. In the same instant we both noticed my chest was inches from her face. Cecilia smiled.

"Do you need some help 'falling into' that brassiere, ma'am?" Her hand crept up and slid open the first button.

I'd slipped into a strange, silky dream. I could feel Alphonse's honky-tonk rhythm in the base of my soles, and an abrupt, muffled guffaw kept shooting off like a distant cannon—Mercy's laugh. We should have been running with the dogs of hell on our heels, yet I was suspended in desire, dangling over the chair with my blouse open. Through half-closed eyes I watched Cecilia suckle my breast, the strong, thrilling pulls of her mouth magnified by the glamour of her painted face. My exquisite lady doll.

With her hand up my skirt. *Oh.* Her fingers polished the length of my stockinged thigh, teased me along the strap of my garter. The lips of my cunt were as juicy as apple slices baking in a pie. Simmering. I writhed, trying to force her to touch my hungry skin. With a deft move, Cecilia slid her hand high and forced aside the damp panel of my panties. I felt my moan more than heard it.

I thought she'd enter me, but her hand closed in a fist between my thighs, index finger bent and jutting up. With that knuckle she pressed hard against my clitoris, made me ride her like a tiny horse. She lifted me up on my toes—what strength! My bronc had bucked and white sparks seemed to burst where we met. I twitched and tried to pull back, but there was nowhere to go. Cecilia boosted me again and my pussy slurped in a moist slide, and once more, and . . . there. Sudden brightness. The orgasm took me so hard and fast it glittered on the edge of pain.

I was gasping. I pulled away at last, my arms aching, legs trembling, trying to find my feet. Cecilia's mascara had smudged to thin crescents under her eyes, but she looked immensely pleased. She licked her knuckle and said, "I call that 'short order.'"

"Good Lord, woman. What the hell's the Blue Plate Special?" We both laughed.

In fifteen minutes we were creeping down the stairs, fine fabric rustling, narrow heels chittering. I'd put all my money into one tiny handbag, hardly bigger than a compact, and clutched it tight. As we drew closer to the busy, jumping room, the music stopped and we heard Mercy's voice. On stage. Cecilia's hand closed around my elbow but in my mind this was good news—the boss was busy.

"Cut through the people standing so she doesn't notice you. Walk in a wide circle but head for the door." I pushed her into the room ahead of me and watched her glide, threading through the suits like a long ribbon of blue silk. Then I took a breath and stepped in, too.

"There she is at last! Ain't it like a dame to keep you waiting?"

The room laughed and chairs scraped. The entire nightclub turned to look at me, faces glowing with good humor and hooch. Abruptly they began to applaud, encouraging.

"Don't disappoint these nice people any more than you already have, Anna-Marie," Mercy called congenially over the noise. She looked to be grinning but I wasn't fooled—she was baring her fangs.

I thought my heart would batter its way out of my chest. What do you do when you're scared shitless and the whole world is watching? Hold your head up and walk like a lady. I made my sunset dress sway like a glittering pendulum and the crowd melted out of the way, giving me a path to the stage. Mercy reached down to help me up, then leaned close and squeezed my arm.

"You ever do this to me again and I'll bend you over until you lick your own cunt," she hissed in my ear.

Hatred speared me upright. I smiled at her. "Oh, sugar, there's no need," I drawled in my best Mobile imitation. "I've got someone else to do that for me."

Brown daggers, the kind that used to give me nightmares. But what could she do in the glare of the spotlight? In a burst of triumph I suddenly knew how to work this. Up on stage, Mercy Lawton was in *my* pocket.

I turned to the audience. "Ladies and gentlemen, the Pan Handle has a rare treat tonight. We've been graced by the finest accompanist in New York. She's only passing through but if you *coax* her, she just might tickle the ivories for us. Ladies and gentlemen, please welcome Miss Cecilia Dumas!"

The room erupted in noise and motion. It was easy to pick out the one stricken face. But I beckoned her up and Cecilia put the shine on, a true performer. You would have thought the shabby club was Carnegie Hall.

Mercy was seething in the wings. I'd just introduced her diva as a piano player. The big "opening" she'd had planned for Friday night was gone in a puff. She'd look like a fool, a liar.

I gave Cecilia a quick embrace on stage.

"Ain't—"

"Misbehavin'," she agreed in a whisper, then sashayed over to the piano.

Alphonse was one fine rhythm man, but Cecilia made that instrument live and breathe. Halfway through her lead-in my stomach flipped, admiration dusted with fear. Damn, I hoped I could be . . . worthy of that sound. That skill. But when I looked over and caught a sliver's glance of her—elegant tigress face and long, dark body frosted in icy blue satin—I felt as if I'd licked a flame. The heat ran down my throat and ignited between my legs, an encore of the sparks we'd made on the second floor. I opened my mouth and let them fly.

I didn't melt Harlem, but I smoked that room. After the last notes died away, there was a full breath of silence, then suddenly the walls were shaking. Thunder. And I finally saw the big man at the back clapping harder than any of them, the one with the slick, seal-shaped body and smudge moustache.

His voice was a velvet rumble. "My, oh, my. You ladies lit that little number up like a Christmas tree. The three of us got some talkin' to do."

Fats Waller was so flattered and impressed with our rendition of his famous song, he found us work—and it paid better than twenty-two dollars a week. Cecilia played the piano and I sang, and between the shows I devoted myself to one particular pocket, the sweet one between the long legs of my lady doll.

ABOUT THE EDITOR

Rachel Kramer Bussel is a professional porn editor and freelance writer. She is the reviser of *The Lesbian Sex Book*, co-editor of *Up All Night: Adventures in Lesbian Sex*, and editor of *First-Timers: True Stories of Lesbian Sex* and *Naughty Spanking Stories from A to Z 1* and *2*. She writes the "Lusty Lady" column in the *Village Voice* and conducts interviews for Gothamist.com and Mediabistro.com. Her writing has been published in over 70 anthologies, including *Best American Erotica 2004* and *2006* and *Best Lesbian Erotica 2001, 2004,* and *2005,* as well as in *Bust,* Cleansheets.com, *Curve, Diva, Girlfriends, On Our Backs,* Oxygen.com, *Rockgrl, The San Francisco Chronicle, Velvetpark,* and other publications. She has appeared on the television shows *Berman and Berman, In The Life,* and *Naked New York.* Find out more at www.rachelkramerbussel.com.

© 2006 by The Haworth Press, Inc. All rights reserved.
doi:10.1300/5328_28

CONTRIBUTORS

Tara Alton's erotica has appeared in *The Mammoth Book of Best New Erotica, Best Lesbian Erotica 2005, Best Women's Erotica, Hot Women's Erotica, Clean Sheets,* and *Scarlet Letters*. She writes erotica because that is what is in her head and it needs to come out. Check out her Web site at www.tara alton.com.

Cheryl B. is a poet and essayist. Her work appears in over two dozen anthologies and literary magazines, including *BLOOM, Pills, Thrills, Chills, and Heartache: Adventures in the First Person* (Alyson), *Naughty Spanking Stories from A to Z 2* (Pretty Things Press), and *Best Lesbian Erotica 2005* (Cleis Press) among many others. She is the recipient of a 2003 poetry fellowship from the New York Foundation for the Arts and a writer's residency from the Virginia Center for the Creative Arts. A native New Yorker, she lives in Brooklyn and online at www .cherylb.com.

Zoe Bishop's writing has appeared in *Good Vibes Magazine* and in the anthology *slave*. She is currently at work on a novel featuring an erotic cross-country road trip and the commission of several federal felonies.

Tania Britton is an erotica writer living in New York City.

Tenille Brown resides in South Carolina with her husband and two children. Her work is featured in *Best Women's Erotica 2004, Chocolate Flava, Swing! Third Party Sex,* and *Naked Erotica*. She is currently compiling a collection of her erotic fiction, tentatively titled *Skin*.

Tulsa Brown is the pseudonym of an award-winning Canadian novelist who would shock librarians right down to their foundations if they knew ALL the things she wrote. Her erotica has appeared in over

© 2006 by The Haworth Press, Inc. All rights reserved.
doi:10.1300/5328_29

249

a dozen anthologies, and her gay romance, *Achilles' Other Heel,* is now available at www.torquerepress.com

Michelle C. lives in New York City and has been told that she has "a lot of clothes." She enjoys Nordstrom's Rack, Daffy's, and sample sales. She was not in a sorority, but she did sleep with a sorority girl when she was in college. All in the name of research, of course.

Diana Cage is a San Francisco-based author and former editor of the world's only lesbian sex magazine, *On Our Backs.* Her books include the best-selling book on the art of oral sex *Box Lunch: The Layperson's Guide to Cunnilingus* (Alyson, 2004), *Bottoms Up: Writing About Sex* (Soft Skull, 2004), *The On Our Backs Guide to Lesbian Sex* (Alyson, 2003), and *On Our Backs: The Best Erotic Fiction 2* (Alyson, 2003). She has two forthcoming books, both from Alyson Press: *The G Word: The Dykes Guide to Dating and Getting a Girlfriend,* and *Threeways: Fulfill Your Ultimate Fantasy.*

Nell Carberry's work has been published in *Salon, The New York Times,* CleanSheets.com, HerCurve.com, and *Libido,* as well as in the anthologies *Best American Erotica* (2000, 2002, 2005), *Exhibitions,* and *Sex Toys.* She also writes under the name Martha Garvey. She thanks Amelia Copeland and Susie Bright and Rachel Kramer Bussel for their inspiration.

Khadijah Caturani is a writer, filmmaker, smut peddler, and rabble-rouser. She's also the force behind the short film *Femme Fatale,* and author of "Ungentlemanly Behavior," which appeared in *Up All Night: Adventures in Lesbian Sex.*

M. Christian is the author of the critically acclaimed and best-selling collections *Dirty Words, Speaking Parts, The Bachelor Machine,* and *Filthy.* He is the editor of *The Burning Pen, Guilty Pleasures, the Best S/M Erotica* series, *The Mammoth Book of Future Cops* and *The Mammoth Book of Tales of the Road* (with Maxim Jakubowski), and *Confessions, Amazons,* and *Garden of Perverse* (with Sage Vivant), as well as 18 other anthologies. His short fiction has appeared in over 200 books and magazines, including *Best American Erotica, Best Gay Erotica, Best Lesbian Erotica, Best Transgendered Erotica, Best Fetish Erotica, Best Bondage Erotica* and—well, you get the idea. He lives in San Francisco and is only some of what that implies.

Jen Collins is a freelance writer who lives in San Francisco. Her work can be found in *Young Wives' Tales: New Adventures in Love and Partnership*, *Best Bi Women's Erotica*, *Tough Girls*, *Best Fetish Erotica*, *Bare Your Soul: The Thinking Girl's Guide to Enlightenment*, and *Back to Basics* (butch-femme erotica, from Bella Books). If you're interested in reading about Bobby's fate (mentioned in "The G-String"), check out "Bedrock" in *Set in Stone: Butch on Butch Erotica*.

Kate Dominic is the author of 2004 Foreword Magazine Book of the Year Finalist *Any 2 People, Kissing* (Down There Press). Her short stories appear in hundreds of erotic publications, including *The Best of Best Women's Erotica*, various volumes of *Ultimate Lesbian Erotica*, and *Naughty Spanking Stories from A-Z*. Her column "The Business End" appears monthly at www.erotica-readers.com. Her Web site is www.katedominic.com.

R. Gay is a writer and graduate student living, quite literally, in the middle of nowhere. Her writing can be found in *Best American Erotica 2004*, *Far From Home: Father Daughter Travel Adventures*, *Shameless: Women's Intimate Erotica*, and many others.

Trish Kelly is the author of more than twenty chapbooks and zines, including the well-known series *The Make Out Club*. She is a contributor to CBC Radio and has had her work anthologized in *Hot + Bothered 4* (Arsenal Pulp Press), *Quickies 3* (Arsenal Pulp Press), and *How to Fuck a Tranny* (forthcoming).

Jessica Melusine lives and writes outside of Washington, DC. Her fiction has appeared in *Shameless: Women's Intimate Erotica*, on Ssspread.com, and other media. She has modeled for Faeriefantasies.com, Thatstrangegirl.com, and Ssspread.com. Her passions include sacred whoredom, ceremonial magick, sex worker rights, and finding the perfect lipstick. Those who want to find out more about her can visit www.jessicamelusine.com.

Ana Slutsky Peril is the pseudonym of a dyke writer whose work has appeared in *The Village Voice, Best Lesbian Erotica 2003* and *2005, Best of Best Lesbian Erotica 2,* and *Hot Lesbian Erotica.* In real life, she's butch.

Shelly Rafferty (b. 1956) is a lesbian parent, activist, writer, and graduate student. Her work has appeared in more than twenty anthologies and journals. She is currently writing her dissertation on teacher diaries, titled "The Necessary Secret: Ambivalence, Silence, Disclosure, and Knowledge in the Personal Writings of Teachers 1905-1935." She lives in upstate New York.

Originally from New York, **Dahlia Schweitzer** has become Berlin's fastest rising ex-pat multitalent, managing to both maintain her public profile as an extroverted, electro-punk diva while keeping up her other, more introverted passions of writing and photography. Her subjects, in all her various media—from performance to photography, writing to music—have consciously run from high and refined to down and dirty in order to explore themes of sexuality and identity, fantasy and gender.

Lori Selke lives in Oakland. She is obsessed with silent movies and vintage pornography. She edits the sassy little litzine Problem Child, and more of her work can be found in *Dyke The Halls* (Circlet Press), *5 Minute Erotica* (Running Press), and *Best S/M Erotica* (Black Books).

Anna South is a UC Berkeley graduate ('99) and the author of numerous children's stories and articles published under a different name. "Zenda" is her first work of erotic fiction.

A. J. Stone was born and raised in New York City. A feature film producer, she currently resides in Los Angeles. This piece, her first crack at erotica, was originally published in *Best Lesbian Erotica 2001.*

Tanya Turner lives in New York City, where she stirs up trouble and writes about it as often as she can. Her erotic fiction also appears in dirty books such as *Ultimate Lesbian Erotica 2005, Show & Tell: True Tales of Lesbian Lust,* and *Naughty Spanking Stories from A to Z.*

Called "a trollop with a laptop," **Alison Tyler** is naughty and knows it. Over the past decade, she has written more than fifteen explicit novels, including *Learning to Love It, Strictly Confidential, Sweet Thing, Sticky Fingers, Something About Workmen*, and *Rumours*. Her stories have appeared in anthologies including *Sweet Life I & II, Taboo, Best Women's Erotica, Best Fetish Erotica*, and in *Wicked Words 4, 5, 6, 8*, and *10*. Ms. Tyler is the editor of *Heat Wave, Best Bondage Erotica, Three-Way, Naughty Stories from A to Z, Down & Dirty, Naked Erotica*, and *Juicy Erotica*. Please visit www.prettythingspress.com.

Kiki Veronika is a skirt-donning skirt chaser who resides in New York City. She is a psychiatric social worker by day and simply psychotic by night. If time and experience permit, she will author more erotica, and she is currently commencing a book about her very unerotic experiences in psychotherapy.

HARRINGTON PARK PRESS®
Alice Street Editions™
Judith P. Stelboum
Editor in Chief

Past Perfect by Judith P. Stelboum

Inside Out by Juliet Carrera

Façades by Alex Marcoux

Weeding at Dawn: A Lesbian Country Life by Hawk Madrone

His Hands, His Tools, His Sex, His Dress: Lesbian Writers on Their Fathers edited by Catherine Reid and Holly K. Iglesias

Treat by Angie Vicars

Yin Fire by Alexandra Grilikhes

Egret by Helen Collins

Your Loving Arms by Gwendolyn Bikis

A Donor Insemination Guide: Written By and For Lesbian Women by Marie Mohler and Lacy Frazer

From Flitch to Ash: A Musing on Trees and Carving by Diane Derrick

To the Edge by Cameron Abbott

Back to Salem by Alex Marcoux

Extraordinary Couples, Ordinary Lives by Lynn Haley-Banez and Joanne Garrett

Cat Rising by Cynn Chadwick

Maryfield Academy by Carla Tomaso

Ginger's Fire by Maureen Brady

A Taste for Blood by Diana Lee

Zach at Risk by Pamela Shepherd

An Inexpressible State of Grace by Cameron Abbott

Minus One: A Twelve-Step Journey by Bridget Bufford

Girls with Hammers by Cynn Chadwick

Rosemary and Juliet by Judy MacLean

An Emergence of Green by Katherine V. Forrest

Descanso: A Soul Journey by Cynthia Tyler

Blood Sisters: A Novel of an Epic Friendship by Mary Jacobsen

Women of Mystery: An Anthology edited by Katherine V. Forrest

Glamour Girls: Femme/Femme Erotica by Rachel Kramer Bussel

The Meadowlark Sings by Helen R. Schwartz

Blown Away by Perry Wynn

Shadow Work by Cynthia Tyler

Dykes on Bikes: An Erotic Anthology edited by Sacchi Green
and Rakelle Valencia

Order a copy of this book with this form or online at:
http://www.haworthpress.com/store/product.asp?sku=5328

GLAMOUR GIRLS
Femme/Femme Erotica

_____ in softbound at $16.95 (ISBN-13: 978-1-56023-534-7; ISBN-10: 1-56023-534-9)

Or order online and use special offer code HEC25 in the shopping cart.

COST OF BOOKS_____

☐ **BILL ME LATER:** (Bill-me option is good on US/Canada/Mexico orders only; not good to jobbers, wholesalers, or subscription agencies.)

☐ Check here if billing address is different from shipping address and attach purchase order and billing address information.

POSTAGE & HANDLING_____
(US: $4.00 for first book & $1.50 for each additional book)
(Outside US: $5.00 for first book & $2.00 for each additional book)

Signature_____

SUBTOTAL_____

☐ **PAYMENT ENCLOSED: $**_____

IN CANADA: ADD 7% GST_____

☐ **PLEASE CHARGE TO MY CREDIT CARD.**

STATE TAX_____
(NJ, NY, OH, MN, CA, IL, IN, PA, & SD residents, add appropriate local sales tax)

☐ Visa ☐ MasterCard ☐ AmEx ☐ Discover
☐ Diner's Club ☐ Eurocard ☐ JCB

Account # _____

FINAL TOTAL_____
(If paying in Canadian funds, convert using the current exchange rate, UNESCO coupons welcome)

Exp. Date_____

Signature_____

Prices in US dollars and subject to change without notice.

NAME_____

INSTITUTION_____

ADDRESS_____

CITY_____

STATE/ZIP_____

COUNTRY_____ COUNTY (NY residents only)_____

TEL_____ FAX_____

E-MAIL_____

May we use your e-mail address for confirmations and other types of information? ☐ Yes ☐ No
We appreciate receiving your e-mail address and fax number. Haworth would like to e-mail or fax special discount offers to you, as a preferred customer. **We will never share, rent, or exchange your e-mail address or fax number.** We regard such actions as an invasion of your privacy.

Order From Your Local Bookstore or Directly From
The Haworth Press, Inc.
10 Alice Street, Binghamton, New York 13904-1580 • USA
TELEPHONE: 1-800-HAWORTH (1-800-429-6784) / Outside US/Canada: (607) 722-5857
FAX: 1-800-895-0582 / Outside US/Canada: (607) 771-0012
E-mail to: orders@haworthpress.com

For orders outside US and Canada, you may wish to order through your local sales representative, distributor, or bookseller.
For information, see http://haworthpress.com/distributors

(Discounts are available for individual orders in US and Canada only, not booksellers/distributors.)

PLEASE PHOTOCOPY THIS FORM FOR YOUR PERSONAL USE.
http://www.HaworthPress.com

BOF06